NEW WORLDS QUARTERLY

#4

EDITED BY
MICHAEL MOORCOCK
Associate Editor: LANGDON JONES
Art Editor: RICHARD GLYN JONES
Literary Editor: M. JOHN HARRISON

A BERKLEY MEDALLION BOOK
PUBLISHED BY
BERKLEY PUBLISHING CORPORATION

This issue is dedicated to Hawkind

Published by arrangement with the editor's agent

SBN 425-02176-9

BERKLEY MEDALLION BOOKS are published by
Berkley Publishing Corporation
200 Madison Avenue
New York, N.Y. 10016

BERKLEY MEDALLION BOOKS ® TM 757,375

Printed in the United States of America

BERKLEY MEDALLION EDITION, JUNE, 1972

CONTENTS

 Additional editorial help was given by Miss Gabi Nasemann and Miss Diane Lambert, to whom acknowledgement is gratefully made.

THE PROBLEM OF SYMPATHY

M. JOHN HARRISON

In Robert Silverberg's critical anthology *The Mirror of Infinity* (Sidgwick & Jackson, £2.50), James Blish, that most erudite and academic of sf authors, can be discovered mourning the loss of the stringent plotting demands of the extinct pulps, and giving a little succinct advice about the art which gave rise to Lester Dent's Master Plot Formula (an invaluable work, to be found on the shelves of all those much loved and sadly departed masters of interplanetary adventure). Who would remember *Whip Queens Of The Scarlet Asteroid,* Mr. Blish implies, if that narrative of courage in extremity had not been founded on a 'sympathetic viewpoint character with whom the reader can identify'?

The literary act of 'identification' has become a peculiar, slippery thing to define; at base, however, it continues to require on the part of the reader a recognition of mutual characteristics: '(to) associate one*self* inseparably *with* . . .' (OED, their italics). This opens two avenues of exploration.

Firstly, there is that familiar reader-identification of popular fiction, which demands that the reader find in this 'sympathetic viewpoint character' some trait or virtue or capability he perceives *or would wish to perceive* in himself—some mental set, quality or compendium of values which he believes to be his own. In this case, it is the word 'sympathetic' which is doing most of the work: it is necessary for the writer to study his market and initiate a feedback system; and it's inevitable that his end-product should be a sop to the most common denominator of popular fantasies and attitudes—a fact that one of Mr. Blish's luminaries, C.S. Lewis, was not slow to point out:

> "(The readers of popular fiction) project themselves into the most enviable or most admirable character; and probably, after they have finished reading, his delights and victories supply hints for further day-dreams."

On the other hand, we have almost the reverse of the above process—a form of identification which requires less in the way of consumer research and a great deal more in terms of ability. It consists, simply, in peopling a novel accurately, and of leading the reader steadily from an external view of its characters to a point where he recognises—in a word or an attitude or an emotional response—an element of himself. He flushes with embarrassment or nods in rueful agreement as he receives a reflection, an abrupt radar echo of his own personality.

At this point, the identification is made.

Both these processes lead to a sympathy between character and reader: the latter, however, leads also to empathy, to an actual insight which the reader may even be able to apply to his own life. While sf is amply provided with hero-identification (indeed, has always taken the greater part of its dynamic from such fantasy fulfilment: as witness the extraordinarily 'ordinary' teenagers of Heinlein, and the things that happen to them), it is relatively —and tragically—free from any sympathy with, for or between real human beings.

An example of the simple sympathetic viewpoint can be found in Mr. Blish's own book *And All The Stars A Stage* (Doubleday, $4.95):

> "You give me a great big fat blue-green fuzzy frozen pain in my starboard rump, Apprentice-Admiral O'Kung," Jorn said, hunching forward over his desk and

glaring up at her. "My math is better than yours and always was, and you know it. If you can find a better navigator, go ahead—I'd rather rub brightwork than be kicking boy for your twitches any longer." (p. 107)

A fairly dreadful piece of writing, but also a classic resignation-fantasy: Jorn is a good worker, but down-trodden. Through him, the reader can pre-live his own possible rebellion against his employee-status; he can work out his resentments via the words on the page. Even the navigators of starships have problems with the boss, or so it seems; at heart, they're just ordinary people like you and me.

This sort of example is easily obtainable. To discover science fiction that provides a more genuine form of identification, it will be necessary to turn elsewhere. Luckily, it's the driving force of Jack Trevor Story's novel *Little Dog's Day*, recently published by Alison & Busby at £1.50.

To the reader who is already familiar with Jack Story's hilarious socio-comic novels, science-fiction might seem something of an abrupt departure. But Story's work has always been concerned with the location, isolation, and subsequent refining of the fantasies implicit in reality; and this is an evolution hinted at some time ago by the serialisation in NEW WORLDS of *The Wind In The Snottygobble Tree.*

Little Dog's Day takes place in the near future and has as its background the landscape, denizens and life-style of what the jacket-notes aptly describe as 'solid Jack Trevor Story country lying between Luton Airport, Welwyn Garden City and the Fens.' That is to say, Story may be writing sf, but he isn't all that interested in the doomy or numinous—he's still aimed accurately at the social strata he's always been involved with; and his touch is still light, vulgar and richly proletarian.

Art Henry, fifty two years old, a 'purchasing and progress manager' and amateur jazz trombonist, recovers from a fatal heart attack (that is not a contradiction in terms—not in Story's universe, which is full of undertakers' jokes made substantial) and returns to his suburban home to discover his relatives bringing back all the things they have 'borrowed' in anticipation of his death. Somebody borrows his job, too: that, and his pet poodle Miffy are the only things that don't return. No other writer could bring it off: I ask you to believe that Story can make you believe in a poodle called Miffy as the object of a grail-search narrative.

In his search for the dog, Art Henry plumbs the depths of a dreadful, jolly, plastic society in which population problems have been solved by means of mysterious holiday camps for the aged, and those who lose their 'social coding' also lose their names. He travels from vet's surgery to slum, playing his trombone; meets the sad, disfigured air-hostess Gwen Rowbottom; joins the dispossessed freelings of Little Hiroshima, witnessing their metamorphosis into four-legged human animals after an experiment in gas warfare.

Now this is almost standard subject matter—half a dozen pale dystopias see the light as paperbacks every couple of months, run off a production line that capitalises on public fear of the political future. Even British commercial television has its own watery vision of future shock, *The Guardians*. What makes *Little Dog's Day* so inestimably more important than any of these flirtings with collective paranoia is Jack Trevor Story's incredible ear for dialogue, his killingly precise observation of character, and his true sympathy for the emotions of working and lower middle class people when faced with tragedy, social uncertainty, and death.

And it is in this area that the word 'identification' really begins to mean something. Consider, for instance, the conversation that ensues when Art Henry returns so unexpectedly to the bosom of his family:

> "I brought your lawnmower back," Harry was saying.
>
> Janet, who was busy with the teapot, swiftly said: "He's had it sharpened for you, Art."
>
> "That's right," Harry said, "I've had it sharpened for you."
>
> "Harry had dad's lawnmower sharpened," Harry's wife Elissa told the others.

"I've got it in the back of the car," Harry said. "I'll just bring it in."

"Got a car now, have you?" Art said; he was quite willing to get him off the hook by changing the subject. But somehow it became the same subject.

"I borrowed yours," Harry said.

Janet said: "I told him to borrow your car to take the mower to the sharpeners. The ironmonger's."

"I've put some juice in it for you," Harry said.

"All ready for you," Elissa said.

"Thanks, Harry," said Art.

Janet was pouring the tea into the sugar basin, he noticed.

Who has not experienced the horrid, grinding embarrassment of post-funeral celebrations? Through his insertion of the corpse—alive, kicking, and amused—into the wake, Story reminds us all of the times we could have bitten off our tongues; of the shuffling depressed conversations, and the motions both physical and mental that are performed mechanically, automatically. The parody is harsh, but so expertly targeted. *We* are Harry. Inevitably, we will become Art Henry, too.

Little Dog's Day doesn't seem as precisely and unerringly constructed as some of Story's previous work: the narration alternates between first and third person—a difficult mixture to juggle with; and at one point Miffy the poodle himself narrates a few hundred words—and although this adds a fresh perspective on the humans-to-animals transformation, it's rather a clumsy means to the end.

But this can't detract from a novel which projects characters like Gwen Rowbottom, who trudges uncomplainingly through what has been a thoroughly miserable sort of life not because she is stupid or insensitive, but because she is a little bemused, a little lonely, a little disconnected. A little *real*.

Dear Mum:

I am thinking of killing myself and Miffy unless you or Dad can get Major Martin or somebody . . . to help me. . . .

Do you remember Yarmouth beauty contest when we had that turkey dinner with Mr. Leason? I am crying for it.

Your loving daughter underground,
Gwen.

We are all crying for it, in some form or another, a fact which Jack Story appreciates perfectly. There is very little difference between a lost happiness and a lost freedom; and it is those freedoms we are already in the process of losing that he mourns through the characters of *Little Dog's Day.*

While Art Henry is out busking, he comes under surveillance from a police helicopter:

> He realised he must be a little unusual but it didn't occur to him that his son had reported him; that advertising executives couldn't have street-trombonist fathers. You could have any disruptive elements, even just social embarrassments removed under the new act, provided you could show steady progress in your career.

It is in touches like these—parodies and extensions of the new brutalities, the mental and psychic curtailments of liberty practised on the aged, the socially inferior, the helpless—which reveal that a change of emphasis has not simply accompanied but motivated Story's shift to this kind of dystopic subject matter. While his novels have always been relevant and genuine pictures of contemporary society, there has been an innocence about them (a knowing, playful innocence, certainly, but innocence all the same) that vanished with *The Wind In The Snotty-gobble Tree.*

Story has come out firmly on the side of humanity in its struggle against petty erosion of freedom, and given his work teeth. Reading the dedication of *Little Dog's Day,* one can guess why. I leave you to discover that for yourself.

The vast distance separting Jorn and his 'big fat blue-green' infantile pain from Gwen Rowbottom's ruined face and pathetic attempts to communicate her sadness to her mother is the perfect measure of the gap of understanding that prevents genre sf from realising any potentiality it possesses. As long as it appeals to writers and readers who can feel more compassion for a machine—Asimov's robots, the sentient bomb of Van Vogt—than a human being, then it is *still* pulp fiction.

The Lensman lives.

It was once fashionable among mainstream critics, teachers and academics to ignore sf: now, the reverse applies, and this has led to the mistaken belief on the part of the genre pundits that the merits of the form have suddenly been recognised—that popularity with a wider audience, obtained simply by the oversell tactics of music halls acts like Kubrick and Clarke, heralds the acceptance of the prodigal relative as a meaningful fiction.

All that has really happened is a sluggish stirring of public interest in pretty hardware.

If the genre as a whole imagines that it has somehow become worthwhile, that its relationship to real life has been consummated, because a few men have walked about on the moon, then it had better stop and think. Because until Lester Dent's Master Plot Formula and Mr. Blish's 'sympathetic viewpoint character' are replaced by a little observation of reality and human understanding, it will never become relevant to anything.

THE EXPLORATION OF SPACE

BARRINGTON BAYLEY

The physical space in which we and the worlds move and have our being may easily be presumed to be a necessary and absolute condition of existence, the only form of the universe that is possible or even conceivable. Mathematicians may invent fictitious spaces of higher dimensions than our own but these, our intuition tells us, are no more than idealistic inventions which could nowhere be translated into reality and do not therefore properly deserve the designation 'space'. The space we know, having the qualities of symmetry and continuity, is intimately and automatically the concomitant of any universe containing things and events, and therefore is inevitable; without space as we know it there could be no existence. The commonplace mind accepts this notion without question; thoughtful philosophers have spoken of the symmetrical, continuous space of three dimensions as an *a priori* world principle whose contradiction would remain a contradiction even in the mind of God. Yet not only has this belief no axiomatic justification but, as I shall attempt to show presently, it is untrue.

I had just smoked my second pipe of opium and was settling into a pleasant reverie. The opium smell, a sweet, cloying and quite unique odour, still hung in the air of my study, mingling with the aroma of the polished mahogany bookcases and the scent of flowers from the garden. Through the open window I could see that garden, with its pretty shrubs and crazy pathways, and beyond, the red ball of the far-off sun sinking through strata of pink and blue clouds.

My attention, however, was on the chessboard before me. Perhaps I should say a few words about myself. I believe that my brief participation in 'orthodox' experimental research may permit me to call myself a man of science, although these days my studies are more mathematical and deductive. It will surprise some that my main interest throughout my life has been alchemy. I have myself practised the Hermetic Art with some assiduity, if only to feel for myself the same numinousness experienced by my alchemistic forebears in manipulating the chemical constituents of the world. Hence I have known what it is to search for the *prima materia* (which others call the Philosopher's stone, being the root of transformation); and I have pondered long and deeply on that profoundly basic manual, the Emerald Table of Hermes Trismegistus.

Unlike most contemporary men I am not inclined to the belief that alchemy has been rendered obsolete by modern science, but rather that its inadequate techniques and theories have been temporarily outstripped, while the essence of the Art remains unapproached. In the not too distant future the reverent search for *prima materia* may once again be conducted with the full charisma of symbology, but employing the best of particle accelerators. If the outlook I am displaying seems to run counter to the spirit of inductive science, let me admit that my thoughts do sometimes wander, for good or ill, outside the pale wherein dwell the more active members of the scientific community. There is value, I believe, in looking back over the history of science as well as forward to future expectations. I am not, for instance, hypnotised by the success of atomic theory, as are practically all of my colleagues. If I may be permitted to say so, the objections to the atomic view of nature listed by Aristotle have never been answered. These objections are still valid, and eventually they will have to be answered—or vindicated—on the level of sub-nuclear physics.

Opium has the happy conjunction of both inducing a feeling of relaxation and well-being and of opening the inner doors of the mind to a realm of colourful creativity. By opium, it is conjectured, Coleridge glimpsed the poem *Kubla Khan,* only fragments of which he managed to remember. By opium I met my new, though sadly soon-departed, friend, the Chessboard Knight.

A chess board, to recapitulate the obvious, consists of 8x8 locations, or 'squares' arranged in a rectilinear grid. To us, the chess board represents a peculiarly restricted world. The entities, or 'pieces' of this world are distinguished from one another only by their power of movement: a pawn can move forward only, one square at a time; a castle can move longtitudinally for up to eight squares, a bishop likewise diagonally, and a knight can move to the opposite corner of a 2x3 rectangle. For all pieces movement is always directly from square to square, with no locations existing between the squares: none of them possesses the power of continuous, non-discrete movement we enjoy in our own world. On the other hand none of us possesses the power of simultaneous transition from location to location enjoyed by chessmen, particularly by the knight, who is unimpeded by intervening obstacles.

A rapid succession of similar thoughts was passing through my head as I gazed at the chessboard, though ostensibly to study the game laid out thereon, which I was playing by letter with a distant correspondent. As sometimes happens when smoking opium, time suddenly slowed down and the thoughts seemed to come with incredible speed and clarity. Normally, I mused, one would unhesitatingly suppose our real physical world to be the superior of the chessboard world, because no limitation is placed upon the number of locations we may occupy. No arbitrary laws restrict me from moving in any way I please about my study, my garden, or the countryside beyond. But is that so important? The significance of chess lies not in the very simplified space-time environment but in the relation the pieces hold to one another. By this latter criterion our own degree of freedom undergoes a drastic reduction: the number of stances I can hold in relation to my wife, to my friends or to my employer (though, being retired, I have no employer) is by no means great; insignificant, in fact, when compared to the infinite number of relationships that would obtain by mathematically permutating all possible locations in our continuum of physical space. Is it an unfounded presumption, then, that our own world of continuous consecutive motions is logically any more basic to nature, or any richer in content, than one based on the principle of the chessboard, comprising discrete transitions between non-continuous locations?

I had reached thus far in my speeding express-train of thought when before my dazed eyes the chess pieces, like a machine that had suddenly been switched on, began flicking themselves around the board, switching from square to square with all the abruptness of the winking patterns of lights on a computer console. After this brief, flurried display they arranged themselves in a formation which left the centre of the board empty and were still—except for the White King's Knight, who went flickering among them in his corner-turning manner, executing a dizzying but gracefully arabesque circuit of the board before finishing up in the centre, where he turned to me, bowed slightly, and lifted his head to speak to me in a distant, somewhat braying tone.

In my drugged state this happening did not induce in me the same surfeit of bewilderment and incredulity that would normally, I believe, have been my reaction.

Astonished I certainly was. It is not every day that one's chess set shows a life of its own, or that the pieces remain so true to their formal nature as laid down by the rules that they move from one position to another without bothering to traverse the spaces between. Not, let me add for the sake of the record, that the pieces showed any carelessness or laziness, or that they took short cuts. In order to move, say, from Qk4 to Kr4, a castle was required to manifest himself in all the intervening squares so as to show that he came by a definite route and that the way was unimpeded—only the knight flashed to his opposite corner unperturbed by whatever might surround him. These manifestations were, however, fleeting in the extreme, and nothing was ever seen of the castle in between adjacent squares—because, naturally, in a game of chess there is no 'between adjacent squares'.

But I jump ahead of myself. My astonishment was so great that I missed the Knight's first words and he was obliged to repeat himself. What he said was:

"We enter your haven with gratitude."

His voice, as I have said, was distant, with a resinous, braying quality. Yet not cold or unpleasant; on the contrary it was cordial and civilised. I replied:-

"I was not aware that you were in need of haven; but that being the case, you are welcome." In retrospect my words might appear to have received weighty consideration, but in fact they were flippant and extemporary, the only response my brain could form to an impossible situation. And so began my conversation with the Chessboard Knight, the strangest and most informative conversation I have ever held.

So total was my bemusement that I accepted with an unnatural calmness the Knight's announcement that he was a space explorer. My sense of excitement returned, however, when he went on to explain that he was not a space explorer such as our imagination might conjure by the phrase, but that he was an explorer of alternative types of spatial framework of which, he assured me, there were a good number in the universe. What we are pleased to call the sidereal universe, that is, the whole system of space-time observable by us on Earth, is merely one among a vast range of various systems. Even more astounding, in the circumstances, was the revelation that the Knight hailed from a system of space identical to that which I had a moment before been contemplating! One analogous to a game of chess, where space, instead of being continuous and homogenous as we know it, was made up of discrete locations, infinite or at any rate indefinite in number, and to which entities can address themselves instantaneously and in any order. There is no extended spatial framework in which these locations are ordered or arrayed and all locations are equally available from any starting point (provided they are not already occupied). An entity may, however, occupy only one location at a time and therein lies the principle of order in this well-nigh incomprehensible world. Structures, systems and events consist of convoluted, arabesque patterns of successive occupations, and of the game-like relationships these manoeuvres hold to one another. The chess-people's analogy of a long distance takes the form of a particularly difficult sequence of locations; alternatively the sequence would correspond to a particularly clever construct or device—the chess-people make little distinction between these two interpretations.

As do the occupants of a chess-board, the entities of this space (which I shall term locational-transitional space) vary in the range and ingenuity of their movements. Primitive organisms can do no more than transfer themselves slowly from one location to another, without pattern or direction, like pawns, while the most evolved intelligent species, like my friend the Knight, had advanced to dizzying achievements as laid down by the possibilities of such a realm. Their most staggering achievement was that of travel to other spaces; this was accomplished by a hazardous, almost infinitely long series of locations executed at colossal speed and comprising a pattern of such subtlety and complexity that my mind could not hope to comprehend it. Indeed, few even in the Knight's spatial realm comprehended it and for their science it constituted a triumph comparable to our release of atomic energy from matter.

The discerning reader who has followed me this far might justly wonder at the coincidence which brought these bizarre travellers to my presence at the very moment when I had been theoretically contemplating something resembling their home space. This question was uppermost in my mind, also, but there was, the Knight told me, no coincidence involved at all. On entering our continuum (which the Knight and the companions under his command did indirectly, via other realms less weird to them) the space explorers had become confused and lost their bearings, seeming to wander in a sea of primaeval chaos where no laws they could hypothesize, not even those garnered in their wide experience of spatial systems, seemed to obtain. Then, like a faint beacon of light in the uncognizable limbo, they had sighted a tiny oasis of ordered space, and with great expertise and luck had managed to steer their ship towards it.

That oasis was my chess board. Not the board alone, of course—tens of thousands of chess games in progress at the same moment failed to catch their attention—but the fact that it had been illumined and made real by the thoughts I had entertained while gazing upon it, imbuing it with conceptions that approached, however haltingly, the conditions of their home world. Hence I owed the visitation to a lesser, more credible coincidence: chess and opium. At any rate, having landed their ship upon the board and thus bringing it under the influence of that vessel's internally maintained alien laws, they had carried out simply manipulations of the pieces in order to signal their presence and establish communication—the real ship and its occupants not being visible or even conceivable to me, since they did not have contiguous spatial extension.

My reader, still suspicious of my truthfulness, will also want to know how it was that the Knight spoke to me in English. The appalling difficulties offered by any other explanation have tempted me to decide that we did not really speak at all, but only telepathically from mind to mind. And yet my grosser, more stubborn recollection belies this evasion: we *did* speak, the air vibrated and brought to me the thin, resinous tones of the Knight's voice. His own remarks on the matter were off-hand and baffling. There was scarcely a language in the universe that could not be mastered in less than a minute, he said, provided it was of the relational type, which they nearly all were. He seemed to find my own mystification slightly disconcerting. The only comment I can contribute, after much reflection, is that for a locational-transitional being what he says may well be the case. Language, as he pointed out, largely concerns relations between things and concepts. To the Knight relations are the stuff of life, and he would find our own comprehension of them far below the level of imbecility. In our world to have but one fraction of his appreciation of relations, which to us are so important but so difficult to manage, would make us past masters of strategy and I believe no power would be able to withstand such knowledge.

But here lies the antinomy: the Knight and his crew were coming to *me* for help. They found the conditions of our three-dimensional continuum as incomprehensible and chaotic as we would find their realm. They had not even been able to ascertain what manner of space it was, and begged me to explain its laws to them in order that they might be able to find their way out of it.

There was a certain irony in being asked to describe the world I knew when I yearned to question the Knight as to *his* world (indeed my imagination was exploding—were there galaxies, stars and planets in the locational-transitional space? No, of course there could not be: such things were products of continuous space. What, then, was there? Some parallel to our phenomena there must be, but try as I might I could not picture what). However, a cry of distress cannot go unanswered and I launched into an exposition.

It was quite a test of the intellect to have to describe the utterly familiar to a being whose conceptions are absolutely different from one's own. At first I had great difficulty in explaining the rules and limitations by which we stereo beings (that is the phrase I have decided upon to describe our spatial characteristics) are obliged to order our lives. In particular it was hard to convey to the Knight that to get from point A to point B the basic strategy is to proceed in a straight line. To give them credit, the chessman crew had already experimented with the idea that continuous motion of some kind might be needed, but they had conceived the natural form of motion to be in a circle. When sighting my chessboard they had proceeded in the opposite direction and approached it by executing a perfect circle of a diameter several times that of the galaxy. I could not help but admire the mathematical expertise that had put both the starting point and the destination on the circumference of this circle.

After a number of false starts the Knight successfully mastered the necessary concepts and was able to identify the class of spaces to which ours belongs, a class some other members of which had been explored previously. They were regarded as dangerous but none, he informed me, had so far proved as hazardous and weird as our own, nor so difficult to move in. He still could not visualise our space, but I had apparently given him enough information for the ship's computer to chart a course homeward (computers, theirs as well as ours, are notoriously untroubled by the limitations of imagination).

During the conversation I had naturally enough sought his opinion on various contemporary theories of the space we inhabit: on Riemannian space, Poincaré space, special and general relativity. Is our space positively or negatively curved? Spherical, parabolic or saddle-shaped—or is it curved at all? Is it finite or infinite? I acquainted him with the equation for the general theory of gravitation and invited his comments:-

$$R_{ik} - 1/2 g_{ik} R = T_{ik}$$

His reply to all this was discouraging. The only definitive datum he would give me was that our space is infinite. As for Einstein's equation, he said that it merely gave an approximate, superficial description of behaviour and did not uncover any law. He told me that in our continuum motion depends on a set of expansion*

Our whole idea of analysing space by means of dimensions is inadequate and artificial, the Knight advised. The notion is an internally generated side-effect, and to anyone from outside, e.g. from another kind of space, it is

*A break in the manuscript occurs here—Ed.

neither meaningful nor descriptive. The essence of a spatial structure is more often expressed by a plain maxim that might appear to be ad hoc and rule of thumb, but that actually contains the nub of its specific law. At this I could not refrain from interrupting with the boast that privately I had once reached the same conclusion; and that if I had to state the basic physical law of our space (which I then thought of as the universe) it would be that in moving towards any one thing one is necessarily moving away from some other thing. The Knight complimented me on my insight; his ship's computer was at that very moment grinding out the implications of a formulation quite close to the one I had come up with.

Following this, the Knight expressed his gratitude and announced his intention to leave. I begged him to stay a while; but he replied that to continue meshing the spatial laws of the ship (i.e. locational-transitional laws) with the pieces on the chessboard was proving to be a drain on the power unit. Guiltily, I confess that I allowed selfishness to come to the fore here. Did he owe me something for the help I had given him, I argued? Could he and his crew not spend a little more energy, and would it truly endanger their lives? My unethical blackmail was prompted solely by my burning desire to learn as much as I could while the opportunity remained. I think he understood my feelings for, after a brief hesitation, he agreed to remain and discourse with me for a short time, or at least until the power drain approached a critical level.

Eagerly I besought him to tell me as much as he could of this vast universe of divers space-times to which he had access but I had not. To begin with, where did the Knight's own spatial realm lie? Was it beyond the boundaries of our own space (beyond infinity!), or was it at right angles to it in another dimension? (I babbled carelessly, forgetting his former objection to the term). Or was it, perhaps, co-extensive with our continuum, passing unnoticed because its own mode of existence is so unutterably different to it? To all these hasty suggestions the Knight replied by chiding me gently for my naivety. I would never know the answer while I persisted in thinking in such a way, he said, for the simple reason that there was no answer *and no question.* While I was still capable of asking this non-existent question the non-answer would never be apparent to me.

Somewhat abashed, I asked a more pertinent question: was each space-time unique, or was each type duplicated over and over? As far as was known, the Knight said, each was unique, but they were classified by similarities and some differed only in details or in the quantitative value of some physical constant. It was to be expected, for instance, that there would be a range of stereo space-times resembling our own but with a different value on the velocity of light. To my next request, that he describe some alien space-times to me, he explained that many would be totally inconceivable to me and that there was no way to express them in my language, mathematical or spoken. The majority of the spaces that were known to the chess-people were variations on the locational-transitional theme. There was a theory in his home world that locational-transitional (or chess-board) space was the basic kind of space in the universe and that all others were permutations and variants of it; but he agreed with me that this theory could be suspected of special pleading and that deeper penetration into the universe by the chess-people's spaceships might well bring home a different story. He would not bore me, he added, by describing meaningless variations on locational-transitional space, but felt that I would be more entertained by those spaces whose qualities made striking comparisons with the qualities of my own realm.

There was, for instance, a space that, though continuous, was not symmetrical in all directions but was hung between two great poles like a magnetic field. Motion along the direction of the axis between the poles was easy as it is for us, but transverse movement was an altogether different phenomenon that required a different type of energy and a different name. This polarisation continued down into every event and structure, which was invariably positioned between two opposing poles of one kind or another. There was stereo space with great cracks of nullity running all through it, chasms of zero-existence which were impossible to cross and had to be gone round. There was space where an entity could travel in a straight line without incident, but where on changing direction he shed similar, though not identical, duplicates of himself which continued to accompany him thereafter. Prior to their rescue by me the Knight and his crew had believed themselves to be in such a space, for they had chanced to catch a glimpse of a woman accompanied by several daughters of various ages who closely resembled her. Also along these lines, there was a space where the image of an object or entity had the same powers and qualities as the original. This space abounded in mirrors and reflecting surfaces, and an entity was liable to project himself in all directions like a volley of arrows.

When you think about it, the necessity to be in only one place at a time is a pretty severe restriction. Many are the spaces where this law has never been heard of, and where an entity may multiply himself simultaneously into disparate situations without prejudice to his psychic integrity, roaming over the world in a number of bodies yet remaining a single individual. Chameleons have caused some puzzlement among biologists because their eyes operate independently of one another; the right eye knoweth not what the left eye is doing but each scans separately for prey or enemies. Does the consciousness of the chameleon give its full attention to both eyes simultaneously? If so, the chameleon is a mental giant which no human being can equal. This feat is a natural function, however, in the space of 'multiple individuality' I have described.

The Knight warned me against a restrictive concept of motion. It was not, he said, an idea of universal validity, but what we understood by motion could be subsumed under a more generalised concept he called 'transformation', a much larger class of phenomenon. Thus there were spaces where to go was to come, where to approach was to recede, where to say goodbye was to say hello. In short, my maxim which says that to approach one point is to recede from another is not a universal law but a local case. Inversely, there were types of transformation that no mangling of the English language could succeed in hinting at. Once again the Knight suggested that I waste none of our precious time in trying to understand these inconceivable variations.

He spent some words in describing spaces that were not totally homogenous. The space with cracks was one of these; another was 'sheaving space' with a quite odd quirk:

the space split itself up into branches not all of which had any possible communication or influence with one another, even though they might all communicate with some common branch. Thus both A and B might communicate with C, but it would still be impossible for any message or particle to pass from A to B even via C. The separate branches usually contained innumerable worlds, with bizarre results.

Space can also vary in the quality of time it contains (The Knight was quite firm in asserting that time is a subsidiary feature of space). Time is not always irreversible, but in some spaces can be revisited by retracing one's steps. The Knight fascinated me by telling of one space which he called 'a space of forking time' where every incident was not one but several possible outcomes, all equally real. Thus space branches continually in this continuum to develop alternate histories; where this space differs from the stock science-fiction notion, however, is that *every past event is recoverable*, and hence *all possible histories communicate*. By retracing his steps in a certain manner a man (or entity) can go back to the crucial moment that determined the shape of events and take a different path. When I reflected on how the fate and happiness of men is tyrannised over in our space by the singleness of time and the cruel dice-throwing of fleeting happenstance, this realm appeared to me to be a perfect abode of happiness.

It will be obvious that casuality is governed by the type of space in which it takes place. The Knight mentioned that our space contains the principle of 'single-instance casuality', which is also the principle obtaining in most space-times, and means that prolonged and complex processes can come to completion only with difficulty. The reason is thus: if A causes B, and B causes C, it still does not follow that A will lead to C because in the interim B might be modified by interceding influences and fail to cause C. There are, claimed the Knight, space-times of extended causality where every process or project reaches completion and no tendency is ever interrupted. As the realising of ambitions is automatic any 'effort to succeed' is quite redundant in this space-time. The struggle and drama of life consists not of trying to actualise intentions but of the struggle to form intentions in the first place.

In this respect the Knight included his only description of a species of locational-transitional space; a space where there was no sequential causality at all, but in which everything happened on a purely statistical basis. Wondering what it could be like on the inside of such a stochastic wonderland, I asked whether there could ever be the slightest possibility of intelligent, conscious entities arising there. To my surprise the Knight averred that it was well stocked with such entities: statistically intelligent, statistically conscious entities.

I have touched but lightly on the role of matter in the space-times I have discussed; it would be needless to tell my intelligent reader that matter and space are inextricably entwined. He will already have guessed that besides the innumerable spaces that form a receptacle for matter, there are also those that are Aristotelian in the sense of complying with that philosopher's erroneous theories: where matter, instead of being atomic, is continuous and identical with the space it occupies, motion being accomplished by a process of compression and attenuation. There is no empty space in these continua, as Aristotle reasons. In at least one such continuum all the matter is dense and solid, so that it consists of a blocked infinity of solid rock or metal (I am not sure which). In this continuum, the Knight admitted, the possibility of conscious intelligences could be discounted. In contrast to such immobility I particularly liked what the Knight called 'folding space' but which I have since named 'origami space' (origami is the Japanese art of paper-folding). Origami space has an inner richness that makes our own space look bland. Objects can be folded so as to develop entirely new qualities. A man (or entity), by folding a piece of paper in the right way, may make of it a chair, a table, an aeroplane, a house, a fruit, a flower, a live animal, another man, a woman, or practically anything. The art of such folding, it need hardly be added, far surpasses anything to be found in our Earthly origami. Mass and size are not constants in this continuum but can be increased (or decreased) by folding, hence a square of paper a foot on the side may end up as an airliner able to carry a hundred people.

After recounting these wonders the Knight paused to allow me to gather my mental breath. As if by way of relaxation he briefly outlined some primitive-sounding space-times that lacked our centreless relativity but were organised around a fixed centre. Remembering that earlier he had referred to our version of stereo space as a particularly rigid and restricted variety, I seized on this latest exposition to remark that at least the world I inhabited had the dignity of being infinite, symmetrical and unconstricted by having a centre. The Knight's amusement was genuine, if gentle. With a dry laugh he instructed me that my mistake was a classic of unsophisticated presumption, and he regretted to have to inform me that my world did not have relativistic symmetry but that *it had a centre.*

Where was this centre? I asked. Once more came the Knight's mocking chuckle. He had neglected to mention so far, he said, that also intimately related to the question of space is the question of *numbers*. Our space might have no identifiable centre in terms of motion and direction, but in its regard to number it was very strongly centred.

At first his meaning escaped me. Number was another way of classifying the innumerable kinds of space in the universe, he explained. There was at least one space for every possible number (a theorem stated that there were more spaces than one for every possible number), and they were arranged in an ascending series, each space having its 'center of gravity' about a particular number. We are near to the bottom of the scale as our 'centre of gravity' is the number One (there are spaces preferring fractions and at least one preferring Zero). The consequences are immediate and self-evident: singleness is what signifies a complete object in our world; integral unity is all, and the state of there being two of a thing is incidental—a thing comes into its own when it is *one*. We all accept this innately. Every entity and thing is itself by assigning the number One to itself. Higher numbers introduce additional qualities, but do not carry the same weight as *one*.*

In the space next above us in the scale completeness attaches to the number *two*. 'Two-ness' is ideal, and

*By way of example, we conceive of Two as 'Two Ones'.

singleness is incomplete in the same way that a fraction or a part is incomplete in our world. I reflected on what a mass migration there would be if communication could be established with that world—for we also have the yearning after *two* in our shadowy, tantalised way. Our lives are full of complementary pairs. The tragedy of lovers is that they are thwarted by the One-ness of the spatial system: each remains alone and solitary, however much they strive and strain to be completely merged as *two*—for the vain yearning of lovers is not to be made One, which would negate the whole proceeding, but to be, as it were, indistinguishably blended as Two. Should a pair of Eros-struck lovers by some magic or science transpose themselves to this other realm where Two is All, then their bliss would be beyond describing.

More remotely, other worlds model themselves on Three, Four, Five, and so on up the scale of integers to infinity. In addition there is a corresponding scale of negative integers, as also of worlds modelled on every possible fraction, or irrational numbers, on imaginary numbers, and on groups, sets and series of numbers, such as on all the primes, all the odd integers, all the even integers, and on arithmetic and geometric progressions. Beyond even these abstruse factualities are the ranges of worlds centred on numbers and number systems not possible or conceivable to us. The only truly symmetrical, non-centred, relativistic space-time, said the Knight, is one giving equal weight to all numbers.

Georg Cantor, wrestling with the enigma of the infinite, discovered a branch of mathematics called transfinite arithmetic, in which he developed a progression of numbers analogous to the positive integers but whose first term was infinity and whose succeeding terms were as qualitatively different from and beyond infinity as are Two, Three, Four, etc., beyond One. In short, he found that there are numbers larger than infinity. As might be expected, the Knight confirmed the reality of this number system and of the transfinite space that goes with it. There is a whole range of transfinite spaces, probably even larger than the range of finite and infinite spaces (since the number of total spaces is both finite, infinite and transfinite). At this point the Knight seemed to think that we were wandering from the type of description from which I might be expected to profit, and proposed to resume expatiating on those nearer to familiarity. I objected; it was diverting, but less challenging, to be presented with nothing but modifications of an existence I already knew. In a sense I could almost have invented these modifications myself. Would not the Knight consent to offer me, or at least attempt to make me understand, worlds having no common ground with my own—for even the Knight's own locational-transitional space-time, I reminded him, was not hard to describe. I longed to hear something so original as to blow my mind free of all its preconceptions. After some hesitation and muttering as to the perplexities engendered by my request, the Knight agreed to make the effort and favoured me with the following amazing descriptions:-*

Suddenly the Knight broke off to warn me that the power drain was now significantly close to tolerable limits and that he would not be able to linger much longer. A brief feeling of panic assailed me. There must be one question that above all others needed to be asked—yes! The choice was obvious, and I did not delay in putting it. Did the chess-people have any single, particular purpose in undertaking their admirable explorations of space?

The instinct of exploration, said the Knight, is a natural one. There was a central quest, however: to try to determine whether, in the multiplicity of space-times, there is a common universal law or principle, and thereby to discover how existence originates and is maintained.

I cursed myself for not having broached this subject sooner, instead of leaving it until it was almost too late. I had given much thought to this Basic Question myself, I tendered. And, if it was of any interest, I had once come to a tentative conclusion, that there *was* a basic law of existence. It is simply: 'A thing is identical to itself'. This

*A second break occurs in the manuscript here. The Narrator pleads that this section was too ephemeral to remember or too abstruse to be outlined in words; The Editor surmises that his invention had run dry—Ed.

principle explained the operation of cause and effect, I claimed. The universe being a unity, it is also identical to itself, and an effect only *appears* to follow a cause. In actuality they are part of the same thing, opposite sides of the same coin.

Once again the Knight had cause to chide me for my lack of imagination. This axiom certainly held in my own space, he conceded, but I shouldn't suppose because of that that it was a universal law. There were numerous space-times where things *were not equal to themselves*. In fact even in my own space the principle adhered only approximately, because things were in motion and motion involved a marginal blurring of self-identity. My axiom held as an absolute law only in those spaces where motion was impossible.

Unabashed, I offered my second contribution, this one concerning the maintenance of existence. There was a theory, I told him, that used an electronic analogy and likened existence to a television screen and a camera. The camera scanned the image on the screen, and fed it back to the screen's input, so maintaining the image perpetually. Thuswise existence was maintained; if the feedback from the camera to the screen should be interrupted, even for a split second, existence would vanish and could never be reconstituted.

A pre-electronic version of the theory replaces the screen and camera by two mirrors, each reflecting the image of existence into the other. It is my belief that this is the meaning of the ancient alchemical aphorism 'As above, so below' found on the Emerald Table of Hermes Trismegistus, it being imagined that the mirrors are placed one above the other. Other authorities unanimously assert that it refers to the supposed similarity between the macrocosm and the microcosm; but I consider that this, besides being of doubtful veridity, is a crude, pedestrian interpretation unworthy of the thought of the Great Master. The full text of the saying runs:-

> That which is above is like to that which is below, and that which is below is like to that which is above, to accomplish the miracles of one thing.

It has to be understood that the mirrors themselves are part of the image, of course, just as the screen and camera are part of the scanning pattern—if it is asked how this could possibly be, I would refer the enquirer to that other Alchemical symbol, the Worm Ouroboros, who is shown with his tail in his mouth, eating himself.

The Knight appeared to look on this exposition with some approval. Hermes Trismegistus, he said, was certainly a king among men of science. I asked what theories or discoveries the chess-people had on the subject; but, the Knight announced, time had run out and he could delay departure no longer. The few seconds remaining would not suffice to tell what he otherwise might have to say; but, he added, he had not so far revealed that the question of space was also intimately bound up with that of *consciousness,* and that it was towards consciousness that the chess-people were now directing their researches. He mentioned a space where an entity, as it might be a man, was forced to enjoy a double consciousness—not only was he conscious in himself, but he was also conscious at every moment of his appearance to the physical world around him, which was also conscious. The Knight invited me to ponder on what existence would be like in such a state—but his words now came in haste and he bade me goodbye.

Again I begged him to stay, just for a little while. But he turned and looked commandingly around him over the chess board. The pieces began to move and to execute their flickering dance pattern around the board. The Knight joined them, gyrating around the board like a dance master directing the others. As the invisible ship lifted away the pieces surged round the board in a circular movement as if caught in a vortex; then they were still. The Knight could no longer speak to me in his resinous, friendly voice: he was only a chiselled piece of dead wood.

I came out of my shocked reverie with a start. On the disappearance of the alien influence the pieces had reverted to their original positions, ready to resume the game. There would be no need, I thought blankly, for me to write to my partner for the details.

I pushed myself away from the table. The sweet opium

smell still hung on the air. The breeze from the garden was only marginally cooler. The far-off sun was still in the act of descending to the horizon through an elegant technicolour sky.

It was hard for me to admit that only a minute or two could have passed, when I was sure that I had been talking and listening for hours. I will never be able to know absolutely, and certainly never be able to prove, that what I say took place really did take place. I can only speak of the compelling veridity of my recollection. But whatever the truth, it has at least brought to my notice that for all our knowledge of the universe, even when we project our giant rockets into space and imagine that at last we are penetrating the basic void that holds all things, we have not even touched or suspected the immensities and the mysteries that existence contains.

SIMON

WILLIAM A. WOODROW

He woke, as animals wake, fully alert; aware but knowing nothing. A voice was whispering. "Simon," it said. "My name is Simon. Simon Adamson." It was his own voice, not as he himself heard it from within—resonant through bones—but as another would when listening. He registered the fact and lapsed into unconsciousness.

Waking again he knew that he was bound, swaddled rather, like a cocoon in foetal position. He could not tell how he knew but it was so. Knowing also that head and neck were free he tried the experiment of moving and turned his head slightly. Sensation ended at the root of the neck. Working his lips he sensed a slight vibration of the larynx.

"Simon," he said. "My name is Simon Adamson."

"Yes, that is your name." A cool voice. Feminine but not, he struggled for the image, not female. He tried again. There was a way of saying it. A word. . . . epicene. The voice came nearer: a shape on the edge of vision.

She was slim and smooth and honey coloured. Young face and honey coloured hair almost concealed by a nun-like habit. Closer. Hands too, that came to him and made some pertinent but insensible gesture at his neck. She leaned across him, not looking at him but beyond, focussing upon a spot that was past him and slightly above. Craning his neck he still saw nothing beyond the downsweep of the habit and the face. Not so much young as ageless. He felt breath on his face, honey scented and cool.

"Simon Adamson." He looked at her, striving to form a question in his mind, struggling to say it. She forestalled him.

"No. We have not names, but you may call me Nurse." She moved back. "You had an accident. Some of the workers went out and brought you in. You are safe here in the Citadel." But was it Citadel? Hospital? . . . Citadel? He tried them over on his tongue; tasting the sounds.

"Nurse?"

"You were severely hurt. Treatment is going on and will continue for six days. Daily you will receive treatment, you will recover and be restored. On the seventh day, made whole, you will go forward to the Blessing that awaits you. In saving you we have saved ourselves. You have redeemed us." For the first time, and then only for an instant, the face shone with emotion. It was an inner glow that emanated from the eyes first and then the whole being. It entered him and remained with him even after the face had resumed its normal serenity.

"Who are you?"

"I am Nurse." It was not the answer. He concentrated and strove for an appropriate collective noun but it eluded him.

"What are you?"

"We are the Remnant of the World. We remain where men have destroyed all else." Like a lesson now, parrot fashion, "all else that was no longer is. We are." Again beyond the line of vision, but returning, she held a hood with fine tremulous antennae. "This is part of the treatment."

"What is it?" Simon was suddenly scared, as a child is scared when ill and faced with inexplicable cures. Gently she fitted it to his head and leaned across him to adjust a flex. He felt her breasts against his face and again the manic moment of infantile fear.

"Mummy," he murmured. "Mummy! Will it hurt?"

He was a child again: ill in bed. The doctor had been and
He was a child again: ill in bed. The doctor had been and
buzzed. Alone in the dark and throbbing room he had cried out; then his mother was there, ample and comforting and smelling of sandalwood. He felt her breast against his face as she rocked him, murmuring nonsense sounds and comforting him until he slept.

And he slept now, comforted. The day droned on and it

the honey-coloured room.
was evening. The memories returned as he slumbered in
And the evening and the morning were the first day.

(ii)

He could move head and shoulders now and his arms were free. Propped on a couch Simon could look about him and freely turn because the intravenous drip that fed him had been transferred from neck to arm. Unswaddled now to the chest he experimented by prodding himself and tugging at his body hair. Sensation had returned but there was no sensory response from that part of his body which was still bound. The task of self-exploration absorbed him entirely so that Nurse returned unnoticed. She leaned across him to adjust the drip.

"What is that?"

"Food." She smiled. "Come Simon, you have been ill. It is time for your treatment." Nurse held out the hood with its slender antennae.

"What is that?"

"When we rescued you and brought you here you were unknown to us, but. . . . looked for. At least, there is One who is looked for. Many have come but we cannot choose the One who Shall Come. The others were false. We made mistakes that were almost fatal. We could not afford to be mistaken again." She held up the apparatus and the antennae quivered before him. "This holds your mind; your memories, thoughts, desires, even those things that you have hidden from yourself. We drained you of your being and now," pausing she smiled again, "we give you back yourself."

Simon felt a sudden surge of feeling as she spoke. Yesterday she had been Nurse, impersonal and remote. Now, glowing and honey-coloured, she was Friend. If the feeling was love, it was a love in which sex played no part. Not love, more than mere love, it was, rather, the deep affinity of like for like.

He submitted to the hood. There was a time at school he remembered. . . . .

. . . . . He was eleven and September was golden all about him. The school, where he was a new boy that day, had a garden. At break, alone and lonely, he found his way to where a groundsman was burning leaves. The scent and taste of the burning leaves seemed to inhabit him as he stood and he was drawn by the crackling flames into a timeless sense of being at one with nature. The fire was himself and he Prometheus, and both were there when the voice sounded and called him as if from a bush that burned. Then another voice and others; yelling.

"There's another . . . New boy . . . You! What's your name?" (And his own voice answering Simon) Simon. Simon . . . Simple Simon Simple Simon Simple . . ." The chanting went on and on. There was no escape. They formed a ring about him and danced. Smoke-blinded and baffled by the noise he frantically struck out at the jeering boys.

"Simple Simon Simple Simon ja. ja. ja. Simon Says Simon says Simon says". . . . "Shut up!" It was a prefect. Silence; and the boys reluctantly drew off as the bell rang for lessons. Then someone murmured "Bloody Yid" and they tittered.

The prefect was talking. "Don't take it so hard, young 'un. They do it to all new boys. It's a kind of tradition." Simon fought back tears, striving to speak. "No," he said. "It's because I'm a Jew." The prefect touched his head, casually as though in passing. "I know that. So am I." It was then that Simon felt the same glow of oneness that stayed with him and grew momentarily as the Nurse, removing his hood, casually touched his head in passing.

(iii)

Free now of all that had bound him, Simon spent time in flexing his limbs and body, discovering his entire person by sight and touch and motion. But he was still confined to his couch. What amazed him was the texture and suppleness of his skin. No longer coarse and callused, no longer showing signs of the wrinkling of age, no longer abraded and ravaged by the stresses of living in the harsh and uncompromising environment he had been used to; his skin had the softness of down and the opalescence of infancy. Even the scar tissue that was legacy of a long past appendectomy had gone.

Gently his fingers explored the spot and strayed without volition to his groin. He cried out. A cry, deadened by the unresponsive and clinical room, that turned inward upon himself and pierced his mind. There was no trace of pubic hair and his genitals were the tentative and improbable appendages of infancy. What had been done to him? The possibility of emasculation came and went, flickering back and forth in his mind like tiny tongues of flame that broke surface as flames do from a raging but subterranean fire, sucking down oxygen to feed upon.

He felt again the skin of his body; its smooth femininity, its supple ambiguousness of gender. "Nurse!" And the call re-called her to mind before she came. Her skin, like his, was smooth and downy. She (was it she at all? But was it? . . . remembering now first doubts and semantic struggles for the word . . . the right word . . . . . . epicene) was not nurse with neutral and professional hands guiding the drip—and the smooth honey-slide of hair beneath the habit, leaning over him—and the delicate breasts gentle against his face; was not Nurse? Simon clutched his own chest with a parody of ecstasy. He fondled the rudimentary nipples, followed the lean line of ribs with trembling fingers. And found relief in the unequivocal but trivial presence of hair.

"Simon." Again unnoticed Nurse had come. Simon lay back exhausted and hostile. "What is the matter?" leaning across him, making routine adjustments to the drip. Hands, hair and fine-boned features, all close enough for him to touch. Roughly he pulled her down onto the couch. Blinded by fine-spun hair, loose tumbled from the hood of her habit, suffocated almost with the honey-scent of that supple and waxlike skin, his hands groped against breasts that were firm and small but feminine. The nipples roused him. Briefly he felt her lips against his own and her tongue, like a sting, in his mouth. Then she drew back and smoothed herself and smiled.

He was stirred by her presence as a precocious boy is stirred by a beautiful woman, but the flicker of response that his loins gave to her kiss reassured him and Simon was suddenly ashamed. "I'm sorry."

She looked at him, once more the professional Nurse. "You are improving but you are not yet well. Not yet," hesitating slightly, "not yet made whole."

The curious formality of her language soothed him and he watched as she deftly replaced the empty drip bottle with another. "This one is different. It is stronger, more nourishing and it will prepare you and give you back what you feel is lost." (Once again the tingle of oneness) "You must grow slowly and," pausing, groping for the nuance, "mature in the fullness of time. And now, the treatment." She began to adjust the headpiece.

"Nurse." She paused. "Shall I be restored in every way?"

"In every way." She touched him briefly on the cheek and moved away. It was a touch that stirred him as the touch of her tongue had done and it had its pale reflection in his groin.

The images raced now and tumbled him through time. First love, poignant but fleeting; passion pure and impure; lust and love. All came and went and wove within him their contrapuntal pattern of desires.

It was like being born anew. And newborn were his memories, for the treatment had restored his mind to the moment of the accident and even that—Nurse promised him—would be revealed at the appropriate stage of treatment. There remained one doubt. One programme of memory eluded him. Something that had been connected with his work in biological sociology. Something about . . . eyes closed, mind searching and turning inward upon himself . . . he almost had it . . . it was? But no. Failing himself he looked about the room for inspiration.

Shaped like an hexagonal prism standing on end, the room was bare and walled throughout with amber coloured glass, transluscent and gleaming equally on all sides so that he found it impossible to tell which walls (if any) looked outside. There was his couch, the intravenous drip and nothing else. He could not even tell the whereabouts of the door. Fighting boredom, the surest sign of all that he was getting well, Simon tried to discover the mechanics of the place. Where was the light source; the heating system? Whence came the energy for his treatment? There were no answers. Only himself and a pulsating but immobile silence. No; not silence. After stopping his ears and then listening Simon realised that what he had taken for silence was really a ceaseless humming, so persistent that its permanency was taken for granted and passed unnoticed. A humming, a buzzing, a noise . . . some fragment of memory stirred and he strove after it. It was the link-thought but it had gone.

(iv)

Nurse came early on the penultimate day. She removed the hood, disconnected the drip and then began to wash him. It was not washing in the usual sense because she rubbed him with a small tablet—like scented wax—and groomed him afterwards by vigorous rubbing with a towel that felt like tissue; dry and papery. It was stimulating, like vibro-massage, and toned his muscles.

She performed the task disinterestedly and with great skill so that standing for the first time Simon felt nothing of the humiliating weakness and debility that usually follows a spell in bed. Standing naked before her, feeling neither embarrassment nor desire, Simon realised for the first time how tiny she was. Barely five feet tall—her head came level with his shoulder—fine boned and fragile looking; her appearance belied the strength she had used in cleansing and massaging him.

Silent still, for she had not spoken since her first perfunctory greeting, Nurse held out a robe for him to wear. It was tawny brown in colour and patterned with irregular darker shapes that were textured with a faint pile of hair. Simon put it on with Nurse's help, but she was not tall enough to adjust the neckline. On tiptoe she stretched to correct the set of the shoulders and Simon, leaning forward, put his arms about her and drew her to him. She came, neither resisting nor responding, her delicate body close to his newfound masculinity. His robe enfolded them both. She was trembling almost imperceptibly, as injured birds tremble when held, the same implicit, though alien, trust. Simon gently kissed her forehead and released her. She stayed against him for a moment and then, the bird-like tremor more pronounced, she moved away.

"We must go now."

"Go?"

"To the ante-room of the High One, where you will receive the final treatment. You will stay there until . . . until . ." She would not look at his face. "Tomorrow is the Seventh Day. Do not delay, Simon. Come."

She brought him to the door of the ante-room by a baffling route through many rooms all exactly similar to his own; and they were all empty. The humming sound persisted and even increased in intensity as they mounted from level to level. They paused at the door and, still not looking at his face, she said, "I must leave you here. Go through."

"Come with me."

"No. I cannot."

"Cannot or will not?"

"I can bring you no further. It is," she hesitated, still not looking, not raising her head, "it is . . . unlawful."

Gently he raised her head but she closed her eyes against the sight of him and he felt the tremor, the captive fluttering.

"Go forward, Simon Adamson. I shall be there at the end. Now go."

(v)

The ante-room was larger than any other room that he had seen. There were two occupants, similar in dress to the Nurse and just as smooth featured and fine boned as she was. But Nurse was unequivocally female; these two—despite an overt effeminacy—had overtones of maleness.

Without greeting him they directed Simon to the couch where he was fitted with the now familiar hood. He lay down, relaxed once more by the normality of the treatment; but this was different. This time he was given a small control box with a single button and a two-way switch. Experiment showed him that the button started and stopped the flow; the switch drove it forward or back in time. He could thus explore without restriction.

Although the imagery was still as vivid as in the early days of his treatment, Simon now retained some faculty that gave him power over thought. He could stop and start the apparatus at will, he could re-run a passage, speed up or slow down, and all without loss of definition. This self-mastery exalted him and external time lost all meaning.

He re-absorbed with all the impact of freshness, yet with the heightened awareness of foreknowledge, books he had read and music he had heard. And also the music making of his own youth, the years before a specialised technology had claimed him, long ago.

Books: *The Magic Mountain, Doktor Faustus,* Tolstoy, Chaucer, Donne. The Bible. He lingered lovingly over the Book of Job, the Song of Solomon, the apocalyptic and terrifying Daniel and Ezekiel.

And music: the formal crystalline purity of Mozart, the songs (those passionate, sad, sick songs) of Mahler, but most often the sonatas of Beethoven and the last quartets.

He came by degrees, logically, inevitably to the last journey and the arrival at the Citadel.

He sensed once more the World in the last days—his World. Even the tortured vision of Hieronymous Bosch could not have envisaged the rioting vegetation; corrupted by radioactivity, stimulated into obscenity by the polluted effluents of mankind: the jungles of flaccid flowerless plants, feeding upon death and decay, and others drawing sustenance from them.

Saprophyte and parasite created He them,
and Simon saw that it was bad.

The swamplands stretched all ways, their turbulence expelling methane and ammonia. The mingling of other gases that burst into flame and swept seething towards him. And he, cabined in a craft designed by the subterranean Institute where he had worked (in the relatively unpolluted southlands of Earth) he had returned to the scene of mankind's primal fall. Finally, through the mist and reek, he saw the Citadel. Hexagonal and faceted, like the compound eye of some huge insect, it stood secure; the last retreat of humanity in a world gone mad.

Reminded of the Nurse's words about the One who Shall Come, he wondered; who am I? The question had bothered him during impressionable adolescence. He had asked the Rabbi. Taking the control box he spun time backwards, seeking himself.

The synagogue, the Rabbi: talking but unheard. His own voice asking but not getting through. "Who am I? Who?WHO?WHO?" The Rabbi smiling, shaking his head. "No no! Not who then. What am I?" . . . The scene crumbled. The Rabbi's face melted within the dissoluti[on] into a pulsating hollow sphere. Around it swarmed uncountable numbers of minute tadpole structures, suspended and swimming in a pervading milkiness. Crossing and forever colliding they swarmed about the sphere 'til one surged forward to penetrate and be absorbed into the mass. The picture changed in his mind and Simon felt drawn upward through a maze of convoluted lines; spiralling upward, folding back upon themselves, always pulsating until the structure gathered shape and became the double helix of DNA. And through it all a voice, felt not heard, saying again and again:

"What is Man, that thou art mindful of him?"

(vi)

The two attendants woke him and cleansed him as the Nurse had done. They dressed him in another robe, similar to the last one but bolder in design and more sumptuous in texture. They also put a cap upon his head. This was round and close fitting and had two tassels that bore a resemblance to the antennae of his treatment hood, but they were merely decorative.

When he was quite ready they brought from some obscure recess in the wall a flask of the amber fluid that had been fed to him throughout his treatment. The flask was fitted with a fine tube and one of the attendants (neither had yet spoken) mimed the suggestion that he should suck up the fluid and swallow it.

It was sweet with the sweetness of honey; of honey made from flowers that Simon thought had been banished forever from the Earth. Each sip stirred memories as vivid and poignant as any that had been stimulated during the treatment: bunches of linden flowers, heavy with scent; rich and spicy gorse and broom and illimitable forests of fragrant clover—for it seemed to Simon as if he were dwarfed by the clover that soared about him—but above all, the murmurous and companionable buzzing of a million bees on summer afternoons. This above all as he drained the last drop and the flask fell from his fingers. The buzzing remained.

Simon was aware of movement in the room and he turned. The two attendants had been joined by others and l more pressed through the doorways. Each wall had an entrance and through each entrance, jostling and flurrying came a multitude of almost exact copies of those he had already met. Some were larger, almost as large as he, and they had the heavier features of the mute males who had attended him, but they were outnumbered many to one by slender and delicate bodies and placid features that were a many times multiplied copy of the Nurse. The buzzing increased in pitch and intensity as they swarmed towards him, and always there were more pushing and jostling at the doors.

Simon backed away until he was against the only remaining intact wall. Still they came. The foremost ones were almost touching him. Their clothes brushed his, their bodies blundered against him as the pressure of the masses increased. They seemed to be performing some unfathomable dance; hands waving, bodies swaying, back and forth, retreating and advancing with each wave coming closer and each time the pressure of their bodies greater against himself.

He could no longer move and still they packed in through open doors. They writhed and swarmed about him, pressing him backwards against the wall. The buzzing in his ears increased, he gasped for air—the heavy scented and fragrant air compounded of the many mingled breaths. With a heave he tried to force them back and his feet left the floor. Carried by the pressure against him, the wall at his back tore down and he was flung into the room beyond.

(vii)

He was alone. No one had followed him through and Simon saw with astonishment that they were actually sealing the rent in the wall, shutting themselves out. He was alone and the buzzing had dropped to its normal level.

It was the smell that first attracted him. An unplaceable but highly evocative scent; the odour of a woman in love. It roused him, stirred his body, urged his sex. He turned towards the room.

And there she was.

Tall, tall as himself, and female. Not with the delicate doubtful femaleness of the Nurse but fully formed and fully aware too of the physical perfection that invited him. (But it was the smell.) Her hair, honey coloured and unhampered by any hood, hung almost to her waist. It stirred slightly as she moved and her paper-thin garment parted to receive him. The smell. Compound of all the spices he had tasted earlier but borne upon an odour as ancient as life itself: the smell of desire; the smell that draws male moth to female across a dozen miles; that stirs the dog to chase bitches across a score of improbable obstacles, or the tomcat to make terrible the night with noise. There was nothing of love in it; only desire.

He came to her and took her with passion and ritual and seemed again to sense the spiralling upwards, the convolutions of the double helix. And at the last pulsating moment the hollow sphere and the all pervading milkiness . . . "What is Man?"

(viii)

The buzzing, growing now to an intensity, to a frenzy of sound. Across the long ages there came to him the lost programme of memory. His own work; his own book. (The buzzing was upon him.) He struggled to recall (a sharp sting at the neck). Mind and memory blurred as he grasped the hidden text . . .

"Following copulation the drone is slaughtered by the guardians of the Queen."

THE FIRST OF TWO RAPED PROSPECTS

MAREK OBTULOWICZ

This is the man who awakened by that which is at once irrelevant neither slumps nor sighs (as he would have me do yesterday, or on any day before). Nor is he curling up in the hope of a way back to his short-measured dreams, but, having had the idea, he becomes obsessed with the idea. Gradually. To slither out naked from between his sheets and blankets; and he's creeping towards the window.

There's a man. There's an idea. And all else is the variable in locale. A March morning at three o'clock when it's still night—the norm—a bedroom; although this man has been known to sleep in kitchens and in the cupboards under stairs.

I've put a wicker laundry basket in the room and beside that a wheel-backed chair because the man will kick either one or the other (it's too dark for me to see which). He'll hack his toe-nail. And cursing, but not very loudly, he'll hop; in a single step the stealthy follow-up limp. In every sense clandestine as the cracked ceiling is uneven and bent on old-aged secrets. Cottage low, too low and without the space for a hanging.

Old women wear black and kneel on the worn stone flags of ancient cathederals. They have greyed hair which wisps through black lace veils and tarnishes in stained-glass contours. Plaited, tied to doom-beads they have fingers that are gnarled, clenched together and a warp to the unseen weft of metaphors. This is the man's idea—like the tremors in those hands—he thinks to capture Index.

Index?

The Good Agency, which keeps on record extensive and well documented files, will vouch for no mention of this word. Transcripts of the tapes show the man throughout referred to whatever has gone amiss as *him*. (Index has left. Would the man but stop listening—his stumble woke nobody—and look from the window to make out the shapes of paths and bramble bushes whose names he never learned. The shadows of bins and the calor-gas tank glinting white. No Index. No sign, no hint of anything. Would he then report *him* missing. Lost. Would he consider the agencies? and so prepare to commit suicide as is befitting? Not this man. Being possessed by the idea, and self-assuaded of his imminent success, he believes himself to be up early enough to catch Index, to discover the creature in its weakness at rest.) While it's the author who feels a need to introduce proper nouns, the choice no doubt arbitrary but at the same time granting him due inventiveness. After all, captivated by the plot of the story, he allows himself the involvement and opts for its writing, wanting only what the narration must teach.

I must disapprove. But later.

The Agency. The plot. Together they conspire to restrict their author, to quickly make defunct his reality. The Good Agency has misgivings about being questioned and no longer accepted without explanation or justification of its workings. Likewise the plot needs to remain untouched, endless and uninterpreted. Then there's a man who has an idea. And I'm none of these. Apart physically? or psychologically a part? The railway hoarding which reads in opposition to the text, an anti-finish to this fiction. What romantic notions I have of myself! I'm the man's wife? maybe his mistress? lying tucked in a bed surrounded by the slowly vanishing pressure of his warmth, and devising plans, scheming to get a new pair of shoes out of the old goat. Perhaps a daughter or son telling the man that I've become a Christian, hearing the father cry:

—Jesus Christ! my child! Why? My dear child, why in heavens why?

More probably I'm Index. Above all nothing but speculation. And sometimes in sequence.

It's seventy-five minutes past three, (by agreement with the government which, revelling in the easy public reception given decimalisation, now exhausts a logical conclusion. Everything's a multiple of ten. There are a hundred minutes to the hour, ten hours in a day. There are ten days per week and ten weeks in the month. Ten months . . . and so on. Spring, or the harvest, the tides . . . these are outmoded forms of nomenclature. Farmers sow by numbers. And people ask:

—Is this not just a preliminary step towards the eventual binary computation take-over? Surely we're only two—the male and the female.

And much of many a debate centres on the circle. Should it have 500 or 1,000 degrees of arc? Someone unwisely spoke of the moon. But it stays, keeps the twenty-eight day cycle, readily accommodated within a base ten system . . . bearing in mind four seven-sided 50 new penny pieces.) or 9 a.m. on another scale.

The man is dressed. He is drinking coffee from an earthenware mug and sitting in the library. He's confident that Index will be trapped before midday.

—Did you hear?

—Yes . . .

—Shocking business.

—Tragic . . . I find it so hard to believe.

—Yes, I know what you mean. It's as if I expect someone to come over and tell me that it's all been a mistake, an error.

—Do you? That's strange 'cause I keep saying to myself—communications have got to be bad out there, in the styx, eh? someone's slipped up. Got the wrong name or something.

—Perhaps. Even so . . . I would never had credited him capable . . .

—To take his own life you mean? no.

—To think I saw his wife on the very day. On a spree in the city . . . a weekend trip, to buy some shoes I believe she said. She was with her sister and the child.

—Yes, I know that trio. . . . and incidentally, just by the way you understand, eh? I hear say they're not sisters at all, that the other one lives with them as a . . . well . . . a comforter, if you like.

Chatted two distinguished-looking and well-dined friends, having their glasses often re-filled with an excellent brandy. But neither was a poet, so I left off my eavesdropping and went home to revise certain popular concepts of sequence.

The man came out of the front door and walked to the side of the house. He stood for a while peering at the top floor windows. Then he stepped back, off the path, as if hoping to see into the bedroom, and a second time that morning almost fell over something.

It was the chain. Heavy and rusted. And with iron links the size of pullet eggs. A chain worn by Index, and in which he bound himself to mock the man. Difficult days when he would bring to brood the irony of his services; a self-whipped pilgrim laughing; a jailer ever-alert to pantomime the man's self-imposed slavery. (Crap! Index merely preferred a weighty and more solid style of jewelry. He was attached to a quarter-mile of chain and how, if not by coiling it about himself, would he hump it from place to place?)

At first the man looked one way along the length of the chain and then the other. And back. He was undecided. Uncertain which way to follow. At last he turned and set off up the hill behind the cottage. He moved awkwardly. The bank was very steep, sheer. Often he stumbled, crawling on all fours and grabbing after branches. His hands were scratched, his knees bruised. The brambles and briars lashed at his face and at his calves, but he tried not to notice, nor to care, wishing instead that he knew what they were all called. It was at once important, (to know which of the bushes flowered, which gave out edible berries or grew leaves and roots that might be cooked). A keen and uncomfortable awareness of his ignorance.

Above the roof line, on a level with the chimney pots,

the slope evened out into a large plateau where thicket fences penned sheep pastures and marked lands for crop rotation. And a lamb bleating. The chain lying between serried turnips, turning, alongside the ditch, and under a rope-bound gate. Then diagonally across a ploughed field. And the man walking beside it, over the newly furrowed clods, his shoes becoming heavier collecting more and more soft mud sticking to the soles. Dough treading—he thought, and smiled; surprised but pleased to be enjoying the soil's richness, a red loam. And the east wind blowing hard.

Roughly in the middle of this lea, the man found the chain anchored to the ground, a wooded clout shot through an end link. He gave the chain a sharp tug, once. The peg jerked out of the earth.

—You little bastard—he mumbled: —You little bastard! But I've got you now.

And he pushed the stake back into its hole.

Straightening up, swinging round, the feeling of being watched. He narrowed his eyes and scanned the hedgerows. But he saw no one.

The man retraced his steps. Cleaning clay from his boots on the lowest rung of the gate, then, swede in hand, half-sliding, half-running down the bank and past the spot where he had discovered the chain, past the kitchen windows, (a woman was waving from inside, yelling something that he couldn't hear) and onto the road where the chain led towards the village.

Some hundred yards further along, over the rise, the road crossed a brook. And the chain disappeared under the bridge, but it didn't come out on the other side. The man chuckled:

—So?

And lying down on the tarmac, he leaned over the water, dangling the turnip bait for whatever was hiding under the bridge.

His arm began to ache.

—Fuck you then!—he cried, jumping up and into the stream. He peered through the tunnel. It was empty. He climbed from the brook and ran across the road. He pulled at the chain. It came easily, and unattached. The link severed. The man stared, the lines on his face alternately smoothed, creased. He laughed. Oddly. All of a sudden letting go of the chain as if he'd held something repulsive. He wiped his palm down his lapel.

He drove his wife, the other woman and the child to Gloucester. He bought tickets for a London train (change at Swindon) and handing them to the women, as well as lots of money, said:

—Stay at least two if not three days. Buy what you will, clothes and shoes, see a show. It'll pass . . . sooner or later.

Neither understood him. But both eagerly left; his wife thinking about her lover and of being alone, of the shows; his mistress dreaming of new shoes, of the hotel room, of her daughter's would-be nagging in the shops. While unperturbed, the child played with her button-eyed teddy bear, talking to him, saying:

—Nex! Bad Nex?

The man went to the nearest supermarket where he started to fill a wire-cage barrow with groceries and provisions. Things selected at random, tins scooped off the shelves by the armful. Hungry, he picked up a pork pie. Peeled away the cellophane wrapping and ostentatiously nibbled at the pastry. He smiled and winked at the superintendants who stared at him, each in a white, name-tagged smock, ready to reproach such a nonchalant manner. But the sight of the muchladen cart made them grin. Foolish grins. And a teenage cashier called out *bon appetit*! (her accent pure).

He finished the pie.

Now he chose carefully, considering the value or need in buying a product, turning the package over in his hands and studying the price. Perhaps sure that the carton would at any minute speak fluent and ample computer-voice reasons why it should be bought. And by him. Gradually he was making his way back to the Spices Counter (this being his fourth or fifth lap of the store). There he picked out a plastic shaker of nutmeg and another of ginger, the two seasonings with which he never flavoured food, and which he disliked. They smelled of soap.

Taking the tube of ginger (ostensibly to examine the label) he pushed it into his trouser pocket. He also tried to steal the nutmeg, but this slipped from his fingers and rolled along the floor. He scurried after it. And caught it. And squatting, he shoved it in under his belt.

The man resumed a circuit of the aisles, but now unloading his goods, returning them to their allotted stacks. The trolley unpacked, he steered it back to the wire-cage train by the entrance and (digging at a piece of pie crust between his teeth) marched through the check-out alley.

He got into his car and drove very fast. Miles across country, to scatter nutmeg and ginger grounds, he shot along the lanes. At a loss. A compulsion to keep steady the wheel, faster, to hold straight on the bends. The next bend . . . the next? . . . etc.

And home.

The room darkens; but he switches on no lights. He waits.

There is a knock at the door. The man clambers laboriously from his armchair to answer it, and says, "Hello."

"Good evening, I represent the Agency."

"O yes. WHAT!"

"The Good Agency, you sent for me, didn't you?"

"Yes yes, but . . ."

"But? O I see . . . you expected a man, well if it bothers you I can find someone else to come, mind you I don't guarantee anybody for tonight."

"No no please, please come in."

AAAGH! I have to, I can't hold off any longer. I would have screamed when I first saw her had not an author clamped his hand over my mouth. I simply had not foreseen a girl and that, without tasks, aids the plot to advantage.

Next to the fireplace the man turns on a single-bulb fixture. He slumps back into his armchair.

There are charred logs in the grate. The ashes unswept, spilled over the fender.

The girl slips a leather strap from her shoulder and puts her carrying-case on the coffee table. She snaps open the lid and drawing out an electric cable, asks, "Where do I plug in?"

The man points at the socket.

What a way to treat a visitor! She's obviously young and beautiful. Had I only known, (I'm getting an erection already) I should have furnished the room altogether differently. A huge king-size bed standing with me in it and for her to fall into as soon as she stepped through the door. And chilled wine in a bucket, an array of snacks and delicacies on a silver tray, but never this arrangement: a coffee table; a couch; an armchair. And this cumbrous 17th century chest. It's a wonder that the thing is still in one piece, though the cracks make useful spy-holes—for where else could I hide both the author and myself to witness this rendezvous. The author, poor fool, has bound the keys of his typewriter in Elastoplast. No noise. Shh! No noise!

The tape recorder runs. The girl sits in front of the man. There's a microphone between them.

"Whenever you're ready," she says. And smiles.

"Yes of course . . . well . . . hagh! Yes. Well, what do I say? Gone? I've been left, forsaken perhaps? How do I begin? I must act to make whole the change because I can't imagine what it was like before, what a hell it's going to be. Now in a void I've no idea where it began . . . but there were days . . . life when . . ."

So he prattles on. Myths reborn, vague as this his hypnagogic poem, (once that too was fine: once I kept a closer watch) to remember the lonely child who years ago saw Index for the first time. Saw no more than an eye. But here digressing with lead-in backdrops of poverty, of mother's struggles to supplement a father's meagre income by stitching brand-tags into shirt collars. And of the sewing machine with yarns, frayed labels strewn over the surface.

He pauses. Peers at the unlit timbers as if to recall evenings seen pass in flames. Then slowly he tells of waking during the night, alone. And an eye gleaming from the corner where the sewing machine had stood. (But the street lamp shining outside and the polished metal plaque stamped with the 'Singer' trade mark are aptly forgotten details.) He isn't afraid. Warm, secure under covers. Again to fall silent.

Spools rotate. The girl glances at them. She recrosses her legs. A static. Movement, sounds to excite me ever further. Still to do nothing? (How vital is it to report speeches? when the girl and the man might better stare at each other. Without words or signs lust after one another until tension reaches a climax. They attack. Shred clothes one from the other's body in an urgent rape of admiration and pity for each other. Soon.)

He pinches the bridge of his nose, pressing down hard on his eyelids and freeing rings of colour. He doesn't look at the girl. Unseen greys in her eyes. There is no blemish on her pale skin. Will he never touch the sheen of her long hair? Full, bell brown. And a crooked tooth, the single flaw that's beauty.

I'm getting cramp, my knees up against the small of the author's back, and no way to stretch.

I want the woman's seduction. Is she a virgin? A thought? sanguine, overpowering as death's scent in the feel of her breasts, sensitive beneath her cotton blouse. Nipples exacting a rubbery firmness between my fingers and thumb. Every handful of flesh hardly a designed guess, but rather stroked to account (were it not for the restraint of the author, ever faithful to the dictated word).

Speaking more, to remember more, more to regret. Passage after passage.

"At this period I refused to acknowledge him and made my intentions plain with rebuffs, and then later a complete ostracism. Other issues made far greater demands and I paid him no heed, or so I believed, but I was quickly to recognise that he still had control, that he would never leave me. Now today . . ."

Is there much more? Does she listen? Looking at any object in the room. Does she see? A poker; a toasting-fork; an unopened envelope on the mantelshelf. I would help her prepare for what's to come, but she's had training. The phlegmatic posture, the smile distant, pleasing. And the typewriter clomp-a clack-clomp.

The man is getting up from his chair. He steps over to the window. A quiet dark, quite night.

"Is that it?" asks the agent.

"No." A whisper. "No, recently things began going wrong you see, he appeared shackled and tied in chains . . . a costume he's since worn frequently. And, and this morning I decided I could take him prisoner. I honestly thought that I could put him in a cage, ha, that's funny you know. He fled of course, and maybe because he feared . . . no . . . it's for me to do something, something in return. It's all over."

A morning before daybreak and a woman is leaving her husband's bed. She tiptoes towards the windows. The man grunts, stirs and sleeps on. His wife looks out on a garden where the faded moon glints along the edge of a large steel cylinder, a fuel supply for the central heating.

If he's going to do anything stupid—she thinks—it won't be that way, the cooker's electric.

Her lover (she who joined the household as an au pair from France, later became the man's mistress and finally his wife's, though sister in name) is walking the path back from the main road. She has fetched a car that'll take her and her daughter and her mate to Gloucester. From there they must travel by train to London—changing at Swindon.

Everybody is readied for a smooth departure, the suitcases packed, the baby wrapped in a shawl without waking, a thermos and blankets for the journey. The boot is loaded. In silence. They drive away.

Am I just—the wife's thinking—in doing this? Has he not become unbearable . . . conceited and selfish? Does he not pervert the child with his wild talk of a love for . . . for something intangible? with his renewed outbursts of religious fervour. Why often he's said that there's comfort in a sensible death and only the other day he stormed into the house shouting, "I have it! I have it! The Fifteenth Station of the Cross!" It's high time for change. It's he who's driving us to Gloucester.

And all of a sudden she insists on going back to speak with him. But when they return to the cottage he's nowhere to be found. Then she sees him rush by the kitchen window and waves, but he takes no notice. He hasn't even read her goodbye letter on the mantelpiece. Already regretting the delay her sentimental folly has caused she asks her lover to drive off once again. For good.

The man spoke no more. The agent looked up.

"How d'you propose it should be done?" she asked.

"Pills, I think."

"Isn't that too long . . . and dull?"

"Well, can I leave it up to you?"

"Of course. Is there anything else, anything I might personally do for you? something special?"

I bite my tongue. Blood seeps from the corners of my mouth. Menstrual.

"No, no thank you."

"Very well, if that's it?" And she paused, and shut off the machine. Then she asked to be shown to the bathroom.

"This way," said the man.

She followed him from the room and up the stairs bringing the sealed polythene pouch which she'd taken out of her case. In the bathroom she showed him the small black cube, holding it in her palm. There was a tiny white circle on one face, and on the opposite, two wire prongs.

"You've probably seen some of these before," she suggested, "but I have to explain how it works. The pins I shall clip here between your eyes. Even then it can be removed by surgery, though you must know of the consequences?"

"An attempted—"
"Punishable under law."
The man nodded.
"When you're ready," the girl continued, "you'll press the white button which in turn does two things. First, an immediate transmission break informing Head Office that my assignment is completed—they'll send someone round. Secondly, the device, as we call it, will become fixed to your skull, permanently. After that it can't be removed unless . . ."
"Yes I know."
"Good, shall we begin?"
Again the man nodded.
The girl set the cube in place on the man's nose and a thin trickle of blood ran down to his nostrils. Onto his lip. She filled the washbowl with steaming water and with a cut-throat razor (also from her kitbag) cleanly slit both her wrists. She plunged them into the basin. The man watched.
The water reddened. The man couldn't watch any longer. He left her.
He paced along the hall, and back, and back, now and then touching the cube.
He needed a piss.
A thud.
He pushed the button with his forefinger.
Downstairs he sat in his armchair. Crossed his legs. Waiting for the Good Agency's undertakers who didn't seem to be coming.
In the bathroom there is a corpse. The man saw it when he went in to relieve himself (a moment ago), when his stomach muscles knotted, bending him double. He almost retched. When his spine arched him up and lurched a last orgasm from his body. Helpless.
Nothing can be done. To aid a marked entity is an offense. And the slightest sign of recognition a crime.

There's a man. He committed suicide; (And the author resigns—extinguished); a murderer condemned to his own resources, on a diet of gingered bread and watered eggnog, in solitary. Deaths to reconciliate the want to create.
Bullshit!
Further histrionics must only hasten ennui for I feel no

more compassion, though for a second, back in the supermarket . . .

There is the man who kills (because his wife and his mistress—who are leaving him—are lovers—who are lovers—are leaving him) himself, (murdering one or other as the unexpected allows him the opportunity in the bathroom) and taking (the fears he has for his daughter's welfare) his own life because he's haunted by pictures of rosaries, of frayed lace and the money mothers squander on eye make-up. Suicide because of his vying sexual desire; (Whenever a woman consents, he mounts her from the rear—not necessarily an anal penetration, but like an animal. Hands kneading and plying, up along the thighs to tug, to tweak at pubic hair and groping be surprised to find no prick. The dismay! Fingers rushing to the breasts make certain that he's with a woman. Not with a boy . . .o Index o! . . . as was his mind.) because to remain impassive etc. renders change unrealised etc.; because to contain a demand etc. requires effort etc.; because etc.

Are these motives sufficient? And:

. . . the plot, limits unexpressed, is laughing.

Yet what of it? None of this concerns me.

The Good Agency charges an appropriate fee which covers the costs of its representative's funeral. I have rid myself of a failing poet. Now I seek out a blacksmith or perhaps a locksmith who would loose the steel collar from around my neck.

THOMAS M. DISCH

334

PART I: LIES

1. The Teevee (2021)

Mrs. Hanson liked to watch television best when there was someone else in the room to watch with her, though Shrimp if the program was something she was serious about—and you never knew from one day to the next what that might be—would get so annoyed with her mother's comments that Mrs. Hanson usually went off into the kitchen and let Shrimp have the teevee to herself, or else to her own bedroom if Boz hadn't taken it over for his erotic activities. For Boz was engaged to the girl at the other end of the corridor, and since the poor boy had nowhere in the apartment that was privately his own except one drawer of the dresser they'd found in Miss Shore's room it seemed the least she could do to let him have the bedroom when she or Shrimp weren't using it.

With Boz when he wasn't taken up with l'amour, and with Lottie when she wasn't flying too high for the dots to make a picture, she liked to watch the soaps. *As the World Turns. Terminal Clinic. The Experience of Life.* She knew all the ins and outs of the various tragedies, but life in her own experience was much simpler: life was a pastime. Not a game, for that would have implied that some won and others lost, and she was seldom conscious of any sensations so vivid or threatening. It was like the afternoons of Monopoly with her brothers when she was a girl: long after her hotels, her houses, her deeds, and her cash were gone, they would let her keep moving her little lead battleship around the board, collecting her $200, falling on Chance and Community Chest, going to Jail and shaking her way out. She never won but she couldn't lose. She just went round and round. Life.

But better than watching with her own children she liked to watch along with Amparo and Mickey. With Mickey most of all, since Amparo was already beginning to feel superior to the programs Mrs. Hanson liked best—the early cartoons and the puppets at five-fifteen. She couldn't have said why. It wasn't just that she took a superior sort of pleasure in Mickey's reactions, since Mickey's reactions were seldom very visible. Already at age 5 he could be as interior as his mother. Hiding inside the bathtub for hours at a time, then doing a complete U-turn and pissing his pants with excitement. No, she honestly enjoyed the shows for what they were—the hungry predators and their lucky prey, the good-natured dynamite, the bouncing rocks, the falling trees, the shrieks and pratfalls, the lovely obviousness of everything. She wasn't stupid, but she did love to see someone tiptoeing along and then out of nowhere: Slam! Bang! something immense would come crashing down on the Monopoly board, scattering the pieces beyond recovery. "Pow!" Mrs. Hanson would say, and Mickey would shoot back, "Ding-Dong!" and collapse into giggles. For some reason "Ding-Dong!" was the funniest notion in the world.

"Pow!"

"Ding-Dong!"

And they'd break up.

2. A & P (2021)

It was the best time she could remember in how long, though it seemed a pity none of it was real—the rows and stacks and pyramids of cans, the lovely boxes of detergents and breakfast food—a whole aisle almost of each!—the dairy shelf, and all the meat, in all its varieties. The meat was the hardest to believe. Candy, and more candy, and at the end of the candy a mountain of tobacco cigarettes. Bread. Some of the brands were still familiar, but she passed by these and put a loaf of Wonder Bread in the shopping cart. It was half full. Juan pushed the cart on ahead, moving to the self-heard melodies that hung like a mist in the museum's air. He rounded a corner toward the vegetables, but Lottie stayed where she was, pretending to study the wrapper of a second loaf. She closed her eyes, trying to separate this moment from its place in the chain of all moments so that she'd always have it, like a pocketful of pebbles from a country road. She grappled details from their context—the nameless song, the spongy give of the bread (forgetting for the moment that it wasn't bread), the waxiness of the paper, the chiming of the registers at the checkout counters. There were voices and footsteps too, but there are always voices and footsteps, so she had no use for these. The real magic, which couldn't be laid hold of, was simply that Juan was happy and interested and willing to spend perhaps the whole day with her.

The trouble was that when you tried this hard to stop the flow it ran through your fingers and you were left squeezing air. She would get soggy and say the wrong thing. Juan would flare up and leave her, like the last time, staring at some insane cloverleaf miles from anywhere. So she put the so-called bread back and made herself available, as Shrimp was always saying she didn't, to the sunshine of here and now and to Juan, who was by the vegetables, playing with a carrot.

"I'd swear it's a carrot," he said.

"But it isn't, you know. If it were a carrot you could eat it, and it wouldn't be art."

(At the entrance, while they were waiting for a cart, a voice had told them what they were going to see and how to appreciate it. There were facts about the different companies who'd cooperated, facts about some of the more unusual products such as laundry starch, and what it would have cost the average person shopping for a week's groceries in terms of present-day money. Then the voice warned that it was all fake—the cans, the boxes, the bottles, the beautiful steaks, everything, no matter how realistic it might look, all just imitations. Finally, if you were still thinking of lifting something just for a souvenir, it explained the alarm system, which worked chemically.)

"Feel it," he said.

It felt exactly like a carrot, not that fresh, but edible.

"But it's plastic or something," she insisted, loyal to the Met's tape.

"It's a carrot, bet you a dollar. It feels like a carrot, it smells like a carrot—" He took it back, looked at it, bit into it. It crunched. "It *is* a carrot."

There was a general sense of letdown among the people who'd been watching, of reality having intruded where it didn't belong.

A guard came and told them they'd have to leave. They wouldn't even be allowed to take the items they'd already chosen through one of the check-out counters. Juan got obstreperous and demanded his money back.

"Where's the manager of this store?" he shouted. Juan, the born entertainer. "I want to talk to the manager." At last to get rid of him they refunded the price of both tickets.

Lottie had been wretched through the whole scene, but even at the bar under the airfield afterwards she didn't bother to contradict his version. Juan was right, the guard was a son of a bitch, the museum deserved to be bombed.

He reached into his jacket pocket and took out the carrot. "Is it a carrot," he wanted to know, "or is it a carrot?"

Dutifully she set down her beer and took a bite. It tasted like plastic.

3. The White Uniform (2021)

Shrimp tried to focus on the music—music was the major source of meaning in her life—but she could only think of January. January's face and her thick hands, the pink palms roughened with calluses. January's neck, the tense muscles slowly melting beneath the pressure of Shrimp's fingers. Or, in the opposite direction: January's heavy thighs pressing against the tank of a bike, bare black flesh, bare black metal, its dizzying sound as it idled, waiting for the light, and then before it had gone quite to green its roar as it went tearing down the freeway on the way to. . . . What would be a suitable destination? Alabama? Spokane? South St. Paul?

Or this: January in a nurse's uniform—brisk, crinkly, blinding white. Shrimp would be *inside* the ambulance. The little white cap rubbing against the low ceiling. She would offer her the soft flesh of her inner arm. The dark fingers searching for a vein. A little daub of alcohol, a moment's chill, the hypodermic, and January smiling—"I know this hurts." Shrimp wanted to swoon at that point. Swoon.

She took out the plugs and let the music wind on, unheard, inside the little plastic case, for a car had left the street and pulled up to the little red charger. January lumbered out from the station, took the man's card, and stuck it in the credit slot, which replied, "Ding." She worked like a model in a shop window, never pausing, never lifting her eyes, off in her own universe, though Shrimp knew that she knew that she was here, on this bench, looking at her, longing for her, swooning.

Look at me! she thought at January fiercely. Make me exist!

But the steady flow of cars and trucks and buses and bikes between them dispersed the thought-message as though it were smoke. Perhaps some driver a dozen yards past the station would glance up with momentary panic, or a woman riding the 17 bus home from work would wonder what had reminded her of some boy she had thought she had loved twenty years before.

Three days.

And each day returning from this vigil, Shrimp would pass in front of a drab shop with a painted sign, MYERS' UNIFORMS & BADGES. In the window a dusty mustached policeman from another town (the sprinkles on his jacket were wrong for New York) brandished, in a diffident way, a wooden billy club. Handcuffs and cannisters dangled from his black gunbelt. Touching the policeman, yet seeming not to notice, a fireman decked out in bright yellow rubber striped with black (another out-of-towner) smiled through the streaked glass at, in the opposite window, a tall black girl in a nurse's white uniform. Shrimp would walk past slowly and on as far as the traffic light, then like a boat when its engine conks out and it can no longer fight against the current she would drift back to the window, the white uniform.

The third day she went inside. A bell clanked. The salesclerk asked could he help her.

"I'd like—" She cleared her throat. "—a uniform. For a nurse."

He lifted a slim yellow tape measure off a stack of visored caps. "You'd be. . . . a twelve?"

"It's not—Actually, it isn't for me. For a friend. I said that since I'd be passing by here. . . ."

"What hospital would she be with? Each hospital has its own little requirements, you know."

Shrimp looked up in his young-old face. A white shirt, the collar too tight. A black tie with a small, crisp knot. He seemed, in the same indefinite way as the mannikins in the windows, to be in uniform.

"Not a hospital. A clinic. A private clinic. She can wear . . . whatever she likes."

"Good, good. And what size is she, your friend?"

"A large size. Eighteen? And tall."

"Well, let me show you what we have." And he led Shrimp, enraptured, into the farther twilight of the shop.

4. January (2021)

She'd met Shrimp at one of the open sessions of The Asylum, where having come to recruit she'd found herself, in the most shameful way, recruited—to the point of tears and, beyond tears, of confessions. All of which January reported faithfully at the next meeting of the cell. There were four cell members besides herself, all in their twenties, all very serious, though none were intellectuals or even college dropouts: Jerry and Lee Lighthall, Ada Miller, and Graham X. Graham was the link upward to the organization but not otherwise "leader" since one thing they were against was pyramidal structures.

Lee, who was fat and black and liked to talk, said what they were all thinking, that having emotions and showing them was a completely healthy direction. "Unless you said something about us?"

"No. It was more just sexual things. Or personal."

"Then I don't see why you brought it up here."

"Maybe if you told us something more about it, Jan," Graham suggested, in Graham's gentle way.

"Well, what they do at The Asylum—"

"We've all been to The Asylum, honey."

"Stop being a fucking bully, Lee," his wife said.

"Lee's right, though—I'm taking up all our time. Anyhow I was there early, sort of sizing them up as they came in, and I could tell the minute this one arrived—her name is Shrimp Hanson—that she wasn't one of the regulars. I think she noticed me right away too. Anyhow we started off in the same group, breathing and holding hands and all that." Ordinarily January would have firmed up a narrative of this length with some obscenities, but any resemblance to bluster now would only have made her feel sillier than she did. "Then she started massaging my neck, I don't know, in a particular way. And I started crying. For no reason at all I started crying."

"Were you up on anything?" Ada asked.

January, who was stricter than any of them on that score (she didn't even drink Koffee), could legitimately bridle. "Yeah, on your vibrator!"

"Now, Jan," said Graham.

"But *she* was up," she went on, "very much up. Meanwhile the regulars were swarming around us like a pack of vampires. That's what most of them come there for, the sludge and the blood.

"That kind of thing," Lee echoed, supportively.

January braced herself and took a deep breath. "About my parents I explained about their being Republicans, which is all right of course, but I said that I could never relate sexual feelings with love because of their both being men. It doesn't sound like much now. And about being lonely I said—" She shrugged, but also she closed her eyes. "—that I was lonely. That everyone was lonely. Then I started crying again."

"You covered a lot of ground."

She opened her eyes. No one seemed to be angry with her, though they might have taken the last thing she'd said as an accusation. "We were at it most of the fucking night."

"You still haven't told us anything about her," Ada observed.

"Her name is Shrimp Hanson. She said she's thirty, but I'd say thirty-four, or older even. Lives somewhere on East 11th, I've got it written down, with a mother and I can't remember how many more. A *family*." This was, at root, exactly what the organization was most against. Authoritarian political structures only exist because people are conditioned by authoritarian family structures. "And no job, just her allowance."

"White?" Jerry asked. Being the only non-black in the group, it was diplomatic for her to be the one to ask.

"As fucking snow."

"Political?"

"Not a bit. But I think she could be guided to it. Or on second thought—"

"How do you *feel* about her now?" Graham asked.

He obviously thought she was in love. Was she?

Possibly. But just as possibly not. Shrimp had reduced her to tears; she wanted to pay her back in kind. What were feelings anyhow? Words floating through your head, or hormones in some gland. "I don't know what I feel."

"What is it you want us to tell you then?" Lee asked. "Whether you should see her again? Or whether you're in love? Or if you should be? Lordie, girl!" This, with a heave of all that goodnatured fat. "Go ahead. Have fun. Fuck yourself silly or cry your heart out, whatever you like. No reason not to. Just remember, if you do fall in love—keep it in a separate compartment."

They all agreed that that was the best advice, and from her own sense of being defluttered she knew it was what she'd wanted to be told. Now they were free to go on to basics—quotas and drops and the reasons why the Revolution, though so long delayed, was the next inevitable step. Then they left the benches and for an hour just enjoyed themselves. You would never have thought, to look at them, that they were any different from any other five people on the roller rink.

5. Richard M. Williken (2024)

They would sit together in the darkroom, officially the bedroom of his son, Richard M. Williken, Jr. Richard Jr. existed for the sake of various files in offices about the city, though upon need a boy answering to the name could be got on loan from his wife's cousin. Without their imaginary son the Willikens could never have held on to a two-bedroom apartment now that their real children had left home.

They might listen to whatever tapes were being copied, usually since they were his speciality to Alkan or Gottschalk or Boagni. The music was the ostensible reason, among other ostensible reasons such as friendship, that she hung around. He would smoke, or doodle, or watch the second hand simplify another day. His ostensible reason was that he was working, and in the sense that he was copying tapes and taking messages and sometimes renting out, for next to nothing an hour, his fictitious son's bed, he was working. But in the sense that counted he was not.

The phone would ring. Williken would pick it up and say, "One-five, five-six." Shrimp would wrap herself in her thin arms and watch him until by the lowering of his eyes she knew the call wasn't from Seattle.

When the lack of some kind of mutual acknowledgement became too raw they would have pleasant little debates about Art. Art: Shrimp loved the word (it was right up there with "epithesis", "mystic", and "Tiffany"), and poor Williken couldn't leave it alone. Despite that they tried never to descend to the level of honest complaint, their separate, secret unhappiness would find ways to poke up their heads into the long silences or to become, with a bit of camouflage, the real subjects of the little debates, as when Williken, too worn out to be anything but serious, had announced: "Art? Art's just the opposite, trueheart. It's patchwork. It's bits and pieces. What you think is all flow and force—"

"—and fun," she added.

"—are an illusion. But the artist can't share it. He knows better."

"The way prostitutes aren't supposed ever to have orgasms? I talked to a prostitute once, mentioning no names, who said she had orgasms all the time."

"It doesn't sound very professional. When an artist is being entertained, his work suffers."

"Yes, yes, that's certainly true," brushing the idea from her lap like crumbs, "for *you*. But I should think that for someone like—" She gestured toward the machinery, the four slowly revolving mandalas of "From Sea to Shining Sea." "—John Herbert MacDowell, for instance. For him it must be like being in love. Except that instead of loving one person, *his* love spreads out in every direction."

Williken made a face. "I'll agree that art is like love. But that doesn't contradict what I said before. It's all patchwork and patience, art and love both."

"And passion? Doesn't that come in at all?"

"Only for the very young." Charitably he left it for her to decide if that shoe fit.

This went on, off, and on for the better part of a month, and in all that time he indulged in only one conscious cruelty. For all his personal grubbiness—the clothes that looked like dirty bandages, the skimpy beard, the smells—Williken was a great fusspot, and it was his style of fuss (in housekeeping now as it had been in art) to efface the evidences of his own undesirable presence, to wipe away the fingerprints and baffle his pursuers. Thus each object that was allowed to be visible in the room came to possess a kind of heightened significance, like so many skulls in a monk's cell: the pink telephone, Richard Jr.'s sagging bed, the speakers, the long silvery swan-neck of the water faucet, the calendar with lovers tumbling in the heavy snows of "January 2024." His cruelty was simply not changing the month.

She never said, as she might have, "Willy, it's the tenth of *May,* for Christ's sake." Possibly she found some grueling satisfaction in whatever hurt his reminder caused her. Certainly she gnawed on it. He had no first-hand knowledge of such feelings. The whole drama of her abandonment seemed ludicrous to him. Anguish for anguish's sake.

It might have gone on like that till summer, but then one day the calendar was gone and one of his own photographs was in its place.

"Is it yours?" she asked.

His awkwardness was sincere. He nodded.

"I noticed it the minute I walked into the room."

A photograph of a glass half full of water resting on a wet glass shelf. A second, empty glass outside the picture cast a shadow across the white tiles of the wall.

Shrimp walked up close to it. "It's sad, isn't it?"

"I don't know," Williken said. He felt confused, insulted; anguished. "Usually I don't like having my own things hanging about. They go dead on you. But I thought—"

"I like it. I do."

6. Amparo (2024)

On her birthday, the 29th of May, she had realized that she hated her mother. Her eleventh birthday. It was a horrible realization, but Geminis can't deceive themselves. There was simply nothing about Mama you could admire and so much to loathe. She bullied herself and Mickey mercilessly, but what was worse were the times she'd miscalculate her stupid pills, slime off into a glorious depression and tell them sob-stories about her wasted life. It was, certainly, a wasted life, but Amparo couldn't see that she'd ever made any effort not to waste it. She didn't know what work was. Even around the house she let poor old Grummy do everything. She just lay about, like some animal at the zoo, snuffling and scratching her smelly cunt. Amparo hated her.

Shrimp, in the way she sometimes had of seeming telepathic, said to her, before the dinner, that they had better have a talk, and she concocted a thin lie to get her out of the apartment. They went down to 15, where a Chinese lady had opened a new shop, and Shrimp bought the shampoo she was being so silly about.

Then to the roof for the inevitable lecture. The sunshine had brought half the building up on top, but they found a spot almost their own. Shrimp slipped out of her blouse, and Amparo couldn't help thinking what a difference there was between her and her mother, even though Shrimp was actually older. No sags, no wrinkles, and only a hint of graininess. Whereas Lottie, with every initial advantage on her side, had let herself become a monster of obesity. Or at least ("monster" was perhaps an exaggeration) she was heading down the road lickety-split.

"Is that all?" Amparo asked, once Shrimp had produced her last pious excuse for Lottie's various awfulnesses. "Can we go downstairs now that I'm properly ashamed?"

"Unless you want to tell me your side of the story?"

"I didn't think I was supposed to have a side."

"That's true when you're ten years old. At eleven you're allowed to have your own point of view."

Amparo grinned a grin that said, Good old democratic Aunt Shrimp. Then she was serious. "Mama hates me, it's as simple as that." She gave examples.

Shrimp appeared unimpressed. "You'd rather bully her—is that your point?"

"No." But giggling. "But it would be a change."

"You do, you know. You bully her something dreadful. You're a worse tyrant than Madame Who's-It with the goiters."

Amparo's second grin was more tentative. "Me!"

"You. Even Mickey can see it, but he's afraid to say

anything or you'll turn on him. We're all afraid."

"Don't be a silly. I don't know what you're talking about. Because I say sarcastic things now and then?"

"And then and then. You're as unpredictable as an airplane schedule. You wait till she's down, completely at the bottom, and then you go for jugular. What was it you said this morning?"

"I don't remember anything I said this morning."

"About the hippopotamus in the mud?"

"I said that to Grummy. *She* didn't hear. She was in bed, as usual."

"She heard."

"Then I'm sorry. What should I do, apologize?"

"You should stop making things worse for her."

Amparo shrugged. "She should stop making things worse for me. I hate to always *harp* about it, but I do want to go to the Lowen School. And why shouldn't I? It's not as though I were asking permission to go to Mexico and cut off my breasts."

"I agree. It's probably a good school. But you're *at* a good school."

"But I *want* to go to the Lowen School. It would be a *career*, but of course Mama wouldn't understand that."

"She doesn't want you living away from home. Is that so cruel?"

"Because if I left, then she'd only have Mickey to bully. Anyhow I'd be here officially, which is all she cares anyhow."

Shrimp was silent for a while, in what seemed a considering way. But what was there to consider? It was all so obvious. Amparo writhed.

At last Shrimp said, "Let's make a bargain. If you promise not to be Little Miss Bitch, I'll do what I can to talk her round to signing you up."

"Will you? Will you really?"

"Will *you?* That's what I'm asking."

"I'll grovel at her feet. Anything."

"If you don't, Amparo, if you go on the way you've been going, believe me, I'll tell her I think the Lowen School will destroy your character, what little there is."

"I promise. I promise to be as nice as—as what?"

"As a birthday cake?"

"As nice as a birthday cake, absolutely!"

They shook hands on it and put on their clothes and went downstairs where a real, rather sad, rather squalid birthday cake was waiting for her. Try as she might, poor old Grummy just couldn't cook. Juan had come by during the time they'd been on the roof, which was, more than any of her crumby presents, a nice surprise. The candles were lit, and everyone sang happy birthday: Juan, Grummy, Mama, Mickey, Shrimp.

Happy birthday to you.
Happy birthday to you.
Happy birthday, dear Amparo.
Happy birthday to you.

"Make a wish," Mickey said.

She made her wish, then with one decisive gust, blew all twelve candles.

Shrimp winked at her. "Now don't tell anyone what it was, or you won't get it."

She hadn't, in fact, been wishing for the Lowen School, since that was hers by right. What she'd wished instead was for Lottie to die.

Wishes never come true the way you think. A month later her father was dead. Juan, who'd never been unhappy a day in his life, had commited suicide.

7. Len Rude (2024)

Weeks after the Anderson debacle, when he'd at last been able to assure himself that there'd be no dire consequences, Mrs. Miller summoned him uptown for "a little talk." Though in the long-range view a nobody (her position scarcely brought her to middle management level), Mrs. Miller would soon be writing up his field summary, which made her, for now, a rather godlike nobody.

He panicked disgracefully. All morning he couldn't think of anything but what to wear, what to wear? He settled on a maroon Perry-Como-type sweater with a forest green scarf peeking out. Wholesome, not sexy, but not pointedly not-sexy.

He had a twenty-minute wait outside the lady's

cubbyhole. Usually he excelled at waiting. Cafeterias, toilets, launderettes—his life was rich in opportunities to acquire that skill. But he was so certain he was about to be axed that by the end of the twenty minutes he was on the brink of acting out his favorite crisis fantasy: I will get up, I will walk out the door. Every door. With never a word of good-bye nor a look backward. And then? Ah, there was the rub. Once he was out the door, where could he go that his identity, the whole immense dossier of his life, wouldn't trail after him like a tin can tied to his tail? So he waited, and then the interview was over, and Mrs. Miller was shaking his hand and saying something bland and anecdotal about Brown, whose book had been decorating his lap. Then, thank you, and thank *you* for coming in. Good-bye, Mrs. Miller. Good-bye, Len.

What had been the point? She hadn't mentioned Anderson except to say in passing that of course the poor man ought to be in Bellevue and that a few like that are statistically inevitable for anyone. It was better than he'd expected and more than he deserved.

Instead of the axe there was only his new assignment: Hanson, Nora/ Apartment 1812/ 334 E. 11th St. Mrs. Miller said she was a nice old lady—"if a little difficult at times." But all the cases he was put on this year were nice and old and difficult, since he was studying, in the catalogue's words, "Problems of Aging." The one odd thing about this Hanson was that she had a sizeable brood under her wings (though not as large as the printout had indicated; the son was married now) and would not seem to be dangerously lonely. However, according to Mrs. Miller, her son's marriage had "unsettled her" (Ominous word!) which was why she stood in need of *his* warmth and attention four hours a week. A stitch in time seemed to be what Mrs. Miller had in mind.

The more he thought about it the more this Hanson woman sounded like an impending disaster. Mrs. Miller had probably called him in to cover herself, so that if and when this one went in the same wrong direction Anderson had gone, it would be his fault, not the nice old difficult lady's, and not absolutely Alexa Miller's. She was probably doing her memorandum for the file right now, if she hadn't done it in advance.

All this for two miserable dollars an hour. Sweet fucking Jesus, if he'd known four years ago what he'd be getting into, he'd never have switched his major from English. Better to teach assholes to read the want ads than be an emotional nursemaid to senile psychotics.

That was the dark side. There was also a bright side. By the fall semester he'd have cleared up his field requirements. Then two years of smooth academic sailing, and then, O happy day, Leonard Rude would be a Doctor of Philosophy, which we all know is the next best condition to out-and-out freedom.

8. The Love Story (2024)

The MODICUM office had sent round an apologetic, shaggy boy with bad skin and a whining midwestern accent. She couldn't get him to explain why he'd been sent to visit her. He claimed it was a mystery just as much to him, some bureaucrat's brainstorm, there was never any sense to these projects, but he hoped she'd go along with it for his sake. A job is a job is a job, and this job in addition was for his degree.

He was going to the university?

Yes, but not, he assured her at once, that he'd come here to *study* her. Students were assigned to these make-work projects because there wasn't enough real work to go around. That was the welfare state for you. He hoped they'd be friends.

Mrs. Hanson couldn't bring herself to feel un-friendly, but what she asked him quite bluntly were they supposed to do, *as* friends? Len—she kept forgetting his name and he kept reminding her it was Len—suggested that he read a book to her.

"Aloud?"

"Yes, why not? It's one I have to read this term anyhow. It's a super book."

"Oh, I'm sure it is," she said, alarmed again. "I'm sure I'd learn all kinds of things. But still." She turned her head sideways and read the golden title of a fat, black book he'd laid down on the kitchen table. Something OLOGY. "Even so."

Len laughed. "Fiddle-dee-dee, Mrs. Hanson, not that one! I can't read *that* one myself."

The book they were to read was a novel he'd been assigned in an English class. He took it out of his pocket. The cover showed a pregnant woman sitting naked on the lap of a man in a blue suit.

"What a strange cover," she said, by way of compliment.

Len took this for another sign of reluctance. He insisted that the story would seem quite commonplace once she accepted the author's basic premise. A love story. That's all. She was bound to like it. Everyone did. "It's a super book," he said again.

She could see he meant to read it, so she led him into the living room and settled herself in one corner of the sofa and Len in the other. She found the Oralines in her purse. As there were only three left, she didn't offer one to him. She began sucking complacently. Then as a humorous afterthought she fit a premium button over the end of the stick. It said, I DON'T BELIEVE IT! But Len took no notice or else he didn't get the joke.

He started reading and right from page one it was sex. That in itself wouldn't have upset her. She had always believed in sex and enjoyed it, and though she did think that *having* sex ought to be a private matter there was certainly no harm in a candid discussion. What was embarrassing was that the whole scene took place on a sofa that was wobbling because one leg was missing. The sofa that she and Len were sitting on also had a missing leg and wobbled, and it seemed to Mrs. Hanson that some sort of comparison couldn't be avoided.

The sofa scene dragged on and on. Then nothing at all happened for a few pages, talk and descriptions. Why, she kept wondering, would the government want to pay college students to come to people's homes and read pornography to them? Wasn't the whole point of college to keep as many young people as possible occupied and out of jobs?

But perhaps this was an experiment. An experiment in adult education! When she thought about it, no other explanation fit the facts half so well. Viewed in this light the book suddenly became a challenge to her, and she tried to pay closer attention. Someone had died, and the woman the story was about—her name was Linda—was going to inherit a fortune. Mrs. Hanson had gone to school with someone called Linda, a dull-witted Negro girl whose father owned two grocery stores. She'd disliked the name ever since. Len stopped reading.

"Oh, go on," she said. "I'm enjoying it."

"So am I, Mrs. Hanson, but it's four o'clock."

She felt obliged to say something intelligent before he went off, but at the same time she didn't want to show that she'd guessed the purpose of the experiment. "It's a very unusual plot."

Len bared small, stained teeth in a smile of agreement.

"I always say there's nothing that can beat a good love story."

And before she could add her little joke ("Except perhaps a bit of smut."), Len had chimed in with: "I'll agree with that, Mrs. Hanson. Friday, then, at two o'clock?" In any case it was Shrimp's joke.

Mrs. Hanson felt she hadn't shown herself at all to advantage, but it was too late. Len was gathering himself together, his umbrella, his black book, talking steadily all the while. He even remembered the wet plaid cap she'd hung up on the hook to dry. Then he was gone.

Her heart swelled up inside her chest, hammering as though it had slipped gears. ker-whop! ker-wham! She went back to the sofa. The cushions at the end where Len had sat were still pressed down. Suddenly she could see the room as he must have seen it: linoleum so filthy you couldn't see the patterns, windows caked, blinds broken, heaps of toys and piles of clothing and tangles of both everywhere. Then, as if to complete the devastation, Lottie came staggering out of her bedroom wrapped in a dirty sheet, and reeking.

"Is there any milk?"

"Is there any milk!"

"Oh Mom. What's wrong now?"

"Do you have to ask? Look at this place. It looks as if a bomb hit it."

Lottie smiled a faint, mussed smile. "I was asleep. *Did* a bomb hit it?"

Poor silly Lotto, who could ever stay angry with her? Mrs. Hanson laughed indulgently, then started to explain about Len and the experiment, but Lottie was off in her own little world again. What a life, Mrs. Hanson thought, and she went out to the kitchen to mix up a glass of milk.

9. The Air Conditioner (2024)

Lottie could hear things. If she were sitting near the closet that used to be the foyer she could understand whole conversations taking place out in the corridor. In her own bedroom anything else happening in the apartment was audible to her—the turbulence of voices on the teevee, or Mickey lecturing his doll in what he imagined was Spanish, or her mother's putterings and sputterings. Such noises had the advantage of being on a human scale. It was the noises that lay behind these that she dreaded, and they were always there, waiting for those first masking sounds to drop, ready for her.

One night in her fifth month with Amparo she'd gone out walking very late, through Washington Square and past the palisades of N.Y.U. and the junior deluxe coops on West Broadway. She stopped beside the window of her favorite shop where the crystals of a darkened chandelier caught glints from the headlights of passing cars. It was four-thirty, the stillest hour of the morning. A diesel roared past and turned west on Prince. A dead silence followed in its wake. It was then she heard that other sound, a sourceless far-off rumble, like the first faint premonition, as one glides down a quiet stream, of the cataract ahead. Since then the sound of those falls had always been with her, sometimes distinctly, sometimes only, like stars behind smog, as a dim presence, an article of faith.

Resistance of a kind was possible. The teevee was a good barrier, when she could concentrate and when the programs weren't themselves upsetting. Or talk, if she could think of something to say and find someone to listen to her. But she'd been submerged by too many of her mother's monologs not to be sensitive to signals of boredom, and Lottie could not, like her mother, keep going regardless. Books demanded too much and were no help. Once she'd enjoyed the stories, simple as tic-tac-toe, in the romance comics that Amparo brought home, but now Amparo had outgrown comic books and Lottie was embarrassed to be buying them for herself. In any case they cost too much for her to get addicted.

Mostly she had to get by with pills, and mostly she could.

Then, in the August of the year Amparo was to start at the Lowen School, Mrs. Hanson traded off the second teevee, which hadn't worked for years, for a King Kool air conditioner of Ab Holt's that also hadn't worked for years except as a fan. Lottie had always complained about how stuffy her bedroom was. Sandwiched between the kitchen and the main bedroom, its only means of ventilation was an ineffective transom over the door to the living room. Shrimp, who was back home again, got her photographer friend from downstairs to take out the transom and install the air conditioner.

The fan made a gentle purring sound all through the night with every so often a tiny hiccoughing counterbeat, like an amplified heart murmur. Lottie could lie in bed for hours, long after the children were asleep in the bunks, just listening to the lovely syncopated hum. It was as calming as the sound of waves, and like the sound of waves it sometimes seemed to be murmuring words, or fragments of words, but however closely she strained to hear exactly what those words were, nothing ever clearly emerged. "Eleven, eleven, eleven," it would whisper to her, "thirty-six, three, eleven."

10. Lipstick (2026)

She assumed it was Amparo who was messing about in her makeup, had even gone so far as to mention the matter once at dinner, just her usual word to the wise. Amparo had sworn she hadn't so much as opened a drawer, but thereafter there were no more lipstick smudges on the mirror, no spilled powder, no problem. Then one Thursday coming back wasted and wornout from one of Brother Cary's periodic nonappearances, she found Mickey sitting at the dresser carefully laying on a foundation. His goggly dismay at her return was so ludicrous in the present blanked-out condition of his face that she simply burst out laughing. Mickey, without ever losing his look of comic horror, began laughing too.

"So—it was you all along, was it?"

He nodded, and reached for the cold cream, but Lottie, misinterpreting, caught hold of his hand and gave it a squeeze. She tried to remember when she'd first noticed things out of place, but it was one of those trivial details, like when a particular song was popular, that wasn't arranged chronologically in her memory. Mickey was ten, almost eleven. He must have been doing this for months without her being aware.

"You said," in a self-justifying whine, "that you used to do the same thing with Uncle Boz. You'd dress up in each other's clothes and pretend. You said."

"When did I say that?"

"Not to me. You said it to him, and I heard you."

She tried to think of the *right* thing to do.

"I've seen men wear makeup. Lots of times."

"Mickey, have I said anything against it?"

"No, but—"

"Sit down." She was brisk and business-like, though looking at his face in the mirror she felt close to breaking up all over again. No doubt the people who worked in beauty shops had that problem all the time. She turned him round, with his back to the mirror, and wiped at his cheeks with a hankie.

"Now to start with, a person with your fair skin doesn't need a foundation at all, or next to none. It isn't the same, you know, as frosting a cake."

She continued a stream of knowledgeable patter as she made him up: how to shape the lips so there always seems to be a little smile lurking in the corners, how to blend in the shadows, the necessity, when drawing on the brows, of studying their effect in profile and three-quarter views. All the while, in contradiction to her own sensible advice, she was creating a doll mask of the broadest exaggerations. When she put on the last brushstroke she framed the result with pendant earrings and a stretch wig. The result was uncanny. Mickey demanded to be allowed to look in the mirror. How could she say no?

In the mirror her face above his and his face below hers melted together and became one face. It was not simply that she had drawn her own features on his blank slate, or that one was a parody of the other. There was a worse truth—that this was the whole portion Mickey stood to inherit, nothing but these marks of pain, and terror, and certain defeat. If she'd written the words on his forehead with the eyebrow pencil it couldn't have been any clearer. And on hers, and on hers. She lay down on the bed and let slow, depthless tears rise and fall. For a while Mickey stared at her, and then he went outside, down to the street.

11. Crossing Brooklyn Ferry (2026)

The whole family was there for the program—Shrimp and Lottie on the sofa with Mickey between them, Mrs. Hanson in the rocker, Milly, with little Peanut in her lap, in the flowered armchair, and Boz beside them being a nuisance on one of the chairs from the kitchen. Amparo, whose triumph this was to be, was everywhere at once, fretting and frothing.

The sponsors were Pfizer and the Conservation Corporation. Since neither had anything to sell that everybody wasn't buying already, the ads were slow and heavy, but no slower and heavier, as it turned out, than *Leaves of Grass*. Shrimp tried gamely for the first half hour to find aspects to admire—the costumes were ultra-authentic, the brass band went oomp-pa-pa very well, and there was a pretty sequence of some brawny blacks hammering a wooden house together. But then Don Hershey would reappear as Whitman, bellowing his dreadful poems, and she would just shrivel up. Shrimp had grown up idolizing Don Hershey, and to see him reduced to this! A dirty old man slobbering after teenagers. It wasn't fair.

"It makes a fella kinda glad he's a Democrat," Boz drawled, when the ads came on again, but Shrimp gave him a dirty look: no matter how dreadful it was they were obliged, for Amparo's sake, to praise it.

"I think it's wonderful," Shrimp said. "I think it's *very* artistic. The colors!" It was the utmost she could manage.

Milly, with what seemed honest curiosity, filled up the rest of station identification with classroom-type questions about Whitman, but Amparo brushed them aside. She no longer kept up a pretense that the show was about anyone but herself.

"I think I'm in the next part. Yes, I'm sure they said part two."

But the second half hour concerned the Civil War and Lincoln's assassination:

> O powerful western fallen star!
> O shades of night!—O moody, tearful night!
> O great star disappear'd—O the black murk that hides the star!

For half an hour.

"You don't suppose they've cut out your scene, do you, Amparo?" Boz teased. They all came down on him together. Clearly it was what they'd all thought to themselves.

"It's possible," Amparo said dourly.

"Let's wait and see," Shrimp advised, as though they might have done anything else.

The Pfizer logo faded away, and there was Don Hershey again in his Santa Claus beard roaring off into a vast. new poem:

> The impalpable sustenance of me from all things at all hours of the day,
> The simple, compact, well-joined scheme, myself disintegrated, every one disintegrated yet part of the scheme,
> The similitudes of the past and those of the future,
> The glories strung like beads on my smallest sights and hearings, on the walk on the street and the passage over the river. . . .

And so on, endlessly, while the camera roved about the streets and over the water and looked at shoes—floods of shoes, centuries of shoes. Then, abrupt as flipping to another channel, it was 2026, and an ordinary crowd of people mulled about in the South Ferry waiting room.

Amparo rolled herself into a tight ball of attention. "This is it, coming up now."

Don Hershey rolled on, voice-over:

> It avails not, time nor place—distance avails not,

I am with you, you men and women of a generation, or ever so many generations hence,
Just as you feel when you look on the river and sky, so I felt,
Just as any of you is one of a living crowd, I was one of a crowd,
Just as you are refreshed by the gladness of the river. . . .

The camera panned past conglomerations of smiling, gesturing, chattering people, filing into the boat, pausing now and then to pick out details—a hand picking nervously at a cuff, a yellow scarf lifting in a breeze and falling, a particular face.

Amparo's.

"There I am! There!" Amparo screamed.

The camera lingered. She stood at the railing, smiling a dreamy smile that none of them watching could recognize. As Don Hershey lowered his volume and asked:

What is then between us?
What is the count of the scores or hundreds of years between us?

Amparo regarded, and the camera regarded, the moving surface of the water.

Shrimp's heart splattered like a bag of garbage dropped to the street from a high rooftop. Envy spilled out through her every vein. Amparo was so beautiful, so young and so damnably beautiful, she wanted to die.

PART II: TALK

12. The Bedroom (2026)

In cross-section the building was a swastika with the arms revolving counterclockwise, the Aztec direction. 1812, the Hansons' apartment, was located halfway along the inner forearm of the swastika's northwest limb, so that its windows commanded an uninterrupted view of several degrees southwestwards across the roofs of the lower buildings as far as the windowless, megalithic masses of the Cooper Union complex. Above: blue sky and roving clouds, jet trails and smoke wreathing up from the chimneys of 320 and 328. However one had to be right at the window to enjoy this vista. From the bed Shrimp could see only a uniformity of yellow brick and windows variegated with different kinds of curtains, shades, and blinds. May—and from two until almost six, when she needed it most, there was direct, yellow sunlight. It was the only advantage of living so near the top. On warm days the window would be opened a crack and a breeze would enter to ruffle the curtains. Lifting and falling, like the shallow erratic breathing of an asthmatic, billowing, collapsing, the curtains became, as anything watched intently enough will, the story of her life. Did any of those other curtains, shades, or blinds conceal a sadder story? Ah, she doubted it.

But sad as it was, life was also irrepressibly comic, and the curtains caught that too. They were a mild, elaborate joke between Mrs. Hanson and her daughter. The material was a sheer spun chintz in sappy ice cream colors patterned with sprigs and garlands of genitalia, his and hers, raspberry, lemon, and peach. A present from January, some ages ago. Loyally Shrimp had brought it home for her mother to make her a pajama suit from, but Mrs. Hanson, without overtly disapproving. had never got round to the job. Then, while Shrimp was in the hospital, Mrs. Hanson had made the material up into a pair of curtains and hung them in their bedroom as homecoming surprise and peace offering. Shrimp had to admit that the chintz had met its just reward.

Shrimp seemed content to float through each day without goals or ideas, just watching the cunts and cocks wafted by the breeze and whatever other infinitesimal events the empty room presented her with. Teevee annoyed her, books bored her, and she had nothing to say to visitors. Williken brought her a jigsaw puzzle, which she worked on an upside-down dresser drawer, but once the border was assembled she found that the drawer, though it had been measured in advance, was an inch too short. Surrendering with a sigh, she swept the pieces back in the box. In every way her convalesence was inexplicable and calm.

Then one day there was a tapping at the door. She said, prophetically, "Come in." And January came in, wet with rain and breathless from the stairs. It was a surprise. January's address on the West Coast had been a well-kept secret. Even so, it wasn't a large enough surprise. But then what is?

"Jan!"

"Hi. I came yesterday too, but your mother said you were asleep. I guess I should have waited, but I didn't know whether—"

"Take off your coat. You're all wet."

January came far enough into the room to be able to close the door, but she didn't approach the bed and she didn't take off her coat.

"How did you happen to—"

"Your sister mentioned it to Jerry, and Jerry phoned me up. I couldn't come right away though, I didn't have the money. Your mother says you're all right now, basically."

"Oh, I'm fine. It wasn't the operation, you know. That was as routine as taking out a wisdom tooth. But impatient me couldn't stay in bed, and so—" She laughed (always bearing in mind that life is comic too) and made a feeble joke. "I can now, though. *Quite* patiently."

January crinkled her eyebrows. All yesterday, and all the way downtown today, all the way up the stairs, feelings of tenderness and concern had tumbled about in her like clothes in a dryer. But now, face to face with Shrimp and seeing her try the same old ploys, she could feel nothing but resentment and the beginnings of anger, as though only hours had intervened since that last awful meal two years before. A Betty Crocker sausage and potatoes.

"I'm glad you came," Shrimp said half-heartedly.

"Are you?"

"Yes."

The anger vanished, and guilt came glinting up at the window of the dryer. "The operation, was it for—Was it because of what I said about having children?"

"I don't know, January. My reasons, when I look back, are still confused. Surely I must have been influenced by things you said. Morally I had no *right* to bear children."

"No, it was me who had no right. Dictating to you that way. Because of my principles! I see it now."

"Well." Shrimp took a sip from the water glass. It was a heavenly refreshment. "It goes deeper than politics. After all, I wasn't in any immediate *danger* of adding to the population, was I? *My* quota was filled. It was a ridiculous, melodramatic gesture, as Dr. Mesic was the first—"

January had shrugged off her raincoat and walked nearer the bed. She was wearing the nurse's uniform Shrimp had bought for her how many years ago. She bulged everywhere.

"Remember?" January said.

Shrimp nodded. She didn't have the heart to tell her that she didn't feel sexy. Or ashamed. Or anything. The horrorshow of Bellevue had taken it out of her—feeling, sex, and all.

January slipped her fingers under Shrimp's wrist to take her pulse. "It's slow," she observed.

Shrimp pulled her hand away. "I don't want to play games."

January began to cry.

13. Shrimp, In Bed (2026)

"You know?"

"I'd like to see it *working* again, the way it was meant to. That may sound like less than the *whole* revolution, but it's something that I can do, that I can try for. Right? Because a building is like. . . . It's a symbol of the life you lead inside it.

"One elevator, one elevator in working order, and not even all day long necessarily. Maybe just an hour in the morning and an hour in the early evening, when there's power to spare. What a difference it would make for people like us here at the top. Think back to all the times you decided not to come up to see me because of these stairs. Or all the times I stayed in. That's no way to live. But it's the older people who suffer most. My mother, I'll bet she doesn't get down to the street once a week nowadays, and Lottie's almost as bad. It's me and Mickey who have to get the mail, the groceries, everything else, and that's not fair to us. Is it?

"What's more, do you know that there are *two* people working full time running errands for the people stranded in their apartments without anyone to help. I'm not exaggerating. They're called auxiliaries! Think what that must cost.

"Or if there's an emergency? They'll send the doctor into the building rather than carry someone down so many steps. If my hemorrhaging had started when I was up here instead of at the Clinic, I might not be alive today. I was lucky, that's all. Think of that—I could be dead just because nobody in this building cares enough to make the fucking elevators *function*! So I figure, it's my responsibility now. Put up or shut up. Right?

"I've started a petition, and naturally everyone will sign it. *That* doesn't take any effort. But what does is I've started sounding out a couple of the people who might be helpful, and they agree that the auxiliary system is a ridiculous waste, but they say that even so it would cost more to keep the elevator running. I told them that people would be willing to pay for *tickets,* if money's the only problem. And they'd say yes, no doubt. absolutely. And then—fuck off, Miss Hanson, and thank you for your concern.

"There was one, the worst of them so far, a toadstool at the MODICUM office called R. M. Blake, who just kept saying what a *wonderful* sense of responsibility I have. Just like that: What a wonderful sense of responsibility you have, Miss Hanson. What big guts you have, Miss Hanson. I wanted to say to him, Yeah, the better to crush you with, Grandma. The old whitened sepulchre.

"It's funny, isn't it, the way we've switched round? The way it's so symmetrical. It used to be I was religious and you were political, now it's just the reverse. It's like, did you see THE ORPHANS the other night? It was sometime in the Nineteenth Century and there was this married couple, very cozy and very poor, except that each of them has *one thing* to be proud of. The man has a gold pocket watch, and the woman, poor darling, has her *hair*. So what happens? He pawns his watch to buy her a comb, and she sells her hair to get him a watch chain. A real ding-dong of a story.

"But if you think about it, that's what we've done. Isn't it? January?

"January, are you asleep?"

14. Lottie, At Bellevue (2026)

"They talk about the end of the world, the bombs and all, or if not the bombs then about the oceans dying, and the fish, but have you ever looked at the ocean? I used to worry, I did, but now I say to myself—so what. So what if the world ends? My sister though, she's just the other way—if there's an election she has to stay up and watch it. Or earthquakes. Anything. But what's the use?

"The end of the world. Let me tell you about the end of the world. It happened fifty years ago. Maybe a hundred. And since then it's been lovely. I mean it. Nobody tries to bother you. You can relax. You know what? I *like* the end of the world."

15. Lottie, At The White Rose Bar (2024)

"Of course there's that. When people want something so badly, say a person with cancer, or the problems I have with my back, then you tell yourself you've been cleared. And you haven't. But when it's the real thing you can tell. Something happens to their faces. The puzzlement is gone, the aggression. Not a relaxing away like sleep, but suddenly. There's someone else there, a spirit, touching them, soothing what's been hurting them so. It might be a tumor, it might be mental anguish. But the spirit is very definite, though the higher ones can be harder to understand sometimes. There aren't always words to explain what they experience on the higher planes. But those are the ones who can heal, not the lower spirits who've only left our plane a little while ago. They're not as strong. They can't help you as much because they're still confused themselves.

"What you should do is go there yourself. She doesn't mind if you're skeptical. Everybody is, at first, especially men. Even now for me, sometimes I think—she's cheating us, she's making it all up in her own head. There are no spirits, you die, and that's it. My sister, who was the one who took me there in the first place—and she practically had to drag me—she can't believe in it any more. But then she's never received any real benefit from it, whereas I—Thank you, I will.

"Okay. The first time was at a regular healing service I went to, about a year ago. This wasn't the woman I was talking about though. The Universal Friends—they were at the Americana. There was a talk first, about the Ka, then right at the start of the service I felt a spirit lay his hands on my head. Like this. Very hard. And cold, like a washcloth when you've got a fever. I concentrated on the pain in my back, which was bad then, I tried to feel if there were some difference. Because I knew I'd been healed in *some* way. It wasn't till after the meeting and out on Sixth Avenue that I realized what had happened. You know how you can look down a street late at night when things are quieter and see all the traffic lights changing together from red to green? Well, all my life I've been colorblind, but that night I could see the colors the way they really are. So bright, it was like—I can't describe it. I stayed up all that night, walking around, even though it was winter. And the sun, when it came up? I was on top of the bridge, and God! But then gradually during the next week it left me. It was too large a gift. I wasn't ready. But sometimes when I feel very clear, and not afraid, I think it's come back. Just for a moment. Then it's gone.

"The second time—thanks.

"The second time wasn't so simple. It was at a message service. About five weeks ago. Or a month? It seems longer, but—Anyhow.

"The arrangement was, you could write down three

questions and then the paper's folded up, but before Reverend Ribera had even picked up mine he was there and—I don't know how to describe it. He was shaking her about. Violently. Very violently. There was a kind of struggle whether he'd use her body and take control. Usually, you see, she likes to just talk *with* them, but Juan was so anxious and impatient, you see. You know what he was like when his mind was set on something. He kept calling my name in this terrible strangled voice. One minute I'd think, Yes, that's Juan, he's trying to reach me, and the next minute I'd think, No, it can't be, Juan is dead. All this time, you see, I'd been trying to reach him—and now he was there and I wouldn't accept it.

"Anyhow.

"At last he seemed to understand that he needed Reverend Ribera's cooperation, and he quieted down. He told about the life on the other side, and how he couldn't adjust to it. There were so many things he'd left unfinished here. At the last minute, he said, he'd wanted to change his mind, but by then it was too late, he was out of control. I wanted so much to believe that was true, and that he was really there, but I couldn't.

"Then just before he left Reverend Ribera's face changed, it became much younger, and she said some lines of poetry. In Spanish—everything had been in Spanish of course. I don't remember the exact words, but what it said, basically, was that he couldn't stand losing me. Even though this would be the last heartbreak that I'd ever cause him—*el ultimo dolor*. Even though this would be the last poem he'd write to me.

"You see, years ago Juan used to write poems to me. So when I went home that night I looked through the ones I'd saved, and it was there, the same poem. He'd written it to me years before, after we first broke up.

"So that's why when somebody says there's no scientific reason to believe in a life after this one, that's why I can't agree."

16. Mrs. Hanson, In Apartment 1812 (2024)

"April. April's the worst month for colds. You see the sunshine and you think it's short-sleeve weather already and by the time you're down on the street it's too late to change your mind. Speaking of short sleeves, you've studied psychology, I wonder what you'd say about this. Lottie's boy, you've seen him, Mickey, he's eight now—and he *will not* wear short sleeves. Even here in the house. He doesn't want you to see any *part* of his body. Wouldn't you have to call that morbid? I would. Or neurotic? For eight years old?

"There, drink that. I remembered this time and it's not so sweet.

"You wonder where children get their ideas. I suppose it was different for you—growing up without a family. Without a home. Such a regimented life. I don't think *any* child—But perhaps there are other factors. Advantages? Well, that's none of my beans-on-toast. But a dormitory, there'd be no privacy, and you, with all your studying! I wonder how you do it. And who looks after you if you're sick?

"Is it too hot? Your poor throat. Though it's little wonder that you're hoarse. That book, it just goes on and on and on. Don't misunderstand me, I'm enjoying it. Thoroughly. That part where she meets the French boy, or was he French, with the red hair, in Notre Dame Cathedral. That was very. . . . What would you call it? Romantic? And then what happens when they're up on the tower, that was a real shockeroo. I'm surprised they haven't made a movie of it. Or have they? Of course *I'd* much rather be reading it, even if. . . . But it isn't fair to you. Your poor throat.

"I'm a Catholic too, did you know that? There's the Sacred Heart, right behind you. Of course, nowadays! But I *was* brought up Catholic. Then just before I was supposed to be confirmed there was that uprising about who owned the churches. There I was standing on Fifth Avenue in my first woolen suit, though as a matter of fact it was more of a jumper, and my father with one umbrella, and my mother with another umbrella, and there was this group of priests practically screaming at us not to go in, and the other priests trying to *drag* us over the bodies on the steps. That would have been nineteen-eighty. . . . One? Two? You can read about it now in history books, but there I was right in the middle of a regular battle, and all I could think of was—R.B. is going to break the umbrella. My father, R.B.

"Lord, whatever got me started on that track? Oh, the cathedral. When you were reading that part of the story I could imagine it so well. Where it said how the stone columns were like tree trunks, I remember thinking the same thing myself when I was in St. Patrick's.

"You know, I try and communicate these things to my daughters, but *they're* not interested. The past doesn't mean anything to them, you wouldn't catch one of *them* wanting to read a book like this. And my grandchildren are too young to talk with. My son, he'd listen, but he's never here now.

"When you're brought up in an orphanage—but do they call it an orphanage, if your parents are still alive?—do they bother with religion and all of that? Not the government, I suppose.

"I think everyone needs some kind of faith, whether they call it religion or spiritual light or what-have-you. But my Boz says it takes more strength to believe in nothing at all. That's more a man's idea. You'd like Boz. You're exactly the same age and you have the same interests and—

"I'll tell you what, Lenny, why don't you spend tonight here? You don't have any classes tomorrow, do you? And why go out in this terrible weather? Shrimp will be gone, she always is, though that's just between you and me. I'll put clean sheets on her bed, and you can have the bedroom all to yourself. Or if not tonight, some other time. It's a standing invitation. You'll like it, having some privacy for a change, and it's a wonderful chance for me, having someone I can talk to."

17. Mrs. Hanson, At The Nursing Home (2021)

"Is this me? It is. I don't believe it. And who is that with me? It isn't you, is it? Did you have a mustache then? Where are we that it's so green? It can't be Elizabeth. Is it the park? It says 'July the Fourth' on the back, but it doesn't say where.

"Are you comfortable now? Would you like to sit up more? I know how to. Like this. There, isn't that better?

"And look—this is that same picnic, and there's *your*

father! What a comical face. The colors are so funny on all of these.

"And Bobby here. Oh dear.

"Mother.

"And who is this? It says, 'I've got more where that came from!' but there's no name. Is it one of the Schearls? Or somebody that you worked with?

"Here he is again. I don't think I ever—

"Oh, that's the car we drove to Lake Hopatcong in, and George Washington was sick all over the back seat. Do you remember that? You were so angry.

"Here's the twins.

"The twins again.

"Here's Gary. No, it's Boz! Oh, no, yes, it's Gary. It doesn't look like Boz at all really, but Boz had a little plastic bucket just like that, with a red stripe.

"Mother. Isn't she pretty in this?

"And here you are together, look. You're both laughing. I wonder what about. Hm? That's a lovely picture. Isn't it? I'll tell you what. I'll leave it in here, on top of this letter from. . . . ? Tony? Is it from Tony? Well, that's thoughtful. Oh, Lottie told me to be sure to remember to give you a kiss for her.

"I guess it's that time. Is it?

"It isn't three o'clock. I thought it was three o'clock. But it isn't. Would you like to look at some more of them? Or are you bored? I wouldn't blame you, having to sit there like that, unable to move a muscle, and listening to me go on. I *can* rattle. I certainly wouldn't blame you if you were bored.

PART III: MRS. HANSON

18. The New American Catholic Bible (2021)

Years before 334, when they'd been living in a single dismal basement room on Mott Street, a salesman had come round selling The New American Catholic Bible, and not just the Bible but a whole course of instructions that would bring her up to date on her own religion. By the time he'd come back to repossess she'd filled in the front pages with all the important dates of the family's history: (See p. 94) The salesman let her keep the Bible in exchange for the original deposit and an additional five dollars but took back the study plans and the looseleaf binder.

That was 1999. Whenever in later years the family enlarged or contracted she would enroll the facts faithfully in The New American Catholic Bible the very day it happened.

On June 30, 2001, Jimmy Tom was clubbed by the police during a riot protesting the ten o'clock curfew that

Name	Relation	Born	Died
Nora Ann Hanson		Nov. 15, 1967	
Dwight Frederick Hanson	Husband	Jan. 10, 1965	Dec. 20,1997
Robert Benjamin O'Meara	Father	Feb. 2, 1940	
Shirley Ann O'Meara (born Schearl)	Mother	Aug. 28, 1943	July 5, 1978
Robert Benjamin O'Meara, Jr.	Brother	Oct. 9, 1962	July 5, 1978
Gary William O'Meara	Brother	Sept. 28, 1963	
Barry Daniel O'Meara	Brother	Sept. 28, 1963	
Jimmy Tom Hanson	Son	Nov. 1, 1984	
Shirley Ann Hanson	Daughter	Feb. 9, 1986	
Loretta Hester Hanson	Daughter	Dec. 24, 1989	

the President had imposed during the Farm Crisis. He died the same night.

On April 11. 2003, six years after his father's death, Boz was born in Bellevue Hospital. Dwight had been a member of the Teamsters, the first union to get sperm preservation benefits as a standard feature of its group life policy.

On May 29, 2013, Amparo was born, at 334. Not until she'd mistakenly written down Amparo's last name as Hanson did she realize that as yet the Bible possessed no record of Amparo's father. By now, however, the official listing had acquired a kind of shadow of omitted relatives: her own stepmother Sue-Ellen, her endless in-laws, and Shrimp's two federal contract babies who had been called Tiger (after the cat he'd replaced) and Thumper (after Thumper in *Bambi*). Juan's case was more delicate than any of these, but finally she decided that even though Amparo's name was Martinez, Lottie was still legally a Hanson, and so Juan was doomed to join the other borderline cases in the margin. The mistake was corrected.

On July 6, 2016, Mickey was born, also at 334.

Then, on March 6, 2011 the nursing home in Elizabeth phoned Williken, who brought the message upstairs that R. B. O'Meara was dead. He had died peacefully and voluntarily at the age of 81. Her father—dead!

As she filled in this new information it occurred to Mrs. Hanson that she hadn't looked at the religious part of the book since the company had stopped sending her lessons. She reached in at random and pulled out, from *Proverbs*:

"Scorn for the scorners, yes; but for the wretched, grace."

Later she mentioned this message to Shrimp, who was up to her eyebrows in mysticism, hoping that her daughter would be able to make it mean more than it meant to her.

Shrimp read it aloud, then read it aloud a second time. In her opinion it meant nothing deeper than it said: "Scorn for the scorners, yes; but for the wretched, grace."

A promise that hadn't been and obviously wouldn't be kept. Mrs. Hanson felt betrayed and insulted.

19. A Desirable Job (2021)

Lottie had dropped out in tenth grade after her humanities teacher, old Mr. Sills, had made fun of her legs . . . Mrs. Hanson never lectured about her going back, certain that the combination of boredom and claustrophobia (these were the Mott Street days) would outweigh wounded pride by the next schoolyear, if not before. But when fall came Lottie was unrelenting, and her mother agreed to sign the permission forms to keep her home. She only had two years of high school herself and could still remember how she'd hated it, sitting there and listening to the jabber or staring at books. Besides it was nice having Lottie about to do all the little nuisance chores, washing, mending, keeping off the cats, that Mrs. Hanson resisted. With Boz Lottie was better than a pound of pills, playing with him and talking with him hour after hour, year after year.

Then, at eighteen, Lottie was issued her own MODICUM card and an ultimatum: if she didn't have a full-time job by the end of six months, dependant benefits would stop and she'd have to move to one of the scrap heaps for hard-core unemployables like Roebling Plaza. Coincidentally the Hansons would lose their place on the waiting list for 334.

Lottie drifted into jobs and out of jobs with the same fierce indifference that had seen her through a lifetime at school relatively unscarred. She waited on counters. She sorted plastic beads for a manufacturer. She wrote down numbers that people phoned in from Chicago. She wrapped boxes. She washed and filled and capped gallon jugs in the basement of Bonwit's. Generally she managed to quit or be fired by May or June, so that she could have a couple months of what life was all about before it was time to die again into the death of a job.

Then one lovely rooftop just after the Hansons had got into 334, she had met Juan Martinez, and the summertime became official and continuous: she was a mother! A wife! A mother again! Juan worked in the Bellevue morgue with Ab Holt, who lived at the other end of the corridor, which was how they'd happened to coincide on that July roof. He had worked at the morgue for years, and it seemed that he would go on working there for more years, and so Lottie could relax into her wife-mother identity and let life be a swimming pool with her season ticket paid in full. She was happy, for a long while.

Not forever. She was a Capricorn, Juan was Sagittarius: from the beginning she'd known it would end, and how. Juan's pleasures became duties. His visits grew less frequent. The money, that had been so wonderfully steady for three years, for four, almost for five, came in spurts and then in trickles. The family had to make do with Mrs. Hanson's monthly checks, the supplemental allowance stamps for Amparo and Mickey, and Shrimp's various windfalls and makeshifts. It reached the point, just short of desperation, where the rent instead of being a nominal $37.50 became a crushing $37.50, and it was at that point that the possibility developed of Lottie getting an incredible job.

Cece Benn, in 1438, was the sweep for 11th Street for the block between First and Second Avenues, a concession good for twenty to thirty dollars a week in tips and scroungings plus a shower of goodies at Christmas. But the real beauty of the job was that since your earnings didn't have to be declared to the MODICUM office, you lost none of your regular benefits. Cece had swept 11th Street since before the turn of the century, but now she was edging up to retirement and had decided to opt for a home.

Lottie had often stopped at the corner in decent weather to chat with Cece, but she'd never supposed the old woman had regarded these attentions as a sign of real friendship. When Cece hinted to her that she was considering letting *her* inherit the license Lottie was flabbergasted with gratitude.

"If you want it, that is," Cece had added with a shy, small smile.

"If I want it! If I *want* it! Oh, Mrs. Benn!"

She went on wanting it for months, since Cece wasn't about to forfeit a consideration like Christmas. Lottie tried not to let her high hopes affect the way she acted toward Cece, but she found it impossible not to be more actively cordial, to the extent eventually of running errands for her up to 1438 and back down to the street. Seeing how Cece's apartment was done up, imagining what it must have cost, made her want that license more than ever. By December she was grovelling.

Over the holidays, Lottie was down with flu and a cold. When she was better, there were new people in 1438, and Mrs. Levin, from 1726, was out on the corner with the broom and the cup. Lottie found out later from her mother, who had heard it from Leda Holt, that Mrs. Levin had paid Cece six hundred dollars for her license.

She could never pass Mrs. Levin on the street without feeling half-sick with the sense of what she had lost. For thirty-three years she had kept herself above actually desiring a job. She had worked when she had had to work, but she'd never let herself want to.

She had *wanted* Cece Benn's job. She still did. She always would. She felt ruined.

20. A & P, continued (2021)

After their beers under the airport, Juan took Lottie to Wollman Rink and they skated for an hour. Around and around, waltzes, tangoes, perfect delight. You could scarcely hear the music over the roar of the skates. Lottie left the rink with a skinned knee and feeling ten years younger.

"Isn't that better than a museum?"

"It was wonderful." She pulled him close to her and kissed the brown mole on his neck.

He said, "Hey."

And then: "I've got to go to the hospital now."

"Already?"

"What do you mean already? It's eleven o'clock. You want a ride downtown?"

Juan's motive in going somewhere was so he could drive there and then drive back. He was devoted to his car, and Lottie pretended she was too. Instead of telling the simple truth that she wanted to go back to the museum by herself, she said, "I'd *love* to go for a ride, but not if it's only as far as the hospital. Then I'd have nowhere to go but home. No, I'll just plop down on a bench."

Juan went off, satisfied, and she deposited the butt of the souvenir carrot in a trash bin. Then through a side entrance behind the Egyptian temple (where she'd been led to worship the mummies and basalt gods in second, fourth, seventh, and ninth grades) into the museum.

A cast of thousands was enjoying the postcards, taking them out of the racks, looking at them, putting them back in the racks. Lottie joined. Faces, trees, people in costumes, the sea, Jesus and Mary, a glass bowl, a farm, stripes and dots, but nowhere a card showing the replica of the A & P. She had to ask, and a girl with braces on her teeth showed her where there were several hidden away. Lottie bought one that showed aisles disappearing at the horizon.

"Wait!" said the girl with braces, as she was walking away. She thought she'd had it then, but it had only been to give her the receipt for 25¢.

Up in the park, in a baffle away from the field, she printed on the message side: "I Was here today + I Thout this woud bring back the Old Times for you." Only then did she consider who she'd send it to. Her grandfather was dead, and no one else she could think of was old enough to remember anything so far back. Finally she addressed it to her mother, adding to the message: "I never pass throuh Elizebeth without Thinking of you."

Then she emptied the other postcards out of her purse—a set of holes, a face, a bouquet, a saint, a fancy chest-of-drawers, an old dress, another face, people working out of doors, some squiggles, a stone coffin, a table covered with more faces. Eleven in all. Worth, she jotted the figures on the back of the card with the coffin—$2.75. A bit of shoplifting always cheered her up.

She decided that the bouquet, "Irises", was the nicest and addressed it to Juan:

Juan Martinez
Abingdon Garage
312 Perry St.
New York 10014

21. Juan (2021)

It wasn't because he disliked Lottie and his offspring that he wasn't regular with his weekly dues. It was just that Princess Cass ate up his money before he could pay it out, Princess Cass being his dream on wheels, a virginal '15 replica of the last great muscle car, Chevy's '79 Vega Fascination. About the neck of his little beauty he had hung five years of sweat and tears: punched out power with all suitable goodies; a '69 vintage Weber clutch with Jag floorbox and Jag universals; leather leather insides; and the shell and glory of her was seven swarthy perspectivized overlays with a full five-inch apparent depth of field. Just touching her was an act of love. And when it moved? Brm brm? You came.

Princess Cass resided on the third floor of the Abingdon Garage on Perry Street, and as the monthly rent plus tax, plus tax, was more than he would have to pay at a hotel, Juan lived there with, and in, the Princess. Besides cars that were just parked or buried at the Abingdon, there were three other members of the faith: a Jap ad man in a newish Rolls Electric, 'Gramps' Gardiner in a self-assembled Uglicar that wasn't much more, poor slut, than a mobile bed; and, stranger than custom, a Hillman Minx from way back and with zero modifications, a jewel belonging to Liz Kreiner, who had inherited it from her father Max.

Juan loved Lottie. He did love Lottie, but what he felt for Princess Cass went beyond love—it was loyalty. It went beyond loyalty—it was symbiosis. ('Symbiosis' being what it said in little gold letters on the fender of the Jap junior executive's Rolls.) A car represented, in a way that Lottie would never understand for all her crooning and her protests, a way of life. Because if she had understood, she wouldn't have addressed her dumb card in care of the Abingdon. A blurry mess about some dumb flower that was probably extinct! *He* didn't worry about an inspection, but the Abingdon's owners had shit-fits when anyone used the place as an address, and he didn't want to see the Princess sleeping on the street.

If Princess Cass was his pride, she was secretly also his shame. Since 80% of his income was extra-legal, he had to buy her basic necessities, gas, oil, and glass fiber, on the black market—and there was never enough, despite his economies in every other direction. Five nights out of seven she had to stay indoors, and Juan would usually stay there with her, puttering and polishing, or reading poems, or sharpening his brains on Liz Kreiner's chessboard, anything rather than have some smart-ass ask. "Hey, Romeo, where's the royal lady?"

The other two nights justified any suffering. The very best and happiest times were when he met someone who could appreciate largeness and they'd set off down the turnpike. All through the night, not stopping except to fill the tank, on and on and on and on. That was colossal, but it wasn't something he could do all the time, or even with the same someone again. Inevitably they would want to know more, and he couldn't bear to admit that this was it—the Princess, himself, and those lovely white flashes coming down the center of the road: All. Once they found out, the pity started flowing, and Juan had no defences against pity.

Lottie had never pitied him, nor had she ever been jealous of Princess Cass, and that's why they could be, and had been, and would be, man and wife. Eight fucking years. Like Liz Kreiner's Hillman, she'd lost the flower of youth, but the guts were still sound. When he was with her and things went right, it was like butter on toast. A melting. The edges vanished. He forgot who he was or that there was anything in particular that had to be done. He was the rain, and she was a lake, and slowly, softly, effortlessly, he fell.

Who could ask for more?

Lottie might have. Sometimes he wondered why she didn't. He knew the kids cost her more than he provided, yet the only demands she tried to make were on his time and presence. She wanted him living, at least part of the time, at 334, and not so far as he could tell for any other reason than because she wanted him near. She kept pointing out ways he'd save money and other kinds of advantages, like having all his clothes in one place instead of scattered over five boroughs.

He loved Lottie. He did love her, and needed her too, but it wasn't possible for them to live together. It was hard to explain why. He'd grown up in a family of seven, all living in one room. It turned people into beasts living that way. Human beings need privacy. But if Lottie didn't understand that, Juan didn't see what else he could say. Any person had to have some privacy, and Juan just needed more than most.

22. Leda Holt (2021)

While she was shuffling, Nora hatched the egg that she had so obviously been holding in reserve. "I saw that colored boy on the steps yesterday."

"Colored boy?" Wasn't that just like Nora, to find the worst possible way to put it? "When did you start keeping company with colored boys?"

Nora cut. "Milly's fellow."

Leda swam round in pillows and comforters, sheets and blankets, until she was sitting almost upright. "Oh yes," archly, "*that* colored fellow." She dealt the cards out carefully and placed the pack between them on the emptied-out cupboard that served as their table.

"I practically—" Nora arranged the cards in her hands. "—had to split a gasket. Knowing that the two of them were in my room the whole while, and him wasting away for it." She plucked out two cards and put them in the crib, which was hers this time. "The droop!"

Leda was more careful. She had a 2, a pair of 3's, a 4, and a pair of 7's. If she kept the double run, she had to give Nora the 7's. But if she kept her two pairs and the starter didn't offer additional help. . . . She decided to risk it and put the 7's in the crib.

Nora cut again, and Leda turned up the Queen of Spades for the starter. She dissembled her satisfaction with a shake of her head, and the opinion, "Sex!"

"Do you know, Leda?" Nora laid down a 7. "I can't even remember what that was all *about*."

Leda played the 4. "I know what you mean. I wish Ab felt that way about it."

A 6. "Seventeen. You say that, but you're young, and you've got Ab."

If she played a 3, Nora could take it to 31 with a face card. She played the 2 instead. "Nineteen. I'm *not* young."

"And five makes twenty-four."

"And three. Twenty-seven?"

"No, *I* can't."

Leda laid down her last card. "And three is thirty." She advanced a hole.

"Five," and Nora took her hole. Then, at last, came the contradiction Leda was waiting for. "I'm fifty-four, and you're, what? Forty-five? It makes all the difference." She spread her cards beside the Queen. "And another crucial difference—Dwight has been dead for twenty years now. Not that I haven't had my opportunities now and then—Let's see, what have I got? Fifteen-two, fifteen-four, and a pair is six, and two runs is six, is twelve." She jumped the second matchstick forward. "But now and then is not the same thing as a habit."

"Are you bragging or complaining?" Leda spread her own cards.

"Bragging, absolutely."

"Fifteen-two, fifteen-four, and a pair is six, and two runs, it's just the same as yours, look—twelve."

"Sex makes people crazy. Like that poor fool on the steps. It's more trouble than it's worth. I'm well out of it."

Leda plugged her matchstick into a hole just four short of game. "That's what Carney said about Portugal, and you know what happened then."

"There's more important things," Nora maundered on, undeterred.

Here it comes, Leda thought, the themesong. "Oh, count your crib," she said.

"There's only the pair you gave me. Thanks." She went ahead two holes. "The family—that's the important thing. Keeping it together."

"True, true. Now get on with it, my dear."

But instead of taking the cards and shuffling, Nora picked up the cribbage board and studied it. "I thought you said you had twelve?"

"Did I make a mistake?" Sweetly.

"No, I don't think so." She moved Leda's matchstick back two holes. "You cheated."

23. Len Rude, continued (2024)

After his initial incredulity, when he realized she really did want him to move in, he thought: Arggh! But after all, why *not*? Being her lodger couldn't be much worse than living in the middle of a motherfucking marching band the way he did now. He could trade in his meal vouchers for food stamps. As Mrs. Hanson herself had pointed out, it didn't have to be official, though if he played his cards right he might be able to get Fulke to give him a couple credits for it as an individual field project. Fulke was always bitching at him for scanting case work. He'd have to agree. It was only a matter, really, of finding the right ribbon to tie around it. Not "Problems of Aging" again, if he didn't want to be sucked down the drainhole of a geriatrics specialty. "Family Structures in a Modicum Environment." Too vast, but that was the direction to aim in. Mention his institutional upbringing and how this was an opportunity to understand family dynamics from the inside. It was emotional blackmail, but how could Fulke refuse?

It never occurred to him to wonder why Mrs. Hanson had extended the invitation. He knew he was likeable and was never surprised when people, accordingly, liked him. Also, as Mrs. Miller had pointed out, the old lady was upset about her son marrying and moving away. He would replace the son she had lost. It was only natural.

24. The Love Story, continued (2024)

"Here's the key," and she handed Amparo the key. "No need to bring it up here, but if there's a *personal* letter inside—" (But mightn't he write to her on office stationery?) "No, if there's anything at all, just wave your arms like this—" Mrs. Hanson waved her arms vigorously and the dewlaps went all quivery. "I'll be watching."

"What are you expecting, Grummy? It must be awfully important."

Mrs. Hanson smiled her sweetest, most Grummy-like

smile. Love made her crafty. "Something from the MODICUM office, dear. And you're right, it could be quite important—for all of us."

Now run! she thought. *Run* down those stairs!

She took one of the chairs from the table in the kitchen and set it by the living room window. She sat down. She stood up. She pressed the palms of her hands against the sides of her neck as a reminder that she must *control* herself.

He'd promised to write whether he came that night or not, but she felt sure he'd forget his promise if he didn't intend to come. If a letter were there, it could mean only one thing.

Amparo *must* have reached the mailboxes by now. Unless she'd met a friend of hers as she went down. Unless she—Would it be there? Would it? Mrs. Hanson scanned the gray sky for an omen, but the clouds were too low for planes to be visible. She pressed her forehead against the cool glass, willing Amparo to come round the corner of the building.

And she was there! Amparo's arms made a V, and then an X, a V, and an X. Mrs. Hanson signaled back. A deadly joy slithered across her skin and shivered through her bones. He *had* written! He *would* come!

She was out the door and at the head of the stairs before she recollected the purse. Two days ago, in anticipation, she'd taken out the credit card from where she kept it hidden in The New American Catholic Bible. She hadn't used it since she'd bought her father's wreath, when, two years ago? Nearer three. $225, and even so it was the smallest he got. What the twins must have paid for theirs! It had taken over a year to pay it back, and all the while the computer kept making the most awful threats. What if the card weren't valid now!

She had her purse, and the list and the card were inside. A raincoat. Was there anything else? And the door, should she lock it? Lottie was inside asleep, but Lottie could have slept through a gang bang. To be on the safe side she locked the door.

I mustn't run, she told herself at the third landing down, that was how old Mr.—I *mustn't* run, but it wasn't running that made her heart beat so—it was love! She was alive and miraculously she was in love again. Even more miraculously, somebody loved her. Loved *her*! Madness.

She had to stop on the ninth floor landing to catch her breath. A temp was sleeping in the corridor in a licensed MODICUM bag. Usually she would only have been annoyed, but this morning the sight affected her with a delicious sense of compassion and community. Give me your tired, she thought with elation, your poor, your huddled masses yearning to breathe free, the wretched refuse of your teeming shore. How it all came pouring back! Details from a lifetime ago, memories of old faces and old feelings. And now, poetry!

By the time she was on one the backs of her legs were trembling so she could barely stand up straight. There was the mailbox, and there, slantwise inside it, was Len's Letter. It had to be his. If it were anything else she would die.

The mailbox key was where Amparo always left it behind the scarecrow camera.

His letter said:

"Dear Mrs. Hanson—You can set an extra plate for dinner Thursday. I'm happy to say I can accept your kind invitation. Will bring my suitcase. Love, Len."

Love! There was no mistaking it, then: Love! She had sensed it from the first, but who would have believed—at her age, at fifty-seven! (True, with a bit of care her fifty-seven could look younger than someone like Leda Holt's forty-six. But even so.) Love!

Impossible.

Of course, and yet always when that thought had come to her there were those words beneath the title on the cover of the book, words that, as if by accident, his finger had pointed to as he read: "The Tale of an Impossible Love." Where there was love *nothing* was impossible.

She read the letter over and over. In its plainness it was more elegant than a poem: "I'm happy to say I can accept your kind invitation." Who would have suspected, reading that, the meaning which for *them* was so obvious?

And then, throwing caution to the winds: "Love, Len"!

Eleven o'clock, and everything still to be done—the groceries, wine, a new dress, and, if she dared—Did she? Was there anything she didn't dare now?

I'll go there first, she decided. When the girl showed her the chart with the various swatches she was no less decisive. She pointed to the brightest, carroty orange and said, "That."

25. The Dinner (2024)

Lottie opened the door, which hadn't been locked after all, and said, "Mom!"

She had figured out, coming up the stairs, just what tone to take and now she took it. "Do you like it?" She dropped the keys into her purse. Casualness itself.

"Your hair."

"Yes, I had it dyed. Do you *like* it?" She picked up her bags and came in. Her back and shoulders were one massive ache from hauling the bags up the stairs. Her scalp was still all pins and needles. Her feet hurt. Her eyes felt like the tops of lightbulbs covered with dust. But she *looked* good.

Lottie took the bags, and she looked, but only looked, at the mercy of a chair. Sit down now and she'd never get up.

"It's so startling. I don't know. Turn around."

"You're supposed to say yes, stupid. Just 'Yes, Mom, it looks *fine.*' " But she turned round obediently.

"I *do* like it," Lottie said, taking the recommended tone. "Yes, I do. The dress too is—Oh Mom, don't go in there yet."

She paused with her hand on the knob of the living room door, waiting to be told of whatever catastrophe she was about to confront.

"Shrimp's in your bedroom. She's feeling very, very bad. I gave her a bit of first aid. She's probably sleeping now."

"What's wrong with her?"

"They've busted up. Shrimp went and got herself another subsidy—"

"Oh Jesus."

"That's what I thought."

"A third time? I didn't think that was legal."

"Well, her scores, you know. And I suppose the first two must have their own scores by now. Anyhow. When she told January, there was a row. January tried to stab her—it's nothing bad, just a scratch on her shoulder."

"With a knife?"

Lottie snickered. "With a fork, actually. January has some kind of political idea that you shouldn't have babies for the government. Or maybe not at all, Shrimp wasn't too clear."

"But she hasn't come here to stay. Has she?"

"For a while."

"She can't. Oh, I know Shrimp. She'll go back. It's like all their other arguments. But you shouldn't have given her pills."

"She'll have to stay here, Mom. January's gone to Seattle and she gave the room up to some friends. They wouldn't even let Shrimp in to pack. Her suitcase, her records, everything was sitting in the hall. I think that's what she was upset about more than anything else."

"And she's brought that all *here*?" A glance into the living room answered the question. Shrimp had emptied herself out everywhere in layers of shoes and underwear, keepsakes and dirty sheets.

"She was looking for a present she'd got me," Lottie explained. "That's why it's all out. Look, a Pepsi bottle, isn't it pretty?"

"Oh my God."

"She bought us all presents. She has money now, you know. A regular income."

"Then she doesn't have to stay here."

"Mom, be reasonable."

"She can't. I've rented the room. I told you I might. The man is coming tonight. That's what those groceries are for. I'm cooking a nice simple meal to start things off on the right foot."

"If it's a question of money, Shrimp can probably—"

"It's not a question of money. I've *told* him that the room is his, and he's coming tonight. My God, look at this mess! This morning it was as neat as a, as a—"

"Shrimp could sleep here on the couch," Lottie suggested, lifting off one of the cartons.

"And where will *I* sleep?"

"Well, where will *she* sleep?"

"Let her be a temp!"

"Mother!"

"Let her. I'm sure it wouldn't be anything new. All the

nights she didn't come home, you don't suppose she was in somebody's *bed,* do you? Hallways and gutters, that's where she belongs. She's spent half her life there already, let her go there now."

"If Shrimp hears you say that—"

"I hope she does." Mrs. Hanson walked right up to the door of the bedroom and shouted. "Hallways and gutters! Hallways and gutters!"

"Mom, there's no need to—I'll tell you what. Mickey can sleep in my bed tonight, he's always asking to, and Shrimp can have his bunk. Maybe in a day or two she'll be able to find a room at a hotel or somewhere. But don't make a scene now. She is very upset."

"*I'm* very upset!"

But she let herself be mollified on condition that Lottie cleared away Shrimp's debris.

Mrs. Hanson, meanwhile, started the dinner. The dessert first, since it would have to cool after it cooked. Cream-style Strawberry Granola. Len had mentioned liking Granola as a boy in Nebraska, before he'd been sent to a home. Once it was bubbling she added a packet of Juicy Fruit bits, then poured it into her two glass bowls. Lottie licked the pot.

Then they transported Shrimp from the front bedroom to Mickey's bunk. Shrimp wouldn't let loose of the pillow Mrs. Hanson had put out for Len, and rather than risk waking her she let her keep it. The fork had left four tiny punctures like squeezed pimples all in a row.

The stew, which came in a kit with instructions in three languages, would have taken no time at all, except that Mrs. Hanson intended to supplement it with meat. She'd bought eight cubes at Stuyvesant Town for $3.20, not a bargain but when was beef ever a bargain? The cubes came out of two Baggies dark red and slimy with blood, but after a fry in the pan they had a nice brown crust. Even so she decided not to add them to the stew till the last minute so as not to upset the flavor.

A fresh salad of carrots and parsnips, with a small onion added for zest—she'd been able to get these with her regular stamps—and she was done.

It was seven o'clock.

Lottie came into the kitchen and sniffed at the fried cubes of beef. "You're certainly going to a lot of trouble." Meaning expense.

"First impressions are important."

"How long is he going to stay here?"

"It probably depends. Oh, go ahead—eat one."

"There'll still be a lot left." Lottie chose the smallest cube and nibbled at it delicately. "Mm. Mmm!"

"Are you going to be late tonight?" Mrs. Hanson asked.

Lottie waved her hand about ("I can't talk now") and nodded.

"Till when do you think?"

She closed her eyes and swallowed. "Till morning sometime if Juan is there. Lee made a point of inviting him. Thanks. That was good."

Lottie set off. Amparo had been fed some snaps and sent up to the roof. Mickey, plugged into the teevee, was as good as invisible. In effect, till Len came, she was alone. The feelings of love that she had felt all day on the street and in stores returned, like some shy child who hides when there is company but torments you afterwards. The little rascal frolicked through the apartment, shrieking, sticking his tongue out, putting tacks on chairs, flashing images at her, like the glimpses you'd catch switching past Channel 5 in the afternoon of fingers sliding up a leg, of lips touching a nipple, of a cock stiffening. Oh, the anxiety! She delved into Lottie's makeup drawer, but there wasn't time for more than a dab of powder. She returned a moment later to put a drop of Molly Bloom beneath each earlobe. And lipstick? A hint. No, it looked macabre. She wiped it off.

It was eight o'clock.

He wasn't going to come.

He knocked.

She opened the door, and he stood before her, smiling with his eyes. His chest in its furry maroon rose and fell, rose and fell. She had forgotten, amid the abstractions of love, the reality of his flesh. Her erotic fancies of a moment before were all *images*, but the creature who came into the kitchen, hefting a black suitcase and a paper carrier full of books, existed solidly in three dimensions. She wanted to walk around him as though he were a statue in Washington Square.

He shook her hand and said hello. No more.

His reticence infected her. She couldn't meet his gaze. She tried to speak to him, as he spoke to her, in silences and trivialities. She led him to his room.

His hand stroked the bedspread, and she wanted to surrender to him then and there, but his manner didn't allow it. He was afraid. Men were always afraid at the start.

"I'm *so* happy," she said. "To think you'll really be staying here."

"Yeah, so am I."

"You must let me go into the kitchen now. So that I can . . . . We're having stew, and a spring salad."

"That sounds terrific, Mrs. Hanson."

"I think you'll like it."

She put the fried cubes of meat into the simmering paste and turned up the heat. She took the salad and the wine out of the icebox. As she turned round he was in the doorway looking at her. She held up the wine bottle with a gesture of immemorial affirmation. The weariness was gone from her back and shoulders as though by the pressure of his gaze he'd smoothed the soreness from the muscles. What a gift it is to be in love.

"Haven't you done your hair differently?"

"I didn't think you'd noticed."

"Oh, I noticed the moment you came to the door."

She started laughing but stopped short. Her laughter, though its source lay deep in her happiness, had sounded harshly in her ears.

"I like it," he said.

"Thank you."

The red wine spurting from the Gallo tetrahedron seemed to issue from the same depths as her laughter.

"I really do," Len insisted.

"I think the stew must be ready. You sit."

She dished the stew out onto the plates at the burner so that he wouldn't see that she was giving him all of the real meat. But in the end she did take one of the cubes for herself.

They sat down. She lifted her glass. "What shall we drink to?"

"To?" Smiling uncertainly he picked up his own glass. Then, getting her drift: "To life?"

"Yes! Yes, to life!"

They toasted life, ate their stew and salad, drank the red wine. They spoke seldom, but their eyes often met in complex and graceful dialogues. Any words either of them might have spoken at this point would have been in some way untrue; their eyes couldn't lie.

They'd finished the dinner and Mrs. Hanson had set out the chilled pink Granola, when there was a thud and a loud cry from Lottie's room. Shrimp had awakened!

Len looked at Mrs. Hanson questioningly.

"I forgot to tell you, Lenny. My daughter came home. But it isn't anything for you to—"

It was too late. Shrimp had stumbled into the kitchen in one of Lottie's delapidated transparencies, unbuckled and candid as an ad for Pier 19. Not till she'd reached the refrigerator did she become aware of Len, and it took her another little while for her to remember to wrap her attractions in the yellow mists of the nightgown.

Mrs. Hanson made introductions. Len insisted that Shrimp join them at the table and took it on himself to spoon out some Granola into a third bowl.

"Why was I in Mickey's bed?" Shrimp asked.

There was no help for it: Briefly she explained Shrimp to Len, and Len to Shrimp. When Len expressed what polite interest the situation required, Shrimp started in on the sordid details, baring her shoulder to show the tine wounds.

Mrs. Hanson said, "Shrimp, please—"

Shrimp said, "I'm not ashamed, Mother, not any more." And went right on. Mrs. Hanson stared at the fork resting on her greasy dinner plate. She could have taken it and torn Shrimp to pieces.

When Shrimp led Len off into the living room, Mrs. Hanson got out of hearing any more by pleading the dishes.

Len had left three of the cubes of beef on the side of his plate untasted. The ounce of Granola he'd kept for himself was stirred about in the bowl. He'd hated the meal.

His wine glass was three-quarters full. She thought, should she pour it down the sink. She wanted to, but it seemed such a waste. She drank it.

Len came back to the kitchen finally with the news that Shrimp had returned to bed. She couldn't bear to look at him. She just waited for the blade to drop, and it didn't take long.

"Mrs. Hanson," he said. "it should be obvious that I can't stay here now, not if it means putting your pregnant daughter out on the street."

"My daughter! Ha!"

"I'm disappointed and—"

"You're disappointed!"

"Of course I am."

"Oh, of course, of course!"

He turned away from her. She couldn't bear it. She would do anything to keep him. "Len!" she called after him.

He returned in no time with his suitcase and his bag of books, moving at the uncanny, hyped-up speed of the five-fifteen puppets.

"Len!" She stretched out a hand, to forgive him, to beg forgiveness.

The speed! The terrible speed of it!

She followed him out into the corridor, weeping, wretched, *afraid*. "Len," she pleaded, "*look* at me."

He strode ahead, heedless, but at the very first step of the stairs his bag swung into the railing and split open. Books spilled out onto the landing.

"I'll get you another bag," she said, calculating quickly and exactly what might hold him to the spot.

He hesitated.

"Len, please don't go." She grasped handfuls of the maroon sweater. "Len, I love you!"

"Sweet fucking Jesus, that's what I *thought*!"

He pulled away from her. She thought he was falling down the steps and screamed.

Then there were only the books at her feet. She recognized the fat black textbook and kicked it out through the gap in the rails. Then the rest, some down the steps, others into the abyss of the stairwell. Forever.

The next day when Lottie asked her what had become of the boarder, she said, "He was a vegetarian. He couldn't live anywhere where there was meat."

Only one of the
20 best-selling cigarettes
can be lowest
in both tar and nicotine.

True's the one.

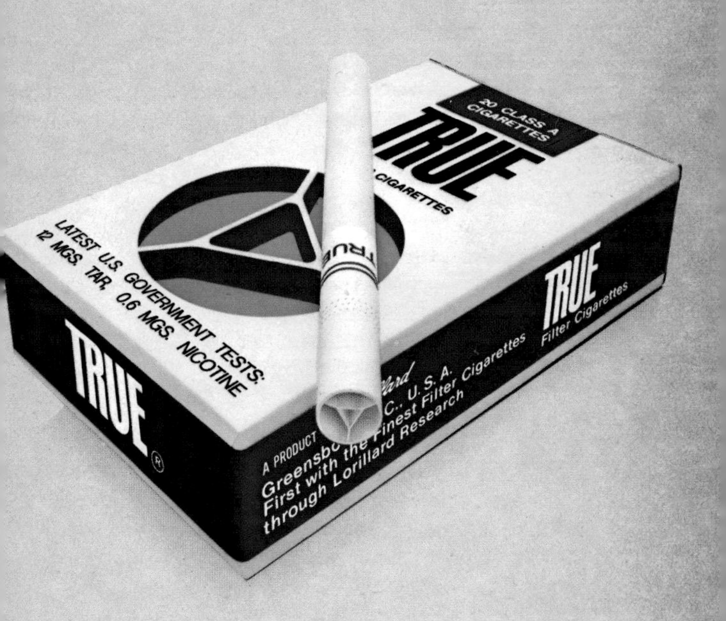

Regular or Menthol.
Doesn't it all add up to True?

Regular: 12 mg. "tar", 0.6 mg. nicotine,
Menthol: 13 mg. "tar", 0.7 mg. nicotine, av. per cigarette, FTC Report, Aug. '71.

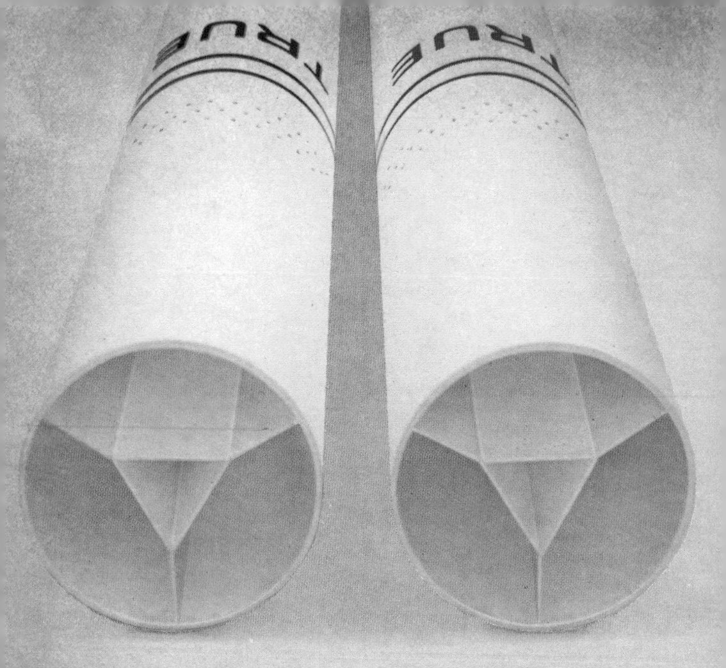
TRUE
TRUE

"He should have told you that before he came."
"Yes," Mrs. Hanson agreed bitterly. "That's what *I* thought."

PART IV: LOTTIE

26. Messages Are Received (2024)

Financially, being a widow was way ahead of being a wife. Lottie was able to phone Jerry Lighthall and tell her that she didn't need her job now, or anyone else's. She was free and then some. Besides the weekly and now completely reliable allotment, Bellevue paid her a lump sum settlement of $5,000. With Lottie's go-ahead the owner of the Abingdon sold what was left of Princess Cass through *Buy-Lines* for $860, off the top of which he skimmed no more than was reasonable. Even after paying out a small fortune for the memorial service that no one came to and wiping up the family's various existing debts, Lottie had over four thousand dollars to do with as she pleased. Four thousand dollars: her first reaction was fear. She put the money in a bank and tried to forget about it.

It was several weeks later before she found out, from her daughter, the probable explanation for Juan's killing himself. Amparo had heard it from Beth Holt who'd pieced it together from scattered remarks of her father's and what she already knew. Juan had been dealing with resurrectionists for years. Either Bellevue had just found out, which didn't seem likely, or the Administration had been pressured, for reasons unknown, to pounce on someone: Juan. He'd had time, apparently, to see it coming, and instead of concurring tamely in his sacrifice (it would have amounted to two or three years at most) he'd found this way to go out of the game with honor unblemished. Honor: for years he'd tried to explain to Lottie the intricacies of his private system of reckoning which squares were black and which white and how to move among them, but it had always made about as much sense to her as the engine under Princess Cass's hood, a man's world of mathematics—arbitrary, finicking, and lethal.

Emotionally it wasn't as bad as she'd expected. She cried a lot, but with a bounded grief. Some of Juan's own affectionate indifference seemed to have rubbed off without her ever realizing. In between the spells of mourning she experienced unaccountable elations. She went for long walks in unfamiliar neighborhoods. Twice she stopped in to visit places where she'd once worked, but she never managed to be more than a source of embarrassment. She increased her evenings with the Universal Friends to two nights a week at the same time that she began to explore in other directions as well.

One day, riding the crest of the highest wave yet, she wandered into Bonwit's for no other reason that it was right there on 14th and might be a bit cooler than the September concrete. Inside the sight of the racks and counters affected her like a lungful of amyl nitrate on top of morbihanine. The colors, the immense space, the noise overwhelmed her—first with a kind of terror, then with a steadily mounting delight. She'd worked here most of a year without being impressed, and the store hadn't noticeably changed. But now! It was like walking into a gigantic wedding cake in which all the desires of a lifetime had become incarnate, beckoning her to touch and taste and ravish. Her hand reached out to stroke the yielding fabrics—sleek blacks, scratchy russets, grays that caressed like a breeze from the river. She wanted all of it.

She began taking things from the racks and off the counters and putting them in her carryall. How strangely convenient that she should have that at hand today! She went to the second floor for shoes, yellow shoes, red shoes with thick straps, frail shoes of silver net, and to four for a hat. And dresses! Bonwit's was thronged with dresses of all descriptions, colors, and lengths, like a great host of disembodied spirits waiting to be called down to earth and named. She took dresses.

Descending a step or two from the heights, she realized that people were watching her. Indeed she was being followed about, and not only by the store detective. There was a ring of faces looking at her, as though from a great distance below, as though they yelled, "Jump! Jump! Why don't you jump!" She walked up to a cash cage in the middle of the floor and emptied her purse out into a hamper. A clerk took off the tags and fed them into a register. The sum mounted higher and higher, dazzling, until the clerk asked, with heavy sarcasm: "Will that be cash or charge?"

"I'll pay cash," she said and waved the brand-new checkbook at his scruffy little beard. When he asked for ID she rummaged among all the scraps and tatters at the bottom of her purse until she found, all munched up and bleached, her Bonwit's Employee Identification Card. Leaving the store she tipped her new hat, a big, good-natured, floppy thing dripping with all widths of (because she *was* a widow) black ribbon, and smiled a big smile for the benefit of Bonwit's detective, who had followed her every inch of the way from the cash cage.

At home she discovered that the dresses, blouses, and other bodywear were all lightyears too small for her. She gave Shrimp the one dress that still looked life-enhancing in the dark of common day, kept the hat for its sentimental value, and sent back all the rest the next day with Amparo, who already, at age 11, had the knack of getting what she wanted from people in stores.

(Since Lottie had signed the forms to let her transfer to the Lowen School, Amparo had been behaving tolerantly toward her mother. In any case she enjoyed the combat of a refund counter. She wasn't able to get cash, but she wangled what for her own purpose was better, a credit slip for any department in the store. She spent the rest of the day selecting a back-to-school wardrobe for herself in careful, mezzo-forte taste, hoping that after the explosion her mother, seeing the sense of sending her out into the world dressed in real clothes, would let her keep as much as half of what she'd pirated. Lottie's explosion was considerable, with screams and a whack or two of the belt, but by the time the late news was over it all seemed to be forgotten, as though Amparo had done nothing worse than to glance in the store's windows. The same night Lottie cleared out one whole drawer of the dresser for the new clothes. Jesus, Amparo thought, what a superannuated ass!)

Not long after this adventure Lottie realized that she was no longer holding steady at 175, which was bad enough; she was gaining. She bought a coke machine and loved to lie in bed and let it fizzle the back of her throat, but noncaloric as this pleasure was, she went on gaining alarmingly. The explanation was physiological: she ate too much. Soon Shrimp would have to give up her polite fiction about her sister's Rubens-like figure and admit that she was just plain fat. Then Lottie would have to admit it too. You're fat, she'd tell herself, looking into the dark mirror of the living room window. Fat! But it didn't help, or it didn't help enough: she couldn't believe that she was the person she saw reflected there. She was Lottie Hanson, the five-dollar tomato; the fat woman was someone else.

Early one morning in the late fall, when the whole apartment smelled of rust (the steam had come on during the night), the explanation—of what was going and had gone wrong—presented itself to her in the plainest terms: "There's nothing left." She repeated the phrase to herself like a prayer, and with each repetition the circumference of its meaning would expand. The terror of it slowly wound its way through the tangle of her feelings until it had merged with its opposite. "There's nothing left": it was cause to rejoice. What had she ever had that it wouldn't be a liberation to lose? Indeed, too much still clinged to her. It would be long before she could say that there was *nothing* left, absolutely, blessedly nothing at all. Then, the way revelations do, the brilliance faded, leaving her with only the embers of the phrase. Her mind grew furry, and she started developing a headache from the smell of the rust.

Other mornings there were other awakenings. Their common feature was that they all seemed to place her squarely on the brink of some momentous event, but facing in the wrong direction, like the tourists in the living room calendar's "Before" view of the Grand Canyon, smiling into the camera, oblivious of what lay behind them. The only thing she knew for sure was that something would be demanded of her, an action larger than any she'd ever been called on to perform, a kind of sacrifice. But what? But when?

Meanwhile her regular religious experience had enlarged to include the message services at the Albert Hotel. The medium, Reverend Inez Ribera from Houston, Texas, was the female side of the coin of Lottie's tenth grade nemesis, old Mr. Sills. She spoke, except when she was in trance, in the same flutey teacherish voice,—broad r's, round vowels, whistling sibilants. Her less inspired messages were the same sour compound of veiled threat and headlong innuendo. However, while Sills had played favorites, Rev. Ribera's scorn withered impartially, which made her, if no more likeable, somewhat easier to take.

Besides, Lottie could understand the bitterness that drove her to lash out in all directions. Rev. Ribera was genuine. She achieved real contact only now and again, but when she did it was unmistakable. The spirits that laid hold on her were seldom gentle, and yet once they'd established their presence, the ridicule, the threats of aneurisms and financial ruin were replaced by mild, rambling descriptions of the other side. Instead of the usual abundance of counsels, the messages of these spirits were uncertain, tentative, even distressed and puzzled. They made little gestures of friendship and reconciliation, then skittered off, as though expecting to be refused. It was invariably during these visitations, when Rev. Ribera was so visibly not herself, that she would pronounce the secret word or mention the significant detail that proved her words weren't just the spiritual outpourings of some vague elsewhere but unique communications from real, known people. The first message from Juan, for instance, had been "his" beyond any doubt, for Lottie had been able to return home and find the same words in one of the letters he'd written to her twelve years before:

Ya no la quiero, es cierto, pero tal vez la quiero.
Es tan corto el amor, y es tan largo el olvido.

Porque en noches como esta la tuve entre mis brazos,
mi alma no se contenta con haberla perdido.

Annque este sea el ultimo dolor que ella me causa,
y estos sean los ultimos versos que yo le escribo.

The poem wasn't Juan's in the sense that he'd written it, though Lottie had never let him know that she'd known that. But even if the words came from someone else, the *feelings* had been his, and were his now more certainly than when he'd copied them into the letter. With all the poems there are in Spanish, how could Rev. Ribera have picked just that one? Unless Juan had been there that night. Unless he'd wanted to find some way to touch her so that she could believe that he *had*.

Later messages from Juan tended to be less other-directed, and more a kind of spiritual autobiography. He described his progress from a plane of existence that was predominantly dark brown to a higher plane that was green, where he met his grandfather Rafael and a woman in a bridal gown, barely more than a girl, whose name came through as Rita or 'Nita. The ghostly bride seemed determined to make contact with Lottie, for she returned on several occasions, but Lottie was never able to see what the connection was between herself and this Rita or 'Nita. As Juan advanced to higher planes, it became harder to distinguish his tone from that of the other spirits. He alternated between wistfulness and hectoring. He wanted Lottie to lose weight. He wanted her to visit the Lighthalls. Finally it became clear to Lottie that Rev. Ribera had lost contact with Juan and was now only faking it. She stopped coming for the private meetings, and shortly thereafter Rafael and other distant relatives began to foresee all kinds of dangers in her path. A person that she trusted was going to betray her. She would lose large sums of money. There was, somewhere ahead, a fire, possibly only a symbolic fire but possibly it was real.

About the money they had been well-informed. By the first anniversary of Juan's death the four thousand dollars had been reduced to little more than four hundred.

It was easier than it might have been to say goodbye to Juan and the rest because she had begun to establish her own, more direct lines of communication with the other side. Off and on over the years Lottie had attended gospel meetings at the Day of Judgement Pentacostal Church, which met in a rented hall on Avenue A. She went there for the sake of the music and the excitement, not being deeply concerned about what seemed to draw in the majority of the others—the drama of sin and salvation. Lottie believed in sin in a general way, as a kind of condition or environment like clouds, but when she felt around inside herself for her own sins she drew a blank. The nearest she could approach to guilt was thinking about the ways she'd messed up Mickey's and Amparo's lives, and even this was a cause rather of discomfort than of out-and-out anguish.

Then one dreadful August night in '25 (an inversion layer had been stifling the city for days, the air was unbreathable) Lottie had stood up in the middle of the prayer asking for spiritual gifts and begun to prophecy in tongues. It lasted only a moment the first time, and Lottie wondered if it might not be just a simple case of heat prostration, but the next time it was much clearer. It began with a sense of constriction, of being covered and enclosed, and then another kind of force struggled against this and emerged through it.

"Like a fire?" Brother Cary had asked her.

She remembered Juan's grandfather's warning about a fire that might be symbolic or might be real.

It was utterly dependable. She spoke in tongues whenever she came to the Day of Judgement Pentacostal Church and at no time else. When she felt the clouds gathering about her, she would stand, no matter what else might be happening, a sermon, a baptising, and the congregation would gather round her in a great circle, while Brother Cary held her and prayed for the fire to come down. When she felt it coming she would begin to tremble, but when it touched her she felt strong, and she spoke in a voice that was loud, and clear with praise:

"Tralla goody ala troddy chaunt. Net nosse betnosse keyscope namallim. Zarbos ha zarbos myer, zarbos roldo teneview menevent. Daney, daney, daney sigs, daney sigs. Chonery ompolla rop!"

Or:

"Dabsa bobby nasa sana dubey. Lo fornival lo fier. Ompolla meny, leasiest mell. Woo—lubba dever ever onna. Woo—molit ule. Nok! Nok! Nok!"

PART V: SHRIMP

27. *Having Babies*

Shrimp's hangup was having babies—first the begetting, with the sperm; then the foetus growing inside her; finally the completed baby coming out. Since the Regents' System had gone into effect it was a fairly widespread syndrome, compulsory contraception having hit many of the old myths and icons with hurricane force, but with Shrimp it took a special form. She had enough psychoanalysis to understand her perversion, but she went on having babies anyhow.

Shrimp had been thirteen years old, and still a virgin, when her mother had gone to the hospital to be injected with a new son. The operation had had a doubly supernatural quality—the sperm had come from a man five years dead, and the result was so clearly intended to be a replacement for the son Mrs. Hanson had lost in the riot: Boz was Jimmie Tom reborn. So when Shrimp had fantasies of the syringe going up into her own womb, it was a ghost that filled her, and its name was incest. The fact that it had to be a woman who did it for her to get excited probably made it even more multiply incest.

The first two, Tiger and Thumper, had not presented any problems on the rational level. She could tell herself that millions of women did it, that it was the only ethical way for homosexuals to procreate, that the children themselves were happier and better off growing up in the country or wherever with professional attention, and so on through a dozen other rationalizations, including the best of all, money. Subsidized motherhood certainly beat the pittance she could get killing herself for Con Ed or the even deadlier fates she'd met after she'd been fired from that. Logically what could be better than to be paid for what you craved?

Even so, through both pregnancies and the contractual months of motherhood she suffered attacks of unreasoning shame so intense that she often thought of donating herself and the baby to the charity of the river. (If her hangup had been feet she'd have been ashamed to walk. You can't argue with Freud.)

The third was another story. January, though she was willing to go along with the thing on the fantasy level, was firmly opposed to the fantasy being acted out. But going in and filling out the forms, what was that but enjoying the fantasy at an institutional level? At her age and having had two already, it didn't seem likely that her application would be approved, and when it was, the temptation to go in for the interview was irresistible. It was all irresistible right up to the moment that she was spread out on the white platform, with her feet in the chrome stirrups. The motor purred, and her pelvis was tipped forward to receive the syringe, and it was as though the heavens opened and a hand came down to stroke the source of all pleasures at the very center of her brain. Mere sex offered nothing to compare.

Not till she was home from her weekend in the Caribbean of delight did she give any thought to what her vacation would cost. January had threatened to leave her when she'd heard about Tiger and Thumper, who were then ancient history. What would she do in this case? She *would* leave her.

She confessed one particularly fine Thursday in April after a late breakfast from Betty Crocker. Shrimp was into her fifth month and couldn't go on much longer calling her pregnancy menopause.

"Why?" January asked, with what seemed a sincere unhappiness. "Why did you do it?"

Having prepared herself to cope with anger, Shrimp resented this detour into pathos. "Because. Oh, you know. I explained that."

"You couldn't stop yourself?"

"I couldn't. Like the other times—it was as though I were in a trance."

"But you're over it now?"

Shrimp nodded, amazed at how easily she was being let off the hook.

"Then get an abortion."

Shrimp pushed a crumb of potato around with the tip of her spoon, trying to decide whether there'd be any purpose in seeming to go along with the idea for a day or two.

January mistook her silence for yielding. "You know it's the only right thing to do. We discussed it and you agreed."

"I know. But the contracts are signed."

"You mean you won't. You *want* another fucking baby!" January flipped. Before she knew what she was doing it was done, and they both stood staring at the four tiny hemispheres of blood that welled up, swelled, conjoined, and flowed down into the darkness of Shrimp's left armpit. The guilty fork was still in January's hand. Shrimp gave a belated scream and ran into the bathroom.

Safe inside she kept squeezing further droplets from the wound.

January banged and clattered.

"Jan?" addressing the crack of the bolted door.

"You better stay in there. The next time I'll use a knife."

"Jan, I know you're angry. You've got every right to be angry. I admit that I'm in the wrong. But wait, Jan. Wait till you see him before you say anything. The first six months are so wonderful. You'll see. I can even get an extension for the whole year if you want. We'll make a fine little family, just the—"

A chair smashed through the paper paneling of the door. Shrimp shut up. When she screwed up the courage to peek out through the torn door, not much later, the room was in a shambles but empty. January had taken one of the cupboards, but Shrimp was sure she'd be back if only to evict her. The room was January's, after all, not Shrimp's. But when she returned, late in the afternoon, from the therapy of a double feature (*The Black Rabbit* and *Billy McGlory* at the Underworld) the eviction had already been accomplished, but not by January, who had gone west, taking love from Shrimp's life, as she supposed, forever.

Her welcome back to 334 was not as cordial as she could have wished, but in a couple of days Mrs. Hanson was brought round to seeing that Shrimp's loss was her own gain. The spirit of family happiness returned officially on the day Mrs. Hanson asked, "What are you going to call this one?"

"The baby, you mean?"

"Yeah, it. You'll have to name it something, won't you? How about Fudge? Or Puddle?" Mrs. Hanson, who'd given her own children unexceptionable names, openly disapproved of Tiger's being called Tiger, and Thumper Thumper, even though the names, being unofficial, didn't stick once the babies were sent off.

"No, Fudge is only nice for a girl, and Puddle is vulgar. I'd rather it were something with more class."

"How about Flapdoodle then?"

"Flapdoodle!" Shrimp went along with the joke, grateful for any joke to go along with. "Flapdoodle! Wonderful! Flapdoodle it'll be. Flapdoodle Hanson."

28. 53 Movies (2024)

Flapdoodle Hanson was born on August 29, 2024, but as she had been a sickly vegetable and was not, as an animal, any healthier, Shrimp returned to 334 alone. She received her weekly check just the same, and the rest was a matter of indifference. The excitement had gone out of the notion of babies. She understood the traditional view that women bring forth children in sorrow.

On September 18 Williken jumped, or was pushed, out of the window of his apartment. His wife's theory was that he hadn't paid off the super for the privilege of operating his various small businesses in the darkroom, but what wife wants to believe her husband will kill himself without so much as a discussion of the theory? Juan's suicide, not much more than two months before, made Williken's seem justifiable by comparison.

She'd never given any thought to how much, since she'd come back to 334 in April, she'd come to depend on Williken to get through the evenings and the weeks. Lottie was off with her spirits or drinking herself blotto on the insurance money. Her mother's endless inanities got to be a Chinese water torture, and the teevee was no defence. Charlotte, Kiri, and the rest were past history—January had seen to that.

Just to escape the apartment she began seeing movies, mostly in the pocket theaters on 1st Avenue or around N.Y.U., since they showed double features. Sometimes she'd sit through the same double feature twice in a row, going in at four o'clock and coming out at ten or eleven. She found she was able to watch the movies totally, any movie, and that afterwards she remembered details, images, lines of dialogue, tunes, with weird fidelity. She'd be walking home through the crowds on Eighth Street and she'd have to stop because some face, or the gesture of a hand, or some luscious, long-ago landscape would have returned to her, wiping out all other data. At the same time she felt completely cut off from everyone and passionately involved.

Not counting second helpings, she saw a total of fifty-three movies in the period from October 1st to November 16th. She saw: *A Girl of the Limberlost* and *Strangers on a Train;* Don Hershey as *Melmoth* and *Stanford White;* Penn's *Hellbottom*; *The Story of Vernon and Irene Castle; Escape from Cuernavaca* and *Singing in the Rain;* Franju's *Thomas l'Imposteur* and *Judex; Dumbo;* Jacquelynn Colton in *The Confessions of St. Augustine;* both parts of *Daniel Deronda; Candide; Snow White and Juliet;* Brando in *On The Waterfront* and *Down Here;* Robert Mitchum in *The Night of the Hunter*; Nicholas Ray's *King of Kings* and Mai Zetterling's *Behold the Man*; both versions of *The Ten Commandments;* Loren and Mastroianni in *Sunflower* and *Black Eyes and Lemonade*; Rainer Murray's *Owens and Darwin*; *The Zany World of Abbott and Costello; The Hills of Switzerland* and *The Sound of Music;* Garbo in *Camille* and *Anna Christie*; *Zarlah the Martian;* Emshwiller's *Walden* and *Image, Flesh, and Voice;* the remake of *Equinox; Casablanca* and *The Big Clock; The Temple of the Golden Pavilion*; *Star * Gut* and *Valentine Vox*; *The Best of Judy Canova*; *Pale Fire*; *Felix Culp; The Green Berets* and *The Day of the Locust;* Sam Blazer's *Three Christs of Ypsilanti; On the Yard; Wednesdays Off;* both parts of *Stinky in the Land of Poop;* the complete ten-hour *Les Vampires*; *The Possibilities of Defeat;* and the shortened version of *Things in the World.* At that point Shrimp suddenly lost interest in seeing any more.

29. The White Uniform, continued (2021)

It was delivered by some derelict messenger. January didn't know what to make of the uniform, but the card that Shrimp had enclosed tickled her pink. She showed it to the people at work, to the Lighthalls, who always enjoyed a good joke, to her brother Ned, and all of them got a chuckle out of it. The outside showed a blithe, vulgar little sparrow. Written underneath in music was the melody he was chirping:

The lyrics of the song were on the inside: *Wanna fuck? Wanna fuck? I do! I do!*

At first January was embarrassed playing nurse. She was a largish girl, and the uniform, even though Shrimp had guessed her size correctly, didn't want to move the way her body moved. Putting it on, she would always feel, as she hadn't for a long time, ashamed of her real job.

As they got to know each other more deeply, January found ways of combining the abstract qualities of Shrimp's fantasies with the mechanics of ordinary sex. She would begin with a lengthy "examination." Shrimp would lie in bed, limp, her eyes closed or lightly bandaged, while January's fingers took her pulse, palpated her breasts, spread her legs, explored her sex. Deeper and deeper the fingers, and the "instruments" probed. January eventually was able to find a medical supply store willing to sell her an authentic pipette that could be attached to an ordinary syringe. The pipette tickled morbidly. She would pretend that Shrimp was too tight or too nervous and had to be opened wider by one of the other instruments. Once the scenario was perfected, it wasn't that much different from any other kind of sex.

Shrimp, while all this was going on, would oscillate between an excruciating pleasure and a no less excruciating guilt. The pleasure was simple and absolute; the guilt was complex. For she loved January and she wanted to perform with her all the acts that any ordinary pair of women would have performed. And, regularly, they did: cunnilingus this way and that, dildoes here and there, lips, fingers, tongues, every orifice and artifice. But she knew, and January knew, that these were readings from some textbook called *Health and Sex*, not the actual erotic lightning bolt of a fantasy that can connect the ankle bone to the shin bone, the shin bone to the leg bone, the leg bone to the thigh bone, the thigh bone to the pelvis, the pelvis to the spine, and onward and upward to that source of all desire and all thought, the head. Shrimp went through the motions, but all the while her poor head sat through yet another screening of those old classics, *Ambulance Story, The White Uniform, The Lady and the Needle,* and *Artsem Baby.* They weren't as exciting as she remembered them, but nothing else was playing, anywhere.

30. Beauty and the Beast (2021)

Shrimp thought of herself as basically an artist. Her eyes saw colors the way a painter's eyes see colors. As an observer of the human comedy she considered herself to be on a par with Deb Potter or Oscar Stevenson. A seemingly offhand remark overheard on the street could trigger her imagination to produce the plot for a whole movie. She was sensitive, intelligent (her Regents scores proved that), and up-to-date. The only thing she was conscious of lacking was a direction, and what was that but a matter of pointing a finger?

Artistry ran in the Hanson family. Jimmie Tom had been well on the way to becoming a singer. Boz, though unfocused as Shrimp herself, was a verbal genius. Amparo, at age 8, was doing such incredibly detailed and psychological drawings at her school that she might grow up to be the real thing.

And not just her family. Many if not most of her closest friends were artists one way or another: Charlotte Blethen had published poems; Kiri Johns knew all the grand operas inside out; Mona Rosen and Patrick Shawn had both acted in plays. And others. But her proudest alliance was with Richard M. Williken, whose photographs had been seen all over the world.

Art was the air she breathed, the sidewalk she walked on to the secret garden of her soul, and living with January was like having a dog constantly shitting on that sidewalk. An innocent, adorable, cuddly puppy—you had to love the little fellow, but oh my.

If January had simply been indifferent to art, Shrimp wouldn't have minded. In a way she'd have liked that. But alas, January had her own horrendous tastes in everything, and she expected Shrimp to share them. She brought home library tapes the like of which Shrimp had never suspected: scraps of pop songs and snatches of symphonies were strung together with sound effects to tell such creaky tales as "Vermont Holiday" or "Cleopatra on the Nile."

January accepted Shrimp's snubs and snide remarks in the spirit of tolerance and good humor in which she thought they were intended. Shrimp joked because she was a Hanson, and all the Hansons were sarcastic. She couldn't believe that anything she enjoyed so much herself could be abhorrent to another person. She could see that Shrimp's music was a better *kind* of music, and she liked listening to it when it was on, but all of the time and nothing else? You'd go nuts.

Her eyes were like her ears. She would inflict well-meaning barbarities of jewelry and clothes on Shrimp, who wore them as tokens of her bondage and abasement. The walls of her room were one great mural of unspeakable, sickly-cute junk and sententious propaganda posters, like this jewel from the lips of a black Spartacus: "A Nation of Slaves is always prepared to applaud the clemency of their Master, who, in the abuse of Absolute Power, does not proceed to the Last extremes of Injustice and Oppression." Bow-wow-wow. But what could Shrimp do? Walk in and rip them from the walls? January *valued* her crap.

What do you do when you love a slob? What she did—try and become a slob herself. Shrimp wallowed diligently, losing most of her old friends in the process. She more than made up for her losses by the friendships January brought with her as a dowry. Not that she ever came to like any of them, but gradually through their eyes she learned that her lover had virtues as well as charms, problems as well as virtues, a mind with its own thoughts, memories, projects, and a personal history as poignant as anything by Chopin or Liszt. In fact, she was a human being, and though it took a day of the very clearest air and brightest sunshine for this feature of January's landscape to be visible, it was such a fine and heartening sight that when it came it was worth every other inconvenience of being, and remaining, in love.

After the sweeping license fell through, Lottie had one of her bad spells, sleeping up to fifteen hours a day, bullying Amparo, making fun of Mickey, living for days on pills and then demolishing the icebox on a binge. In general she fell apart. This time it was her sister who pulled her out. Living with January seemed to have made Shrimp one hundred per cent more human. Lottie even told her so.

"Suffering," Shrimp said, "That's what does it—I suffer a lot."

They talked, they played games. they went to whatever events Shrimp could get freebies for. Mostly, they talked; in Stuyvesant Square, on the roof, in Tompkins Square Park. They talked about growing old, about being in love, about not being in love, about life, about death. They agreed that it was terrible to grow old, though Shrimp thought they both had a long way to go before it got really terrible. They agreed that it was terrible to be in love, but that it was more terrible not to be. They agreed that life was rotten. They didn't agree about death. Shrimp believed, though not always literally, in reincarnation and psychic phenomena. To Lottie death made no sense. It wasn't death she dreaded so much as the pain of dying.

"It helps to talk, doesn't it?" Shrimp said during one magnificent sunset up on the roof with rose-colored clouds zooming by.

"No," said Lottie, with a sour, here-I-am-again type smile to say to Shrimp that she was on her feet and not to worry, "it doesn't."

It was that evening that Shrimp mentioned the possibility of prostitution.

"Me? Don't be silly!"

"Why not? You used to."

"Ten years ago. More! And even *then* I never earned enough to make it worthwhile."

"You weren't trying."

"Shrimp, for God's sake, just look at me!"

"Many men are attracted to large, Rubens-type women. Anyhow I only mentioned it. And I was going to say that *if*—"

"If!" Lottie giggled.

"If you change your mind, January knows a couple who handle that sort of thing. It's safer than doing it as a freelance, so I'm told, and more businesslike too."

The couple that January knew were the Lighthalls, Jerry and Lee. Lee was fat and black and something of an Uncle Tom. Jerry was wraithlike and given to sudden meaningful silences. Lottie was never able to decide which of them was actually in charge. They worked from what Lottie believed for months was a bogus law office, until she found out that Jerry actually belonged to the New York State Bar. The clients arriving at the office behaved in a solemn deliberate way, as though they were after all here for a legal consultation rather than a good time. For the most part they were a sort of person Lottie had had no personal experience with—engineers, programmers, what Lee called 'our technologically *ee*—leete clientele.'

The Lighthalls specialized in golden showers, but by the time Lottie found this out, she had made up her mind to go through with it, come what may. The first time was awful. The man insisted that she watch his face the whole while he kept saying, "I'm pissing on you, Lottie. I'm pissing on you." As though otherwise she might not have known.

Jerry suggested that if she took a pink pill a couple hours beforehand and then sank back on a green at the start of a session it was possible to keep the experience at an impersonal level, as though it were taking place on teevee. Lottie tried it and the result for her was not so much to make it impersonal as to make it unreal. Instead of the scene becoming a teevee screen, she was pissed on *by* one.

The single largest advantage of the job was that her wages weren't official. The Lighthalls didn't believe in paying taxes, and so they operated illegally, even though that meant charging much less than the licensed brothels. Lottie didn't lose any of her regular MODICUM benefits, and the necessity of spending what she made on the black market meant that she bought the fun things she wanted instead of the dull things she ought to have. Her wardrobe trebled. She ate at restaurants. Her room filled with knick-knacks and toys and the fruity reek of Faberge's Molly Bloom.

As the Lighthalls got to know and trust her, she began to be sent out to people's homes, often staying the night.

Invariably this would mean something beyond golden showers. She could see that it was a job that she could grow to like. Not for the sex, the sex was nothing, but sometimes afterwards, especially on assignments away from Washington Street, the clients would warm up and talk about something besides their own unvarying predilections. This was the aspect of the job that appealed to Lottie—the human contact.

32. Lottie, in Stuyvesant Square (2021)

"Heaven. I'm *in* heaven.

"What I mean is, anyone if he just looked around and really understood what he saw. . . . But that's not what I'm supposed to say, is it? The object's to be able to say what you *want.* Instead, I guess what *I* was saying was that I'd better be happy with what I've got, cause I won't get any more. But then if I don't *ask* for more. . . . It's a vicious circle.

"Heaven. What is heaven. Heaven is a supermarket. Like that one they built outside the museum. Full of everything you could ever ask for. Full of fresh meat—I wouldn't live in any vegetarian heaven—full of cake mixes and cartons of cold milk and fizzies in cans. Oh, the works. And *lots* of disposable containers. And I would just go down the aisles with my big cart in a kind of trance, the way they say the housewives did then, without thinking what any of it was going to cost. Without thinking. Nineteen-Fifty-Three A.D.—you're right, that's heaven.

"No. No, I guess not. That's the trouble with heaven. You say something that sounds nice, but then you think, would you really want it a second time? A third time? Like your highway, it would be great once. And then? What then?

"You see, it *has* to come from inside.

"So what *I* want, what I really do want. . . . I don't know how to say it. What I really want is to *really* want something. The way, you know, when a baby wants something? The way he reaches for it. I'd like to see something and reach for it like that. Not to be aware that I couldn't have it, or that it wasn't my turn. Juan is that way sometimes with sex, once he lets loose. But of course heaven would have to be larger than that.

"I know! The movie we saw on teevee the other night when Mom wouldn't shut up, the Japanese movie, remember? Do you remember the fire festival, the song they sang? I forget the exact words, but the idea was that you should let life burn you up. That's what I want. I want life to burn me up.

"So that's what heaven is then. Heaven is the fire that does that, a huge roaring bonfire with lots of little Japanese women dancing around it, and every so often they let out a great shout and one of them rushes into it. Whoof!"

33. Shrimp, in Stuyvesant Square (2021)

"One of the rules in the magazine was that you can't mention other people by name. Otherwise I could just say, 'Heaven would be if I were living with January,' and then describe that. But if you're describing a *relationship*, you don't let yourself imagine all you could, and so you learn nothing.

"So where does that leave me?"

"Visualize, it said.

"Okay. Well, there's grass in heaven, because I can see myself standing in grass. But it isn't the country, not with cows and such. And it can't be a park, because the grass in parks is either sickly or you can't walk on it. It's beside a highway. A highway in Texas! Let's say in Nineteen-Fifty-Three. It's a clear, clear day in 1953, and I can see the highway stretching on and on past the horizon.

"Endlessly.

"Then what? Then I'll want to drive on the highway, I suppose. But not by myself, that would be anxiety-making. So I'll break the rule and let January drive. If we're on a motorcycle, it's scarcely a relationship, is it?

"Well, our motorcycle is going fast, it's going terribly fast, and there are cars and gigantic trucks going almost as fast as we are. Toward the horizon. We weave in and out, in and out. Faster we go, and faster and faster.

"Then what? I don't know. That's as far as I see.

"Now it's your turn."

34. Shrimp, At The Asylum (2024)

"What do I feel? Angry. Afraid. Sorry for myself. I don't know. I feel a bit of everything, but not—Oh, this is silly. I don't want to be wasting everyone's time with—

"Well, I'll try it. Just say the one thing over and over until—What happens?

"I love you. There, that wasn't so bad. I love you. I love you, January. I love you, January. January, I love you. January, I *love* you. If she were here it would be a lot easier, you know. Okay, okay. I love you. I love *you*. I love your big warm boobs. I'd like to squeeze them. And I love your . . . I love your juicy black cunt. How about that? I do. I love *all* of you. I wish we were together again. I wish I knew where you were so you'd know that. I don't want the baby, any babies, I want *you*. I want to be married. To you. For all time. I love you.

"Keep going?

"I love you. I love you. I love you very much. And that's a lie. I *hate* you. I can't stand you. You appall me, with your stupidity, with your vulgarity, with your third-hand ideas that you take off the party-line like—You *bore* me. You bore me to tears. You're dumb nigger *scum*! Nigger bitch. Stupid! And I don't care if—

"No, I can't. It's not there. I'm just saying the words because I know you want to hear them. Love, hate, love, hate—words.

"It isn't that I'm resisting. But I don't *feel* what I'm saying, and that's the truth. Either way. The only thing I feel is tired. I wish I were home watching teevee instead of wasting everyone's time. For which I apologize.

"Somebody else say something and I'll shut up."

35. Richard M. Williken, continued (2024)

"Your problem," he told her, as they were rocking home in the RR after the big non-breakthrough, "is that you're not willing to accept your own mediocrity."

"Oh shut up," she said. "I mean that sincerely."

"It's my own problem, just as much. Even more so, perhaps. Why do you think I've gone so long now without doing any work? It isn't that if I started in nothing would happen. But when I'm all done I look at what I'm left with and I say to myself, 'No, not enough.' In effect that's what you were saying tonight."

"I know you're trying to be nice, Willy, but it doesn't help. There's no comparison between your situation and mine."

"Sure there is. I can't believe in my pictures. You can't believe in your love affairs."

"A love affair isn't some goddamn work of art." The spirit of argument had caught hold of Shrimp. Williken could see her struggling out of her glooms as though they were no more than a wet swimsuit. Good old Shrimp!

"Isn't it?" he prompted.

She plunged after the bait without a thought. "You at least try to *do* something. There's an *attempt*. I've never gone that far. I suppose if I did I would be what you say—mediocre."

"You attempt to—ever so visibly."

"What?" she asked.

She wanted to be torn to pieces (no one at The Asylum had bothered even to scream at her), but Williken didn't rise above irony. "I try to *do* something; you try to *feel* something. You want an inner life, a spiritual life if you prefer. And you've got it. Only no matter what you do, no matter how you squirm to get away from the fact, it's mediocre. Not bad. Not *poor*."

"Blessed are the poor in spirit. Eh?"

"Exactly. But you don't believe that, and neither do I. You know who we are? We're the scribes and Pharisees."

"Oh, that's good."

"You're a bit more cheerful now."

Shrimp pulled a long face. "I'm laughing on the outside."

"Things could be a lot worse."

"How?"

"You might be a loser. Like me."

"And I'm a winner instead? You can say that! After you saw me there tonight?"

"Wait," he promised her. "Just wait."

PART VI: 2026

36. Boz

"Bulgaria!" Milly exclaimed, and it took no special equipment to know that her next words were going to be: "*I've* been to Bulgaria."

"Why don't you get out your slides and show us," Boz said, clamping the lid gently on her ego. Then, though he knew, he asked, "Whose turn is it?"

January snapped to attention and shook the dice. "Seven!" She counted out seven spaces aloud, ending up on Go to Jail. "I hope I stay there," she said cheerfully. "If I land on Boardwalk again that's the end of the game for me." She said it so hopefully.

"I'm trying to remember," Milly said, elbow propped on the table, the dice held aloft, time and the game in suspense, "what it was like. All that comes back is that people told jokes there. You had to sit and listen, for hours, to jokes. About *breasts*." A look passed between them, and another look passed between January and Shrimp.

Boz, though he'd have liked to retaliate with something gross, rose above it. He sat straighter in his chair. while in languid contrast his left hand dipped toward the dish of hot snaps. So much tastier cold.

Milly shook. Four: her cannon landed on the B & O. She paid Shrimp $200, and shook again. Eleven: her token came down on one of her own properties.

The Monopoly set was an heirloom from the O'Meara side of the family. The houses and hotels were wood, the counters lead. Milly, as ever, had the cannon, Shrimp had the little racing car, Boz had the battleship, and January had the flatiron. Milly and Shrimp were winning. Boz and January were losing. C'est la vie.

"Bulgaria," Boz said, because it was such a fine thing to say, but also because his duty as a host required him to lead the conversation back to the interrupted guest. "But why?"

Shrimp, who was studying the backs of her property deeds to see how many more houses she could get by mortgaging the odds and ends, explained the exchange system between the two schools.

"Isn't this what she was being so giddy about last spring?" Milly asked. "I thought another girl got the scholarship then."

"Celeste diCecca. She was the one in the airplane crash."

"Oh!" Milly said, as the light dawned. "I didn't make the connection."

"You thought Shrimp just likes to keep up with the latest plane crashes?" Boz asked.

"I don't know what I thought, trueheart. So now she's going after all. Talk about luck!"

Shrimp bought three more houses. Then the racing car sped past Park Place, Boardwalk, Go, and Income Tax, to land on Vermont Avenue. It was mortgaged to the bank.

"Talk about luck!" said January.

The talk about luck continued for several turns round the board—who had it and who lacked it and whether there was, outside of Monopoly, any such thing. Boz asked if any of them had ever known anyone who'd won on the numbers or in the lottery. January's brother had won $500 three years before.

"But of course," January added conscientiously, "Over the long run he's lost more than that."

"Certainly for the passengers an airplane crash is only luck," Milly insisted.

"Did you think about crashes a lot when you were a hostess?" January asked the question with the same leaden disinterest with which she played at the game.

While Milly told her story about the Great Air Disaster of 2021, Boz snuck around behind the screen to revise the orzata and add some ice. Tabbycat was watching tiny ballplayers silently playing ball on the teevee, and Peanut was sleeping peacefully. When he returned with the tray the Air Disaster was concluded and Shrimp was spelling out her philosophy of life:

"It may look like luck on the surface, but if you go deeper you'll see that people usually get what they've got coming. If it hadn't been this scholarship for Amparo, it would have been something else. She's worked for it."

"And Mickey?" January asked.

"Poor Mickey," Milly agreed.

"Mickey got exactly what he deserved."

For once Boz had to agree with his sister. "People, when they do things like that, are often *seeking* punishment."

January's orzata chose just that moment to spill itself. Milly got the board up in time, and only one edge was wet. January had had so little money left in front of her that that was no loss either. Boz was more embarrassed than January, since his last words seemed to imply that she'd overturned her drink deliberately. God knew, she had every reason to want to. Nothing is quite so dull as two solid hours of losing.

Two turns later January's wish came true. She landed on Boardwalk and was out of the game. Boz, who was being ground into the dust more slowly but just as surely, insisted on conceding at the same time. He went with January out onto the veranda.

"You didn't have to give up just to keep me company, you know."

"Oh, they're happier in there without us. Now they can fight it out between themselves, fang and claw."

"Do you know, I've *never* won at Monopoly? Never once in my life!" She sighed. Then, so as not to seem an ungrateful guest. "You've got a lovely view."

They appreciated the night-view in silence: lights that moved, cars and planes; lights that didn't move, stars, windows, streetlamps. Then, growing uneasy, Boz made his usual quip for a visitor on the veranda: "Yes—I've got the sun in the morning and the clouds in the afternoon."

Possibly January didn't get it. In any case she intended to be serious. "Boz, maybe you could give me some advice."

"Me? Fiddle-dee-dee!" Boz loved to give advice. "What about?"

"What we're doing."

"I thought that was more in the nature of being already done."

"What?"

"I mean, from the way Shrimp talks, I thought it was a—" But he couldn't say 'fait accompli,' so he translated: "—an accomplished fact."

"I suppose it is, as far as our being accepted. They've been very nice to us, the others there. It isn't us that I'm worried about so much as her mother."

"Mom? Oh, she'll get along."

"She seemed very upset last night."

"She gets upset, but she recovers quickly, our Mom does. All the Hansons are great bouncers-back. As you must have noticed." That wasn't nice, but it seemed to slip past January with most of his other meanings.

"She'll still have Lottie with her. And Mickey too, when he gets back."

"That's right." But his agreement had an edge of sarcasm. He'd begun to resent January's clumsy streaks of whitewash. "And anyhow, even if it is as bad as *she* seems to think, you can't let that stand in your way. If Mom didn't have *anyone* else, that shouldn't affect your decision."

"You don't think so?"

"If I thought so, then *I'd* have to move back there, wouldn't I? If it came to the point that she was going to lose the place. Oh, look who's here!"

It was Tabbycat. Boz picked her up and rubbed her in all her favorite places.

January persisted. "But you've got your own. . . . family."

"No, I've got my own *life*. The same as you or Shrimp."

"So you *do* think we're doing the right thing?"

But he wasn't going to let her have it as easy as that.

"Are you doing what you want to? Yes or no."

"Yes."

"Then it's the right thing." Which judgement pronounced, he turned his attention to Tabbycat. "What's going on in there, huh, little fella? Are those people still playing their long dull game? Huh? Who's going to win? Huh?"

January, who didn't know the cat had been watching television, answered the question straightforwardly. "I think Shrimp will."

"Oh?" *Why* had Shrimp ever. . . . . ? He had never understood.

"Yes. She always wins. It's incredible. The luck."

That was why.

37. Mickey

He was going to be a ballplayer. Ideally a catcher for the Mets, but lacking that he'd be content so long as he was in the major leagues. If his sister could become a ballerina, there was no reason he couldn't be an athlete. He had the same basic genetic equipment, quick reflexes, a good mind. He could do it. Dr. Sullivan *said* he could do it, and Greg Lincoln the sports director said he had as good a chance as any other boy, possibly better. It meant endless practice, rigid discipline, an iron will, but with Dr. Sullivan helping him to weed out his bad mental habits there wasn't any reason he couldn't meet those demands.

But how could he explain that in half an hour in the visitors' room? To his mother, who didn't know Kike Chalmers from Opal Nash? His mother who was the source (he could understand that now) of most of his wrong ways of thinking. So he just told her.

"I don't want to go back to 334. Not this week, not next week, not . . ." He pulled up just short of the word 'never'. "Not for a long time."

Emotions flickered across her face like strobes. Mickey looked away. She said, "Why, Mickey? What did I do?"

"Nothing. That's not it."

"Why then? A reason."

"You talk in your sleep. All night long you talk."

"That's not a reason. You can sleep in the living room,

like Boz used to, if I keep you up."

"Then you're crazy. How's that? Is that a reason? You're crazy, all of you are."

That stopped her, but not for long. Then she was pecking away at him again. "Maybe everyone's crazy, a little. But *this* place, Mickey, you can't want to—I mean, look at it!"

"I like this place. The guys here, as far as they're concerned, I'm just like them. And that's what I want. I don't want to go back and live with you. *Ever.* If you make me go, I'll just do the same thing all over again. I swear I will. And this time I'll use enough fluid and *really* kill him too, not just pretend."

"Okay, Mickey, it's your life."

"God damn right." These words, and the tears on which they verged, were like a load of cement dumped into the raw foundation of his new life. By tomorrow morning all the wet slop of feeling would be solid as rock and in a year a skyscraper would stand where now there was nothing but a gaping hole.

38. Father Charmain

Reverend Cox had just taken down Bunyan's *Kerygma,* which was already a week overdue, and settled down for a nice warm dip into his plodding, solid, reassuring prose, when the bell went Ding-Dong, and before she could unfold her legs, again, Ding-Dong. Someone was upset.

A dumpy old woman with a frazzled face, curdled flesh, the left eyelid drooping, the right eye popping out. As soon as the door opened the mismatched eyes went through the familiar motions of surprise, distrust, withdrawal.

"Please come in." She gestured to the glow from the office at the end of the hall.

"I came to see Father Cox." She held up one of the form letters the office sent out: *If you should ever experience the need. . . .*

Charmain offered her hand. "I'm Charmain Cox."

The woman, remembering her manners, took the hand offered her. "I'm Nora Hanson. Are you. . . . ?"

"His wife?" She smiled. "No, I'm afraid I'm the priest. Is that better or worse? But do come in out of this dreadful cold. If you think you'd be more comfortable talking with a man, I can phone up my colleague at St. Mark's, Reverend Gogardin. He's only around the corner." She steered her into the office and into the comfy confessional of the brown chair.

"It's been so long since I've been to church. It never occurred to me, from your letter. . . ."

"Yes, I suppose it's something of a fraud on my part, using only my initials." And she went through her disingenuous but useful patter song about the woman who had fainted, the man who'd snatched off her pectoral. Then she renewed her offer to phone St. Mark's, but by now Mrs. Hanson was resigned to a priest of the wrong sex.

Her story was a mosaic of little guilts and indignities, weaknesses and woes, but the picture that emerged was all too recognizably the disintegration of a family. Charmain began to assemble all the arguments why she wouldn't be able to take an active role in her struggle against the great octopus, Bureaucracy—chief among them that in the nine-to-five portion of her life she was a slave at one of the octopus's shrines (Department of Temporary Assistance). But then it developed that the Church, and even God, *were* involved in Mrs. Hanson's problems. The older daughter and her lover were leaving the sinking family to join the Sodality of St. Clare. In the quarrel that had tumbled the old lady out of her building and into this office the lover had used the poor dear's own Bible as ammunition. From Mrs. Hanson's extremely partisan account it took Charmain some time to locate the offending passage, but at last she tracked it down to St. Mark, third chapter, verses thirty-three to thirty-five:

> And he answered them, saying, Who is my mother, or my brethren?
>
> And he looked round about on them which sat about him, and said, Behold my mother and my brethren!
>
> For whosoever shall do the will of God, the same is my brother, and my sister, and mother.

"Now I ask you!"

"Of course," Charmain explained, "Christ isn't saying

there that one has a license to abuse or insult one's natural parents."

"Of course he isn't!"

"But has it occurred to you that this. . . . is her name January?"

"Yes. It's a ridiculous name."

"Has it occurred to you that January, and your daughter, may be right?"

"How do you mean?"

"Let's put it this way. What *is* the will of God?"

Mrs. Hanson shrugged. "You've got me." Then, after the question had settled, "But if you think that *Shrimp* knows—Ha!"

Deciding that St. Mark had done enough harm already, Charmain stumbled through her usual good counsels for disaster situations, but if she had been a shop clerk helping the woman to pick out a hat she couldn't have felt more futile or ridiculous. Everything Mrs. Hanson tried on made her look grotesque.

"In other words," Mrs. Hanson summed up, "you think I'm wrong."

"No. But on the other hand I'm not sure your daughter is. Have you tried, really, to see things from her side? To think why she wants to join a Sodality?"

"Yes. I have. She likes to shit on me and call it cake."

Charmain laughed without much zest. "Well, perhaps you're right. I hope we can talk again about this after we've both had a chance to think it over."

"You mean you want me to go."

"Yes, I guess that's what I mean. It's late, I have a job."

"Okay, I'm going. But I meant to ask: that book on the floor. . . ."

"*Kerygma*?"

"What does that mean?"

"It's Greek for message. It's supposed to be one of the things that the Church does, it brings a message."

"What message?"

"In a nutshell—Christ is risen. We are saved."

"Is that what *you* believe?"

"I don't know, Mrs. Hanson. But what I believe doesn't matter—I'm only the messenger."

"Shall I tell you something?"
"What?"
"I don't think you're much of a priest."
"Thank you, Mrs. Hanson. I know that."

39. The Five-Fifteen Puppets

Alone in the apartment, doors locked, mind bolted, Mrs. Hanson watched the teevee with a fierce, wandering attention. People knocked, she ignored them. Even Ab Holt, who should have known better than to be playing their game. "Just a discussion, Nora." Nora! He'd never called her Nora before. His big voice kept smashing through the door of the closet that had been a foyer. She couldn't believe that they would really use physical force to evict her. After fifteen years! There were hundreds of people in the building, she could name them, who didn't meet occupancy standards. Who took in any temp from the hallway and called them lodgers. "Mrs. Hanson, I'd like you to meet my new daughter." Oh yes! The corruption wasn't all at the top—it worked its way through the whole system. And when she'd asked, "Why me?" that slut had had the nerve to say, "Che sera sera, I'm afraid." If it had been that Mrs. Miller. There was someone who really did care, not a lot of fake sympathy and "Che sera sera." Maybe, if she phoned? But there wasn't a phone at Williken's now, and in any case she wasn't budging from where she was. They'd have to drag her. Would they dare go that far? The electricity would be shut off, that's always the first step. God knew what she'd do without the teevee. A blonde girl showed her how easy something was to do, just one, two, three. Then four, five, six, and it would be broken? *Terminal Clinic* came on. The new doctor was still in a feud with Nurse Loughtis. Hair like a witch, that one, and you couldn't believe a word she said. That mean look of hers, and then, "You can't fight City Hall, Doctor." Of course, that's what they wanted you to believe, that the individual person is helpless. She switched channels. Fucking on 5. Cooking on 4. She paused. Hands pushed and pulled at a great ball of dough. Food! But the nice Spanish lady—though really you couldn't say she was Spanish, it was only her name—from the Tenants'

Committee had promised her she wouldn't starve. As for water, she'd filled every container in the house days ago.

It was so *unfair*. Mrs. Manuel, if that was her name, had said she was being hung in a loophole. Somebody must have had their eye on the apartment for a long time, waiting for this opportunity. But try and find out from that asshole Blake who was moving in—oh no, that was "confidential." She'd known from one look at his beady eyes that he was getting *his* orange juice.

It was only a matter of holding out. In a few days Lottie would come home. She'd gone off before like this and she'd always come back. Her clothes were all here, except the one little suitcase, a detail she hadn't pointed out to Miss Slime. Lottie'd have her little breakdown or whatever and then come home and there'd be two of them and the department would *have* to grant a statutory six months' stay. Mrs. Manuel had emphasized that—six months. And Shrimp wouldn't last six months at that convent so-called. Religion was a hobby with her. In six months she'd have thrown it all up and started on something new, and then there'd be *three* of them and the department wouldn't have a leg to stand on.

The dates they gave you were just a bluff. She saw that now. It was already a week past the time they'd set. Let them knock on the door all they liked, though the idea of it drove her crazy. And Ab Holt, helping them. Damn!

"I *would* like a cigarette," she said calmly, as if it were something one always says to oneself at five o'clock when the news came on, and she walked into the bedroom and took the cigarettes and the matches from the top drawer. Everything was so neat. Clothes folded. She'd even fixed the broken blind, though now the slats were stuck. She sat on the edge of the bed and lit a cigarette. It took two matches, and then: Phew, the taste! Stale? But the smoke did something necessary to her head. She stopped worrying around in the same circle and thought about her secret weapon.

Her secret weapon was the furniture. Over the years she'd accumulated so much, mostly from other people's apartments when they'd died or moved out, and they couldn't evict her without clearing away every rag and stick of it. That was the law. And not just out into the corridor, oh no, they had to bring it down all the way to the street. So what were they going to do? Hire an army to take it down those stairs? Eighteen floors? No, so long as she insisted on her rights, she was as safe as if she were in a castle. And they'd just keep going on like they'd been going on, exerting psychological pressure so that she'd sign their fucking forms.

On the teevee a bunch of dancers had gotten up a party at the Greenwich Village office of Manufacturers Hanover Trust. The news was over and Mrs. Hanson returned to the living room, with her second awful cigarette, to the tune of "Getting to Know You." It seemed ironic.

At last the puppets came on. Her old friends. Her *only* friends. It was Flapdoodle's birthday. Bowser brought in a present in a gigantic box. "Is it for me?" Flapdoodle squeaked. "Open it," Bowser said, and you knew from the tone of his voice it was going to be something pretty bad. "For me, oh boy! It's something for me!" There was one box inside another box, and then a box inside that, and then still another box. Bowser got more and more impatient. "Go on, go on, open the next one." "Oh, I'm *bored*," said little Flapdoodle. "Let me show you how," said Bowser, and he did, and a gigantic wonderful hammer came out on a spring and knocked him on the head. Mrs. Hanson laughed herself into a fit, and sparks and ashes from the cigarette splashed all over her lap.

40. Hunt's Tomato Catsup

Before it was even daylight the super had let the two of them in through the closet with his key. Auxiliaries. Now they were packing, wrapping, wrecking the whole apartment. She told them politely to leave, she screamed at them to leave, they paid no attention.

On the way down to find the Tenants' Committee woman she met the super coming up. "What about my furniture?" she asked him.

"What *about* your furniture?"

"You can't evict me without my belongings. That's the law."

"Go talk to the office. I don't have anything to do with this."

"You let them in. They're there now, and you should see the mess they're making. You can't tell me that's legal—another person's belongings. Not just mine, a whole family's."

"So? So it's illegal—does that make you feel better?" He turned round and started down the stairs.

Remembering the chaos upstairs—clothes tumbled out of the closet, pictures off the walls, dishes stacked helter-skelter inside cheap carrier cartons—she decided it wasn't worth it. Mrs. Manuel, even if she could find her, wasn't going to stick her neck out on the Hanson's behalf. When she returned to 1812, the red-haired one was pissing in the kitchen sink.

"Oh, don't apologize!" she said, when he started in. "A job is a job is a job, isn't it? You've got to do what they tell you to."

She felt every minute as though she was going to start roaring or spinning in circles or just explode, but what stopped and held her was knowing that none of that would have had any effect. Television had supplied her with models for almost all the real-life situations she'd ever had to face—happiness, heartbreak, and points between—but this morning she was alone and scriptless, without even a notion of what was supposed to happen next. Of what to do. Cooperate with the damned steamrollers? That's what the steamrollers seemed to expect, Miss Slime and the rest of them in their offices with their forms and their good manners. She'd be damned if she would.

She'd resist. Let the whole lot of them try to tell her it wouldn't do her any good, she'd go on resisting. With that decision she recognized that she had found her role and that it was after all a familiar role in a known story: she would go down fighting. Very often in such cases, if you held out long enough against even the most hopeless odds the tide would turn. She'd seen it happen time and again.

At ten o'clock Slime came round and made a checklist of the destruction the auxiliaries had accomplished. She tried to make Mrs. Hanson sign a paper for certain of the boxes and cupboards to be stored at the city's expense—the rest presumably was garbage—at which point Mrs. Hanson pointed out that until she'd been evicted the apartment still belonged to her and so would Miss Slime please leave and take her two sink-pissers with her.

Then she sat down beside the lifeless teevee (the electricity was off, finally) and had another cigarette. Hunt's Tomato Catsup, the matchbook said. There was a recipe inside for Waikiki Beans that she'd always intended to test out but never got around to. Mix up Beef or Pork Chunkies, some crushed pineapple, a tablespoon of Wesson Oil, and lots of catsup, heat, and serve on toast. She fell asleep in the armchair planning an entire Hawaiian style dinner around the Waikiki Beans.

At four o'clock there was a banging and clattering at the door of what was once again the foyer. The movers. She had time to freshen herself before they found the super to let them in. She watched grimly as they stripped the kitchen of furniture, shelves, boxes. Even vacant, the patterns of wear on the linoleum, of stains on the walls, declared the room to be the Hansons' kitchen.

The contents of the kitchen had been stacked at the top of the stairs. This was the part she'd been waiting for. Now, she thought, break your backs!

There was a groan and shudder of faroff machineries. The elevator was working. It was Shrimp's doing, her ridiculous campaign, a final farewell slap in the face. Mrs. Hanson's secret weapon had failed. In no time the kitchen was loaded into the elevator and the movers squeezed in and pressed the button. The outer and then the inner doors closed. The disc of dim yellow light slipped from sight. Mrs. Hanson approached the dirty window and watched the steel cables shiver like the strings of gigantic bows. After a long, long time the massive black counterweight rose up out of the darkness.

The apartment or the furniture? It had to be one or the other. She chose—they must have known she would—the furniture. She returned one last time to 1812 and got together her brown coat, her Wooly cap, her purse. In the dusk, with no lights and the blinds off the windows, with the walls bare and the floor cluttered with big sealed boxes, there was no one to say goodbye to except the rocker, the teevee, the sofa—and they'd be with her on the street soon enough.

She doublelocked the door as she left. At the top of the stairs, hearing the elevator groaning upwards, she stopped.

Why kill herself? She got in as the movers came out. "Any objections?" she asked. The doors closed and Mrs. Hanson was in free fall before they discovered they couldn't get in.

"I hope it crashes," she said aloud, a little afraid it might.

Slime was standing guard over the kitchen which was huddled together beyond the curb in a little island of light under a streetlamp. It was almost night. A sharp wind with dry flakes of yesterday's snow swept down 11th Street from the west. With a scowl for Slime, Mrs. Hanson seated herself on one of the kitchen chairs. She just hoped that Slime would try and sit down too.

The second load arrived—armchairs, the disassembled bunk, cupboards of clothes, the teevee. A second hypothetical room began to form beside the first. Mrs. Hanson moved to her regular armchair and tried, with her hands in the coat pockets, to warm her fingers in her crotch.

Now Miss Slime judged the time had come to really twist and squeeze. The forms came out of the briefcase. Mrs. Hanson got rid of her quite elegantly. She lit a cigarette. Slime backed off from the smoke as though she'd been offered a teaspoonful of cancer. Social workers!

All the bulkiest items came in the third load—the sofa, the rocker, the three beds. the dresser with the missing drawer. The movers told Slime that in one more trip they'd have it all down. When they'd gone back in, she started in again with her forms and her ballpoint.

"I can *understand* your anger, and I sympathize, Mrs. Hanson, believe me. But someone has to attend to these matters and see that things are handled as *fairly* as the situation permits. Now please *do* sign these forms so that when the van comes. . . ."

Mrs. Hanson got up, took the form, tore it in half, tore the halves in half, and handed the scraps back to Slime, who stopped talking. "Now, is there anything else?" she asked in the same tone of voice as Slime.

"I'm only trying to help, Mrs. Hanson."

"If you try to help for one more minute, so help *me,* I'll spread you all over that sidewalk like so much—Like so much catsup!"

"Threats of violence don't solve problems, Mrs. Hanson."

Mrs. Hanson picked up the top half of the lamp pole from the lap of the rocker and swung, aiming for the middle of her thick coat. There was a satisfying *Whap!* The plastic shade that had always been such an eyesore cracked off. Without another word Slime walked away in the direction of First Avenue.

The last boxes were brought out from the lobby and dumped beside the curb. The rooms were all scrambled together now in one gigantic irrational jumble. Two colored brats from the building had begun bouncing on a stack made from the bunk mattresses and the mattress from Lottie's bed. Mrs. Hanson chased them off with the lamp pole. They joined the small crowd that had gathered on the sidewalk, just outside the imaginery walls of the imaginery apartment. Silhouettes watched from the lower windows.

She couldn't let them have it just like that. As though she were dead and they could go through her pockets. This furniture was her own private property and they just stood about, waiting for Slime to come back with reinforcements and take her off. Like vultures, waiting.

Well, they could wait till they dropped—they weren't going to get a thing!

She dug into her freezing purse for the cigarettes, the matches. There were only three left. She'd have to be careful. She found the drawers for the wooden dresser that had come from Miss Shore's apartment when Miss Shore had died. Her nicest piece of furniture. Oak. Before replacing them she used the lamp pole to poke holes through the pasteboard bottoms. Then she broke open the sealed boxes looking for burnables. She encountered bathroom items, sheets and pillows, her flowers. She dumped out the flowers, tore the broken box into strips. The strips went into the bottom drawer of the dresser. She waited until there was no wind at all. Even so it took all three matches to get it started.

The crowd—still mostly of children—had grown, but they kept well back from the walls. She scouted about for the kindling. Pages of books, the remains of the calendar, and Mickey's watercolors ("Promising" and "Shows independence") from the third grade were fed into the dresser. Before long she had a nice little furnace going inside. The problem now was how to get the rest of the furniture started. She couldn't keep pushing things into the drawers.

Using the lamp pole she was able to get the dresser over on its side. Sparks geysered up and were swept along by the wind. The crowd, which had been closing in more tightly around the bonfire, swayed back. Mrs. Hanson placed the kitchen chairs and table on the flames. They were the last large items she still had left from the Mott Street days —Seeing them go was painful.

Once the chairs had caught she used them as torches to start the rest of the furniture going. The cupboards, loosely packed and made of cheap materials, became fountains of fire. The crowd cheered as each one, after smoking blackly, would catch hold and shoot up. Ah! Is there anything like a good fire?

The sofa, armchairs, and mattresses were more obstinate. The fabric would char, the stuffing would stink and smoulder, but it wouldn't burn outright. Piece by piece (except for the sofa, which had always been beyond her), Mrs. Hanson dragged these items to the central pyre. The last mattress, however, only got as far as the teevee and her strength gave out.

A figure advanced toward her from the crowd, but if they wanted to stop her now it was too late. A fat woman with a small suitcase.

"Mom?" she said.

"Lottie!"

"Guess what? I've come home. What are you doing with—"

A clothes cupboard fell apart, scattering flames in modules scaled to the human form.

"I told them. I told them you'd be back!"

"Isn't this *our* furniture?"

"Stay here." Mrs. Hanson took the suitcase out of Lottie's hand, which was all cut and scratched, the poor darling, and set it down on the concrete. "Don't go anywhere, right? I'm getting someone, but I'll be right back. We've lost a battle, but we'll win the war."

"Are you feeling all right, Mom?"

"I'm feeling fine. Just wait here, all right? And there's no need to worry. Not now. We've got six months for certain."

41. *At the Falls*

Incredible? Her mother running off through the flames like some opera star going out for a curtain call. Her suitcase had crushed the plastic flowers. She stooped and picked one up. An iris. She tossed it into the flames in approximately the direction her mother had disappeared in.

And hadn't it been a magnificent performance? Lottie had watched from the sidewalk, awestruck, as she'd set fire to. . . . everything. The rocker was burning. The kid's bunk, in two pieces, was burning propped up against the embers of the kitchen table. Even the teevee, with Lottie's own mattress draped over it, though because of the mattress the teevee wasn't burning as well as it might. The entire Hanson apartment was on fire. The strength! Lottie thought. The strength that represents.

But why strength? Wasn't it as much a yielding? What Agnes Vargas had said years ago at Afra Imports: "The hard part isn't *doing* the job. The hard part is learning how." Such a commonplace thing to say, yet it had always stuck with her.

Had she learned how?

The beauty, that was what was so remarkable. Seeing the furniture standing about on the street, that had been beautiful enough. But when it burned!

The flowered armchair, which had only been smouldering till now, took hold all at once. and all its meaning was expressed in a tall column of orange flames. Glorious!

Could she?

At the very least she could try to approach it.

She fiddled open the locks of the suitcase. Already she'd lost so many of things she'd brought with her, all the little smouldering till now, took hold all at once, and all its worrying at them yielded her one dribble of the feelings they were supposed to hold. Postcards she'd never sent. Baby clothes. The book of autographs (including three celebrities) she'd started keeping in eighth grade. But what junk she had left she'd gladly give.

At the top of the suitcase a white dress. She threw it into the lap of the burning chair. As it touched the flames years of whiteness condensed into a moment's fierce flare.

Shoes, a sweater. They shriveled inside lurid haloes of green flame.

Prints. Stripes.

Most of these things didn't even fit her! She lost patience and dumped the rest in all in a heap, everything except the photographs and the bundle of letters. These she fed to the fire one by one. The pictures winked into flame like the popping of so many flashbulbs, leaving the world as they'd entered it. The letters, on lighter paper, went even more quickly: a single whoosh! and then they rose in the updraft, black weightless birds, poem after poem, lie upon lie—all of Juan's love.

Now she was free?

The clothes she wore were of no importance. As little time as a week ago she might have thought at this moment that she'd have to take her clothes off too.

She herself was the clothing she must remove.

She went to where her own bed had been prepared atop the teevee. All else was in flames now, only the mattress still smoldered. She lay down. It was no more uncomfortable than entering a very hot bathtub, and as the water might have, the heat melted away the soreness and tension of the last sad days and weeks. This was so much more *simple*!

Relaxing, she became aware of the sound of the flames, a roaring all around her, as though she had finally come to the head of the falls she had been listening to so long. As her little boat had drifted towards this moment. But these waters were flames and fell upwards. With her head thrown back she could watch the sparks from the separate fires join, in the updraft, into a single ceaseless flow of light that mocked the static pallid squares of light gouged in the face of the brick. People stood within those squares of light, watching the fire, waiting, with Lottie, for the mattress to go.

The first flames curled around the edge, and through these flames she saw the ring of onlookers. Each face, in its separateness, in the avidity of its gaze, seemed to insist that Lottie's action was directed in some special way at him. There was no way to tell them that this was not for their sake but for the sake, purely, of the flames.

At the very moment that she knew she couldn't go on, that her strength *would* fail, their faces disappeared. She pushed herself up: the teevee collapsed; and she fell, in her little boat, through the white spray of her fear, towards the magnificence below.

But then, before she could see quite through the curtain of the spray, there was another face. A man. He aimed the nozzle of the firehose at her. A stream of white plastic foam shot out, blanketing Lottie and the bed, and all the while she was compelled to watch, in his eyes, on his lips, everywhere, an expression of insupportable loss.

42. Lottie, at Bellevue, continued

"And anyhow the world *doesn't* end. Even though it may try to, even though you wish to hell it would—it can't. There's always some poor jerk who thinks he needs something he hasn't got, and there goes five years, ten years, getting it. And then it'll be something else. It's another day and you're still waiting for the world to end.

"Oh, sometimes, you know, I have to laugh. When I think—Like the first time you're really in love and you say to yourself, Hey! I'm really in love! Now I know what it's about. And then he leaves you and you can't believe it. Or worse than that you gradually lose sight of it. Just gradually. You're in love, only it isn't as wonderful as it used to be. Maybe you're not even in love, maybe you just want to be. And maybe you don't even want to be. You stop bothering about songs on the radio, and there's nothing you want to do but sleep. Do you know? But you can only sleep for so long and then it's tomorrow. The icebox is empty and you have to think who haven't you borrowed any money from and the room smells and you get up just in time to see the most terrific sunset. So it wasn't the end of the world after all, it's just another day.

"You know, when I came here, there was a part of me that was so happy. Like the first day of school, though maybe that was terrifying, I can't remember. Anyhow. I was so happy because I thought, here I am, this is the bottom. At last! The end of the world, right? And then, it was only the next day, I was up on the veranda, and there it was again, this perfectly gorgeous sunset, with Brooklyn all big and mysterious, and the river. And then it was as though I could take a step back from myself, like when you're sitting across from someone in the subway and they don't know you're watching them, I could see myself like that. And I thought, Why you dope! You've only been here one day, and here you are enjoying a goddamned sunset.

"Of course it's also true, what we were saying before, about people. People are shits. In here just as much as out there. Their faces. And the way they grab things. It's like, I don't know if you've ever had children, but it's like that, eating at the same table with children. At first you can enjoy it. Like watching a mouse—nibble, nibble, nibble. But then there's another meal, and another, and if you don't see them other times there doesn't seem to be anything to them but an endless appetite. Well, and that's what I think can be so frightening, when you look at somebody and you can't see anything but their hungry face. Looking at you.

"Do you feel that way ever? When you feel something very strongly, you always suppose other people must have felt the same way, but do you know what? I'm thirty-eight years old, tomorrow I'll be thirty-nine, and I still wonder if that's so. Whether anyone ever feels the same way.

"Oh! Oh, the funniest thing, I have to tell you. This morning when I was on the can Miss What's-It comes in, the nice one, and very matter-of-fact as though it were my office or something she asks did I want a chocolate birthday cake or a white birthday cake? For my birthday! A chocolate birthday cake or a white birthday cake? Because, you see, they had to order it today. God, I laughed. I thought I'd fall off the stool I laughed so hard. 'A chocolate birthday cake or a white birthday cake. Which will it be, Lottie?'

"Chocolate, I told her, and I was very serious about it too, believe me. It had to be chocolate. Nothing else would do."

43. Mrs. Hanson, in Room 7

"I've thought about it. For years. I don't talk about it because I don't think it's something you can discuss. Once. Once I met a lady in the park, that was a long time ago. We talked about it, but I don't think that either of us . . . Not then. Once you're serious, it isn't something you care to talk about.

"Here it's a different situation, I know. I don't mind

discussing it with you. It's your job, and you have to do it. But with my family, you see, that's a different matter. They'd try to argue against it, but only because they felt they ought to. And I understand that. I was the same myself. I can remember visiting my father when he was in the hospital—that would be Twenty-twenty or twenty-one, in there, and talking away at him a mile a minute. Lord. But could I look him in the eye? Not for a moment! I kept showing him photographs, as though. . . . But even then I knew what he must have been thinking. What I didn't know was that it can all seem so possible.

"But I suppose you'll need better reasons than that for the form you're filling out. Well, just put down cancer. You must have a copy of my medical report. I've been cut open just once, to have my appendix taken out, and that was enough. The doctors explained to me what I can expect and that my chances are better than fifty-fifty, and I believe them. It's not the risk I'm afraid of. That would be silly, wouldn't it?

"What I am afraid of is turning into some kind of old vegetable. There's so many like that where I am now. Some of them are just completely. . . . I stare at them sometimes. I know I shouldn't, but I can't help myself.

"And *they* don't realize. They don't have any idea. There's one of them who's gone like that just in the time I've been there. He used to spend every day off somewhere, independent wasn't the word for it, and then—a stroke. And now he can't control himself. They wheel him out on the porch with all the rest of us, and suddenly you hear him in his tin pot, tinkle tinkle tinkle. Oh, you have to laugh.

"Then you think, that could be me. I don't mean to say that *pissing* is so important. But the mental change! Old pisspot used to be such a sharp bastard, crusty, full of fight. But now? I don't care if I wet my bed, but I don't want my *brains* to go soft.

"The attendants are always joking about this one or that one. It's not malicious, really. Sometimes I have to laugh myself at what they say. And then I think. After my operation *I* might be the one they're making jokes about. And then it would be too late. You can see that in their eyes sometimes. The fact that they've let their chance slip by, and that they know it.

"After a certain point you ask yourself why. Why go on?

Why bother? For what reason? I guess it's when you stop enjoying things. The day-to-day things. It's not as though there's all that much *to* enjoy. Not there. The food? Eating is a chore for me now, like putting on my shoes. I do it. That's all. Or the people? Well, I talk to them, they talk to me, but does anyone listen? You—do you listen? Huh? And when *you* talk, who listens to you? And how much are *they* paid?

"What was I talking about? Oh, friendship. Well, I've expressed my thoughts on that subject. So, what's left? What *is* left? Teevee. I used to watch teevee a lot. Maybe if I had my own set again, and my own private room, maybe I could gradually just forget about everything else. But sitting there in that room at Terminal Clinic—that's our name for it—with the others all sneezing and jabbering and I don't know what, I can't connect with the screen. I can't make it take me over.

"And that's it. That's my life, and I say, who needs it? Oh, I forgot to mention baths. Twice a week I get a nice warm bath for fifteen minutes and I love it. Also, when I sleep I enjoy that. I sleep about four hours a night. It's not enough.

"I've made sense, haven't I? I've been rational? Before I came here I made a list of the things I meant to say, and now I've said them. They're all good reasons, every one of them. I checked them in your little book. Have I left any out?

"Oh. Family relationships. Right. Well, I don't have any left that count. After a certain age that's true for everyone, and I've reached that age, I guess. It took a while, but I'm there.

"As I understand it, you've *got* to approve my application. If you don't, I'll appeal. As I have a right to. And eventually I'll win. I'm smart, you know. When I have to be, I am. My whole family was a smart family, with very high scores. I never did much with my intelligence, I have to confess, but I'll do this. I'll get what I want and what I have a right to. And sincerely, Miss Latham, I do want it. I want to die. The way some people want sex, that's how I want death. I dream about it. And I think about it. And it's what I want."

MAN IN TRANSIT

ALAN AUMBRY

My name is Untuar Murti, and having spent all my life in airplanes, apart from short intervals of hours and minutes, I am better qualified than most to judge the state of the world. True, my experience is slight; but that is all to the good: it means that my understanding has not been attenuated or compromised by too close an involvement in life.

This paper comprises, if you like, my last will and testament—not that I hope that anyone will find time to read it. As to myself: 'Murti' was my father's family name, while 'Untuar' has no meaning or derivation but was invented by my father on the principle that it should lack any history or connection with anything else. That, he claimed, was most descriptive of my situation and thus the perfect name for his first, and only child. Let me add that the bitterness which tinged his attitude is not shared by me: the life into which one is born is naturally accepted without rancour, and I have known no other.

My recollection of my parents is unusually sharp—due, no doubt, to the fact that no one has taken their place in my life—if one considers that I was only five years old at the death or my mother, and only eight at the death of my father. They were docile, rather harmless people who were somewhat prone to miscalculation. Their early deaths may be attributed to an inability to adjust to the ordeal which an adverse fate had thrust upon them.

Fortunately enough the circumstances of my own birth are unique. I was born on board an airliner flying from Nairobi to London; I was not, however, permitted to disembark either at the port of arrival or at the port of departure. I have been travelling the same route ever since—a total of thirty-eight years.

My aerial imprisonment disappointed my parents, naturally, but it came as no great surprise to them because they had already been suffering the same indignity for several months. In those days, when the affairs of the world were less settled or rigidified than they are now, large numbers of people were occasionally trapped in pernicious political antinomies. Let me explain: my own parents were of Indian stock, holders of British passports, and residents of East Africa where their families had lived for two generations. Into this heterogeneity of allegiances, arising from the dismantling of a once far-flung empire, the government of their resident country dropped a calamity: seized by a convulsion of nationalism, it pronounced measures against all its 'non-citizens', making it impossible for them to earn a livelihood there. Understandably, the victims of this decision made moves to repair to their putative homeland, the British Isles, there being nowhere else for them to go. Alas, the moral qualities of that previously great nation must already have declined considerably by then; with open impudicity the British government revoked the official passports it had earlier issued, disowning all its guarantees and turned away all who presented themselves for entry.

That was not the end of the matter: there were still some who were prepared to take plane for England in the knowledge that once airborne they would not be let back into East Africa again. These stateless suppliants, capitalising perhaps on the reputed humanitarianism of their prospective hosts, or else desperate enough to try anything, were shuttled back and forth between airports for weeks. Finally, with much grumbling and misgiving, the officials would relent.

Such a course of action was chosen by my parents. They embarked upon it cheerfully enough; others had been successful, and so, they thought, could they. Besides, my mother was pregnant at the time they set out and so . . . ?

On presenting their passports they were immediately returned to Nairobi, and thence back again to London. This occasioned them no dismay: they had expected it. Weeks, months even, might be required to pass before the portals to safety and freedom would at last open.

Yet one factor failed to enter their cogitations: how long can any government allow its decisions to be persistently overruled? Already the draughty wind of change was causing doors to slam shut all round the world. Already the word 'patrial' had entered official usage as an adumbration that in future nations would look after their own and no other. Today, a third of a century later, the maxim is well established: 'Procedures take precedence over persons'. My parents haplessly became the test case that was to prove this rule; the weeks did indeed lengthen into months. I was born over water, in midflight, and was not even entered on the worthless passport which by now, I believe, was stained with my mother's tears. Gradually it became evident that they were not, ever, going to be allowed into any country again.

Sitting here gazing through the fuselage window, I often wonder how long they continued to hope. I have reason to think it was for a long time, and that when they finally lost hope was when they died. Even then my mother clung to the belief (my father knew better) that once I was alone some country would notice me, as an airborne waif, and take me in. But here I remain, the most long-suffering air passenger in history.

For a spell during my early life my situation evoked some interest and an amount of pity, a form of intercourse I find thoroughly distasteful. In my twelfth year there was an abortive attempt to resurrect Human Rights Year and I appeared (to no purpose) on TV (and was able to see the programme on the flight screens). All such public interest has long since washed away and I am left in peace. It is possible that these efforts were doubly futile, for my own image of myself differs fundamentally from the one presented by the well-meaning media; the burden of their consciousness lies on the ground—mine is up here, traversing in this airliner. Mine is the image that once formed in the mind of a pagan English king on seeing a bird, at night, enter his hall by a window; for a few moments to flit over the warmth, the companionship, the light and the feasting that took place below, before passing by a second window, never to return, into the same darkness again. This glyph of human life converted the king to Christianity.

I, let me make it clear, am no convert, for I am not the king but the bird. But does not the legend describe me precisely? Soon I shall pass into that same darkness again.

I have seen a marvellous development in passenger plane services during the time I have spent with the airline. The transports are large and spacious, with plenty of room to walk about. There are showers, bars, TV and restaurants. Businessmen speak to colleagues and transactors over the in-transit viewphone service. And of course the planes are fast, efficient and need little servicing. From my point of view this is a disadvantage for there is only the briefest turn-around time, which allows me almost no time to spend on the ground. Previously the hours I spent between journeys on the older aircraft were like a holiday for me—fresh air has an extraordinary effect on my system. I confess I miss my youthful jaunts to the cafeteria, to the passenger lounge, or along the frontage of the airport buildings. I had, in fact, virtual freedom of access on this side of the customs barrier. But then, perhaps I am getting too old for such exercises.

The airline has been good to me. Once when I was ill they brought me a doctor and several times I have been attended by a dentist. As I grew up pilots and stewardesses gave me new clothes to wear. For all items I am still dependent on these hand-outs, which have been my only way of accumulating property throughout life. Thus I am the possessor of adequate clothing, a toothbrush, an electric shaver, and a very small private collection of books culled over the years. These, together with my legacy (which I shall describe later) constitute my material wealth.

There is also the question of emotional wealth accruing from personal relationships. In these my life could be described as deficient. Yet I did once have a girl friend; to be truthful she was a woman rather than a girl, and was several years older than myself. We met and were drawn to one another when, in the course of her work, she had cause to travel between London and Karachi several times in quick succession (this was during the period when African routes became impassable and I was shuttled instead to Karachi or Delhi). When her intercontinental commuting ceased she took to visiting the airport and we waved to one another through the fence. Infrequently we contrived brief meetings in the passenger lounge. Then one day she failed to appear and I never saw her again. In retrospect I discard my naïvety and suppose that her good will was prompted partly by pity, a thought which spoils in no small measure my memories of the occasion.

Our friendship, while it lasted, was sexually innocent, indeed there has been no occasion for sexual intercourse in my life—not that such things are impossible aboard an airliner; congress can be accomplished with a modicum of ingenuity and commonly is, in the toilets, in the changing room, even in the stewardesses' galley. But my upbringing has given me little initiative in these matters, and I have been obliged to stifle such urges as I do feel.

Enough of these divagations—poor I may be in material and emotional wealth, but they are not everything; there is also intellectual wealth. I have an education!

For this I am indebted to my father, who before he died assiduously taught me to read and instructed me to study carefully the books in the list he drew up. I have not, it is true, finished the list. Contrary to what might be imagined, I am not a voracious reader. Debilitated by an unnatural life, I am very easily fatigued; altogether I am a weak individual, both physically and mentally. I sleep a good deal—fifteen to twenty hours a day—and during the rest of the time reading is a painful effort for me. My progress is further impeded by the difficulty of obtaining the requisite books: I have to rely on chance to place most of the volumes in my hands, and have waited years, for instance, to acquire a copy of the *Timaeus*. This, as with several other volumes, I shall probably never see.

Many would imagine that my fahher, a Vedantist, would have directed me to a study of the Vedas, particularly of the Upanishads, on the grounds that in the doctrine that the world is *maya,* merely illusion, might be found an anodyne to mitigate my plight. Nothing could have been further from his intention. Admittedly, it has fleetingly occurred to me that that *other* world, the world that rolls beneath me scudded with cloud, is only an insubstantial extrapolation, an epiphenomenon, and that the only substantive things in the universe are airliners, airports, and transient passengers who flick in and out of existence on embarkation and debarkation. But that thought cannot be taken seriously. All my father's efforts strove not to obfuscate with recondite metaphysics but to exacerbate realities and make the apprehension of my condition all the sharper. He believed in science, a product of the West; all the books he specified are by Western writers, and I take their point of view: that the world exists in reality (insofar as it is perceived between conception and death), that everything happening in it has really happened, that I really am trapped in this airliner, the only man in history never to be allowed to descend to earth.

No, my father's feeling for me did not lead him to compromise the facts. His educational programme was a work of genius—genius born, I tender, of intense emotional pain. I am convinced that his aim was to lead me by my own efforts towards a truth which he had wrested from the world but which otherwise is known to few, if any: the secret nature of that explosive, perdurable, many-headed hydra: the Christian religion.

How much is implied—how much is masked—by the phrase 'Christian civilization'! To penetrate to the arcane core of what its existence on Earth means was the achievement of my father's booklist.

The list is extensive, but its greater part is introductory only, being designed to facilitate the process of intussusception by means of adroit acquaintanceship with vocabulary and ideas. At the centre of the system, like a centre of gravity, lie two major works around which all else revolves:-

1. The Socratic Dialogues.
2. The Gospel according to St. Matthew, St. Mark, St. Luke and St. John.

From the comparison of these two, the objective historical perspective of the world is obtained.

A brief word concerning their acquisition. My tiny pocket copy of the New Testament, Authorized Version, was given to me by a kindly English lady on her way to perform missionary work in India, and has been with me for many years. The more bulky Socratic Dialogues present a greater problem and therefore I lack a complete collection. They are, however, a lesser counterpoint to the Christian theme, so the gaps do not matter so much.

One volume that I do have is worth comment: a collection of some of the dialogues, including the Apology of Socrates, it was given to me rather offhandedly by a brash, untidily dressed young man of about eighteen who I remember for his piercing blue eyes. The book is entitled 'Plato's Divine Dialogues' and is a very old one, being published in 1841 by Cornish & Co., 126 Newgate Street, London. Its pages are yellow and brittle, held together by sticky tape.

The edition is remarkable for its spiritual chauvinism. By means of a wordy introduction and copious footnotes the editor strives to impress on the reader the superiority of the Christian world and how unlikely it is that anything worthwhile could ever take place outside its confines. He puts forward a tenuous and wandering argument to show that Plato owed such wisdom as he did possess to Moses, 'from whom he has borrowed that which is most rational and substantial in his works'. Noting that during his trial Socrates could have saved himself by withholding the truth but declined to do so, he exclaims passionately: 'What a noble example is this in a pagan!'

Noble in a pagan, indeed! And is it commonplace in a Christian? I cannot help but find these and other commentaries bizarre. For it is from Socrates that I have learned the qualities of rationality, coolness of mind, balanced feeling, justice—in short, the qualities of a sane and good-humoured civilization. By contrast the extraordinary story of Jesus gives witness to the creation of the sinister *un*civilization that has conquered humanity, encompassed the globe, raised to unfeeling heights science and the technique of bureaucratic civilization—that has built airplanes.

The tide of history must have tussled uncertainly with these two men as it decided which of them to cast up on the shore. For observe: both were sentenced to death as a result of unjust accusations (though Socrates with a lighter heart). History is rarely arbitrary about these matters. Further, observe the curious affinity between the valedictions of their biographers—not in content, it is true, but in mood, in tone, in feeling—as if they comprised two strands of a single chord.

Thus Plato has Phedon say: 'This, Echecrates, was the exit of our friend, a man who, as it appears to me, was the best man of our time with whom we were acquainted, and besides this the wisest and most just.'

St. John concludes: 'There were many other things which Jesus did, which if they were to be written down every one, I suppose that even the world itself could not contain the books that should be written.'

But to my thesis:- my contention is that not merely some, but every particle of the common conception of Christ and his role in the world is false. We are told that he entered the world as a moral force to save the world, that all who heed him will be redeemed. That if the world opens its heart to him, mankind will be transformed. If now we find that doors are closed, that some are excluded from the feast, it is because Christ has not yet touched the hearts of all men. To this I counter that, by holding to this creed, the Christians are looking into a reversed mirror image of their religion, the obverse of which is *the world as it exists today*. Compare: other teachings exhibit an open-ended liberation; in contrast to the smile of Buddha, the systemless jokes of the Zen masters, the story of Christ is one of persecution; of a series of progressively closing traps: the last supper; the betrayal in the garden of Gethsemane; the nailing to the cross; the descent into Hell. Is that not descriptive of the modern world, which progressively encloses the individual?

Again, where other teachers inspire detachment, wisdom, justice and friendship, Christ invoked not abstract qualities but *deeds*—and so inaugurated the tumultuous industriousness of the modern world. There are other close parallels too numerous to be ignored: the refusal of a petition to authority when in dire distress ('Father, all things are possible unto thee; take away this cup from me.'—St. March Ch. 14, verse 36); the washing of hands; the freeing of the guilty in order that the innocent may be punished

(‘Away with this man and give us Barabbas’—St. Luke Ch. 23 verse 18).

Has it not come to pass that ‘to him that hath, more shall be given, while to him that hath little even that which he hath shall be taken away’?

And am I not the seed that, not even falling on stony ground, fails to reach earth at all?

Mankind *has* absorbed the message of Jesus, absorbed it fully and without omission; the story of the passion has been blended into the world and transformed into vaster fact, like a mustard seed that grows into a monstrous bush. Alone among the cheerful smiling reason of other world teachers Christ never laughed but groaned and wept. Perhaps he wept because he saw the consequences of his mission, much as my mother wept to realize that her actions had condemned me to the life of an air passenger.

Once these correspondences are marshalled the genesis of the present-day world culture becomes all too clear. Only one point remains obscure: what was Christ’s origin? Possibly he was indeed an incarnation of the Creator, sent to scourge mankind. Pursuing the Christian cosmology, I would be more inclined to name him as an agent of Satan, despatched to corrupt the soul of humanity and destroy for all time the Socratic civilization which might otherwise have flourished in Western Europe.

These scanty comments must suffice to outline my thesis, for I become too weary to expatiate further. How the world would judge my intellectual offering I cannot know; perhaps it is unscholarly, naive, jejune even, when placed against better-considered world systems. But for me it carries the inner conviction of a truth revealed. Besides—my role in the world drama, miniscule though it may be, gives me one thing in common with Jesus: I also am pinned to a cross, this flying cross which whines ceaselessly to and fro across the face of the globe.

The hebetude into which my parents sank claims me also. I shall not live much longer now. Most of my time, when not sleeping, I spend gazing through the fuselage window. At night the unbreakable glass becomes a mirror which returns my tired face. To be honest it is a handsome face. The nose is strong, the lips are full, the eyes are sensitive—but withdrawn. And the hair, brushed neatly back, is prematurely white. In fact the whole face looks about thirty years older than it really is and its calmness, one sees after a while, is a forced, resigned calmness. Anyway, now that, with a frank feeling of relief, I contemplate my approaching death, I will go through the formality of setting forth final arrangements. To anyone who can use it I bequeath the legacy left to me by my father: two second-class one-way air tickets from Nairobi to London, still valid. For my epitaph I choose yet another quotation from that prophetic New Testament, and one which demonstrates even more clearly the applicability of the gospels to our time: 'The birds have their nests, the foxes have their holes, but the Son of Man has no place to lay his head.'

THE LOCKED ROOM

ANOTHER FENTON WORTH MYSTERY

by John Sladek

Fenton Worth instructed his valet Bozo to turn away all callers for the rest of the evening.

"I mean to spend a quiet evening with a good book," said the popular private detective, and indicated a new, calf-bound volume on the library table.

Bozo smirked, knowing what usually happened to all such "quiet evenings" in the life of a famous sleuth. "I imagine, sir," he said, "that a beautiful lady will burst in, begging you to save her life. That, or else Inspector Grogan will ask you to help recover the Stilton diamonds."

The well-known private dick smiled. "Not tonight, Bozo. I mean it: No calls of any kind. If it is a matter of life and death, as is usual, refer our caller to the police. Other cases I can look into in the morning. For now, I'm going to lock myself in the library, and I don't want to be disturbed."

With that, the eminent criminologist shooed his servant from the room, turned the key and settled into his favorite Morris chair with the "good book". It was a detection novel, entitled *The Locked Room.*

"*The Locked Room,* eh? That should be of considerable interest," he mused, toying with his letter opener. This curious instrument was actually a Moro weapon, an example of that knife with a wavy blade familiar to crossword buffs as a *kriis*. Opening the volume, Fenton used the *kriis* to slit a few pages, then began to read.

The plot of this novel, shorn of its ornaments, misdirections and other fanciful elements, was simple: A man was found dead in a sealed room, locked from the inside. No one else was found in the room, and though the death was certainly a homicide, no weapon could be found. Suspects were abundant, yet how could any of them have done it?

Fenton had met a great many such cases in real life; indeed, they formed the bulk of his murder investigations. He had opened locked rooms containing corpses which had been done to death by strangulation, shooting, stabbing, poison, smothering, drowning, burning, being chopped to bits, electrocution; by the action of deadly snakes and spiders—and far worse.

A few of such cases involved rooms which were not really locked at all. These included rooms with secret panels and one room where the midget assassin lay hidden in a chest. Fenton had left all such "cheating" cases to the police.

More interesting were the cases where the rooms were really locked, but ingeniously locked from the outside. One killer, having simply locked the door and concealed the key in his hand, helped smash a panel of the door to get into the room. Then he reached through the panel and "found" the key in the lock. Others relied on clever systems of string, pins, wires and so on, to drop latch-bars, shoot bolts and turn locks from outside the door. One killer simply removed the door hinges, replacing them after his grim business inside.

In other cases the room was locked, and from the inside, but it was not utterly unimpregnable. Poison gas might be introduced by a ventilator, as, indeed, might an adder. Ice bullets might be fired through the keyhole to kill, then melt, leaving no trace of the weapon. Others used poison darts fired through an otherwise inaccessible window, bombs down the chimney and so on. In one curious case a man was stabbed through the wall itself, with a very long, thin, sharp sword.

There were a number of "funny contrivance" cases. These invariably concerned machines, hidden about the rooms which, having done their deeds, became to all appearances innocent furniture again. Some were set off by the victims themselves, some by remote control and some by clockwork. Men were shot by telephones, blown up by hearing aids, stabbed by clocks, strangled by stethoscopes and ripped to pieces by typewriters. In this category Fenton placed his interesting "Case of the Freudian Outlook", where a man was crushed to death between the red-hot iron walls of a gimmicked room.

He paused to cut a few more pages. This mystery, *The Locked Room,* was the most baffling he'd yet encountered, and nothing like any of the others.

It was certainly not like the elaborate suicide in "The Mystery of the Yellow Step", where the victim hanged himself with an especially knotted and weighted rope. When the door to the room was broken in, this noose undid itself, deposited the body on the floor, and vanished out the window into (for this was in Venice) the Grand Canal.

Nor did this case resemble "The Orchid Piano Mystery", where the victim locked himself in a room coincidentally full of broken furniture and other signs of a struggle, fainted and cracked his head on the fender. That case had given Fenton some food for thought, as had the related "Mauve Marimba Mystery". There the supposed victim had merely suffered an epileptic seizure, smashed up the room, and ended by kicking himself in the face until dead (this epileptic was also a dancer).

Fenton's meditations were here interrupted by Bozo, who came in with a tray of toast and cocoa.

"I was just thinking over some of my old 'locked-room' cases, Bozo," said the reknowned gumshoe. "I must confess that real-life cases are a whale of a lot easier than detective fiction. This novel has me stymied, so far." And he outlined the story for his valet.

"It sounds tough, sir," said Bozo. "Reminds one of the 'Case of the Bashful Bimbo'."

"No, I think you're thinking of the 'Vast Duck Mystery', aren't you, Bozo? Where it finally turned out that the victim had been stabbed with a hatpin at the ambassador's reception, amid a roomful of people. He wasn't even aware of the stabbing himself. He'd gone into another room, locked himself in, and then the slow leakage from his heart finally caught up with him."

"Like I've caught up with you," laughed Inspector Grogan, strolling in. "I came over on the chance of getting you to help on the Stilton diamonds case. I found this young lady outside. Claims her life's in danger."

The young lady, a beautiful blonde with a black eye, seemed too frightened to speak. Next came Claude Elliott, the millionaire playboy, attired in his customary black evening wear, a monocle twinkling in his eye. "I say, old sport," he drawled, "d'you think you could do anything about it? Someone seems to have kidnapped Pater. His entire private car has vanished from its train. Deucedly awkward, what?" Young Elliott expected no answer to this question.

"Scuse me, mistah Wort'," said a jockey, ducking into view from behind Elliott's scarlet-lined cape. "Honeymarch has been heisted!"

"Honeymarch stolen!" echoed the astonished shamus. This famous filly had won many times her weight in gold, as had her sire, My White Dream, which Fenton had earlier saved from doping in—

"The Case of the Mona Lisa Moth", breathed Bozo.

"Exactly," Fenton said. "Get rid of some of these people—all of them, Bozo. I want to do some hard thinking."

Bozo gently but firmly pushed them all from the library: the debutante and the B-girl, the Brovnian ambassador and the gum-chewing taxi driver, the business tycoon and the spirit medium, the jockey, the playboy, the cop and the black-eyed blonde.

"In 'The Case of the Oddest Occurrence,'" Fenton mused, "the trick was to make it seem as if the victim were dead before he really was. The killer got him into a room and drugged, and managed to get the room locked. Then he feigned alarm, convinced us there was something afoot, and broke the door down to get in. He rushed in ahead of us, I recall, exclaiming at the (fictitious) sight of the victim's throat, cut from ear to ear. And even while he was exclaiming, he was cutting that throat—an instant before the rest of us saw it!"

"It was another kettle of fish, sir," said Bozo, "in the case you called 'Murder Galore'."

"True enough, Bozo. In that, as in many cases, the ruse was to get the rest of us believing the victim to be still alive, when he had already been done to death. In the case you mention, this was accomplished by means of a phonographic recording of the victim's voice. Other cases involved the use of mirrors, disguises, death-masks and even ventriloquism. Yet *The Locked Room* is not one of this type.

"Nor does it resemble the more bizarre cases, such as 'The Wrong Hotel Room Mystery', or the simpler ones, such as 'The Case of the Gunsel's Gardenia'. In the former the whole plot hinged upon an elaborate switch of door number plates; in the latter, the killer only *pretended* the door was locked, and held it shut as he feigned battering it open."

Bozo withdrew, and the celebrated crime-solver locked and bolted the door. There remained only the pages of the final chapter to be cut, but he could not yet bring himself to break their seal. Surely he could guess the ending in advance of reading it! Surely, in all his experience, there must be one case relevant to solving this tangle.

Yet he had covered all categories: the secret passage or panel; the string-locked door; the ice bullet; and so on. There remained for consideration only one case, the strange "Case of the Parched Adjutant."

THE CASE OF THE PARCHED ADJUTANT

Another Fenton Worth Mystery

The victim was a retired military gentleman of sober and regular habits, an ardent anti-vivisectionist. He spent several hours each day in his study, writing his memoirs and anti-vivisection pamphlets, or perhaps just gazing out over the vast heath of which his window commanded an excellent prospect. When he was not writing, he could generally be found upon that heath, strolling and meditating. He had no relatives living, very little money, and a devoted housekeeper who was a chimpanzee.

On the day in question a circus had pitched on the heath, and the adjutant had, according to the housekeeper, gone to see it—for the second time. Worried at his absence, she finally called the police and Fenton Worth. No one at the circus had seen him. In search of the house, they broke in the door of his study.

The study had only one door, to which the adjutant had the only key, and its only window was inaccessible. The furniture consisted of a desk, a chair and a sofa. The adjutant was found lying on the sofa, strangled to death—with finger marks clear on his throat—and oddly parched. The door key was in his pocket.

The study window was open, but Fenton soon proved that it was inaccessible, for it lay forty feet above a mire of wet sand. This mire would neither support a ladder nor any climbing device, and its unbroken surface indicated that nothing had come within a hundred feet of the house on that side. It was further impossible to lower oneself from the roof by a rope, for the roof was made of treacherous rotten thatching—which likewise had not been disturbed.

A great deal of suspicion fell upon the housekeeper, as the adjutant's only heir. But an examination of the corpse, together with evidence from the adjutant's pamphlets and memoirs, established the true circumstances, as Fenton explained:

The adjutant had been strangled at the circus, bundled into a cannon, and fired through the window to land upon the sofa. This was confirmed by the parching, and powder burns on the corpse's feet. Certain details in the adjutant's memoirs and pamphlets showed that he had uncovered a vicious vivisection racket running behind the scenes at the circus, and was about to subject this sordid business to the light of public scrutiny. On his first visit to the circus, he had recognized an old enemy, an ex-Nazi artillery officer notorious during the war for his torture of animals, chiefly puppies and kittens. The adjutant's discovery of what the lions were fed completed his inquiry; the rest was duck soup, as he'd have said.

Confronted with this evidence, the Human Cannonball broke down and confessed, sobbing in half-coherent German.

*

"Hmmm" said Fenton. "Even that case doesn't help me here. Maybe I should re-read the novel, to see what clues I've missed." The well-known peeper leafed back through the book.

"Say, here's an anomaly!" he exclaimed. "The author

tells us on page one the door is locked, and here on page three it so manifestly isn't! What can be the explanation of that?"

Suddenly the world-famed private eye sat bolt upright. "Aha! The author says the door is locked, *but we have only his word for it*. The pieces of the jigsaw are beginning to fall into place, now. The author may in fact have *staged* the entire murder to make money from his own fictionalization of it! So the name of the killer must be—"

But the publicly-acclaimed private investigator will never name me. He'll be found tomorrow morning, stabbed to death, in a room locked from the inside. The *kriis* will have vanished.

Thus begins my novel of detection, another Fenton Worth Mystery,

THE END

KEITH ROBERTS

Weihnachtabend

The big car moved slowly, nosing its way along narrowing lanes. Here, beyond the little market town of Wilton, the snow lay thicker. Trees and bushes loomed in the headlights, coated with driven white. The tail of the Mercedes wagged slightly, steadied. Mainwaring heard the chauffeur swear under his breath. The link had been left live.

Dials let into the seatback recorded the vehicle's mechanical wellbeing; oil pressure, temperature, revs, k.p.h. Lights from the repeater glowed softly on his companion's face. She moved, restlessly; he saw the swing of yellow hair. He turned slightly. She was wearing a neat, brief kilt, heavy boots. Her legs were excellent.

He clicked the dial lights off. He said, "Not much farther."

He wondered if she was aware of the open link. He said, "First time down?"

She nodded in the dark. She said, "I was a bit overwhelmed."

Wilton Great House sprawled across a hilltop five miles or more beyond the town. The car drove for some distance beside the wall that fringed the estate. The perimeter defences had been strengthened since Mainwaring's last visit. Watchtowers reared at intervals; the wall itself had been topped by multiple strands of wire.

The lodge gates were commanded by two new stone pillboxes. The Merc edged between them, stopped. On the road from London, the snow had eased; now big flakes drifted again, lit by the headlights. Somewhere, orders were barked.

A man stepped forward, tapped at the window. Mainwaring buttoned it open. He saw a GFP armband, a hip holster with the flap tucked back. He said, "Good evening, Captain."

"Guten Abend, mein Herr. Ihre Ausweis Karte?"

Cold air gusted against Mainwaring's cheek. He passed across his identity card and security clearance. He said, "*Richard Mainwaring. Die rechte Hand zu dem Gesanten. Fräulein Hunter, von meiner Abteilung.*"

A torch flashed over the papers, dazzled into his eyes, moved to examine the girl. She sat stiffly, staring ahead. Beyond the Security officer Mainwaring made out two steel-helmeted troopers, automatics slung. In front of him, the wipers clicked steadily.

The GFP man stepped back. He said, "*In einer Woche, Ihre Ausweis Karte ist ausgelaufen. Erneuen Sie Ihre Karte.*"

Mainwaring said, "*Vielen Dank, Herr Hauptmann. Frohe Weihnacht.*"

The man saluted stiffly, unclipped a walkie-talkie from his belt. A pause, and the gates swung back. The Merc creamed through. Mainwaring said, "*Bastard . . .*"

She said, "Is it always like this?"

He said. "They're tightening up all round."

She pulled her coat round her shoulders. She said,

"Frankly, I find it a bit scary."

He said, "Just the Minister taking care of his guests."

Wilton stood in open downland set with great trees. Hans negotiated a bend, carefully, drove beneath half-seen branches. The wind moaned, zipping round a quarterlight. It was as if the car butted into a black tunnel, full of swirling pale flakes. He thought he saw her shiver. He said, "Soon be there."

The headlamps lit a rolling expanse of snow. Posts, buried nearly to their tops marked the drive. Another bend, and the house showed ahead. The car lights swept across a facade of mullioned windows. crenellated towers. Hard for the uninitiated to guess, staring at the skilfully-weathered stone, that the shell of the place was of reinforced concrete. The car swung right with a crunching of unseen gravel, and stopped. The ignition repeater glowed on the seatback.

Mainwaring said, "Thank you, Hans. Nice drive."

Hans said, "My pleasure, sir."

She flicked her hair free, picked up her handbag. He held the door for her. He said, "OK, Diane?"

She shrugged. She said, "Yes. I'm a bit silly sometimes." She squeezed his hand, briefly. She said, "I'm glad you'll be here. Somebody to rely on."

Mainwaring lay back on the bed and stared at the ceiling. Inside as well as out, Wilton was a triumph of art over nature. Here, in the Tudor wing where most of the guests were housed, walls and ceilings were of wavy plaster framed by heavy oak beams. He turned his head. The room was dominated by a fireplace of yellow Ham stone; on the overmantel, carved in bold relief, the *hakenkreuz* was flanked by the lion and eagle emblems of the Two Empires. A fire burned in the wrought-iron basket; the logs glowed cheerfully, casting wavering warm reflections across the ceiling. Beside the bed a bookshelf offered required reading; the Fuehrer's official biography, Shirer's *Rise of the Third Reich*, Cummings' monumental *Churchill: the Trial of Decadence*. There were a nicely-bound set of Buchan novels, some Kiplings, a Shakespeare, a complete Wilde. A side table carried a stack of current magazines; *Connoisseur, The Field, Der Spiegel, Paris Match*. There was a washstand, its rail hung with dark blue towels; in the corner of the room were the doors to the bathroom and wardrobe, in which a servant had already neatly disposed his clothes.

He stubbed his cigarette, lit another. He swung his legs off the bed, poured himself a whisky. From the grounds, faintly, came voices, snatches of laughter. He heard the crash of a pistol, the rattle of an automatic. He walked to the window, pushed the curtain aside. Snow was still falling, drifting silently from the black sky; but the firing pits beside the big house were brightly lit. He watched the figures move and bunch for a while, let the curtain fall. He sat by the fire, shoulders hunched, staring into the flames. He was remembering the trip through London; the flags hanging limp over Whitehall, slow, jerking movement of traffic, the light tanks drawn up outside St. James. The Kensington Road had been crowded, traffic edging and hooting; the vast frontage of Harrods looked grim and oriental against the louring sky. He frowned, remembering the call he had had before leaving the Ministry.

Kosowicz had been the name. From Time International; or so he had claimed. He'd refused twice to speak to him; but Kosowicz had been insistent. In the end, he'd asked his secretary to put him through.

Kosowicz had sounded very American. He said, "Mr. Mainwaring, I'd like to arrange a personal interview with your Minister."

"I'm afraid that's out of the question. I must also point out that this communication is extremely irregular."

Kosowicz said, "What do I take that as, sir? A warning, or a threat?"

Mainwaring said carefully, "It was neither. I merely observed that proper channels of approach do exist."

Kosowicz said, "Uh-huh. Mr. Mainwaring, what's the truth behind this rumour that Action Groups are being moved into Moscow?"

Mainwaring said, "Deputy-Fuehrer Hess has already issued a statement on the situation. I can see that you're supplied with a copy."

The phone said, "I have it before me. Mr. Mainwaring, what are you people trying to set up? Another Warsaw?"

Mainwaring said, "I'm afraid I can't comment further, Mr. Kosowicz. The Deputy-Fuehrer deplored the necessity of force. The *Einsatzegruppen* have been alerted; at this time, that is all. They will be used if necessary to disperse militants. As of this moment, the need has not arisen."

Kosowicz shifted his ground. "You mentioned the Deputy-Fuehrer, sir. I hear there was another bomb attempt two nights ago, can you comment on this?"

Mainwaring tightened his knuckles on the handset. He said, "I'm afraid you've been misinformed. We know nothing of any such incident."

The phone was silent for a moment. Then it said, "Can I take your denial as official?"

Mainwaring said, "This is not an official conversation. I'm not empowered to issue statements in any respect."

The phone said, "Yeah, channels do exist. Mr. Mainwaring, thanks for your time."

Mainwaring said, "Goodbye." He put the handset down, sat staring at it. After a while he lit a cigarette.

Outside the windows of the Ministry the snow still fell, a dark whirl and dance against the sky. His tea, when he came to drink it, was half cold.

The fire crackled and shifted. He poured himself another whisky, sat back. Before leaving for Wilton, he'd lunched with Winsby-Walker from Productivity. Winsby-Walker made it his business to know everything; but he had known nothing of a correspondent called Kosowicz. He thought, 'I should have checked with Security.' But then, Security would have checked with him.

He sat up, looked at his watch. The noise from the ranges had diminished. He turned his mind with a deliberate effort into another channel. The new thoughts brought no more comfort. Last Christmas he had spent with his mother; now, that couldn't happen again. He remembered other Christmases, back across the years. Once, to the child unknowing, they had been gay affairs of crackers and toys. He remembered the scent and texture of pine branches, closeness of candlelight; and books read by torchlight under the sheets, the hard angles of the filled pillowslip, heavy at the foot of the bed. Then, he had been complete; only later, slowly, had come the knowledge of failure. And with it, loneliness. He thought, 'She wanted to see me settled. It didn't seem much to ask.'

The Scotch was making him maudlin. He drained the glass, walked through to the bathroom. He stripped, and showered. Towelling himself, he thought, "Richard Mainwaring, Personal Assistant to the British Minister of

Liaison.' Aloud he said, "One must remember the compensations."

He dressed, lathered his face and began to shave. He thought, 'Thirty five is the exact middle of one's life.' He was remembering another time with the girl Diane when just for a little while some magic had interposed. Now, the affair was never mentioned between them. Because of James. Always, of course, there is a James.

He towelled his face, applied aftershave. Despite himself, his mind had drifted back to the phone call. One fact was certain; there had been a major security spillage. Somebody somewhere had supplied Kosowicz with closely-guarded information. That same someone, presumably, had supplied a list of ex-directory lines. He frowned, grappling with the problem. One country, and one only, opposed the Two Empires with gigantic, latent strength. To that country had shifted the focus of Semitic nationalism. And Kosowicz had been an American.

He thought, 'Freedom, schmeedom. Democracy is Jew-shaped.' He frowned again, fingering his face. It didn't alter the salient fact. The tipoff had come from the Freedom Front; and he had been contacted, however obliquely. Now, he had become an accessory; the thought had been nagging at the back of his brain all day.

He wondered what they could want of him. There was a rumour—a nasty rumour—that you never found out. Not till the end, till you'd done whatever was required from you. They were untiring, deadly and subtle. He hadn't run squalling to Security at the first hint of danger; but that would have been allowed for. Every turn and twist would have been allowed for.

Every squirm, on the hook.

He grunted, angry with himself. Fear was half their strength. He buttoned his shirt remembering the guards at the gates, the wire and pillboxes. Here, of all places, nothing could reach him. For a few days, he could forget the whole affair. He said aloud, "Anyway, I don't even matter. I'm not important." The thought cheered him, nearly.

He clicked the light off, walked through to his room, closed the door behind him. He crossed to the bed and stood quite still, staring at the bookshelf. Between Shirer and the Churchill tome there rested a third slim volume. He reached to touch the spine, delicately; read the author name, Geissler, and the title. *Toward Humanity.* Below the title, like a topless Cross of Lorraine, were the twin linked F's of the Freedom Front.

Ten minutes ago, the book hadn't been there.

He walked to the door. The corridor beyond was deserted. From somewhere in the house, faintly, came music; *Till Eulenspiegel.* There were no nearer sounds. He closed the door again, locked it. Turned back and saw the wardrobe stood slightly ajar.

His case still lay on the sidetable. He crossed to it, took out the Luger. The feel of the heavy pistol was comforting. He pushed the clip home, thumbed the safety forward, chambered a round. The breech closed with a hard snap. He walked to the wardrobe, shoved the door wide with his foot.

Nothing there.

He let his held breath escape with a little hiss. He pressed the clip release, ejected the cartridge, laid the gun on the bed. He stood again looking at the shelf. He thought, 'I must have been mistaken.'

He took the book down, carefully. Geissler had been banned since publication in every Province of the Two Empires; Mainwaring himself had never even seen a copy. He squatted on the edge of the bed, opened the thing at random.

> 'The doctrine of Aryan co-ancestry, seized on so eagerly by the English middle classes, had the superficial reasonableness of most theories ultimately traceable to Rosenberg. Churchill's answer, in one sense, had already been made; but Chamberlain, and the country, turned to Hess . . .'
>
> 'The Cologne settlement though seeming to offer hope of security to Jews already domiciled in Britain, in fact paved the way for campaigns of intimidation and extortion similar to those already undertaken in history, notably by King John. The comparison is not inapt; for the English *bourgeoisie,* anxious to construct a rationale, discovered many unassailable precedents. A true Sign of the Times, almost certainly, was the resurgence of interest in the novels of Sir Walter Scott. By 1942 the

lesson had been learned on both sides; and the Star of David was a common sight on the streets of most British cities.'

The wind rose momentarily in a long wail, shaking the window casement. Mainwaring glanced up, turned his attention back to the book. He leafed through several pages.

'In 1940, her Expeditionary Force shattered, her allies quiescent or defeated, the island truly stood alone. Her proletariat, bedevilled by bad leadership, weakened by a gigantic depression, was effectively without a voice. Her aristocracy, like their *Junker* counterparts, embraced coldly what could no longer be ignored; while after the Whitehall *Putsch* the Cabinet was reduced to the status of an Executive Council . . .'

The knock at the door made him start, guiltily. He pushed the book away. He said, "Who's that?"

She said, "Me. Richard, aren't you ready?"

He said, "Just a minute." He stared at the book, then placed it back on the shelf. He thought, 'That at least wouldn't be expected.' He slipped the Luger into his case and closed it. Then he went to the door.

She was wearing a lacy black dress. Her shoulders were bare; her hair, worn loose, had been brushed till it gleamed. He stared at her a moment, stupidly. Then he said, "Please come in."

She said, "I was starting to wonder . . . Are you all right?"

"Yes. Yes, of course."

She said, "You look as if you'd seen a ghost."

He smiled. He said. "I expect I was taken aback. Those Aryan good looks."

She grinned at him. She said, "I'm half Irish, half English, half Scandinavian. If you have to know."

"That doesn't add up."

She said, "Neither do I, most of the time."

"Drink?"

"Just a little one. We shall be late."

He said, "It's not very formal tonight." He turned away, fiddling with his tie.

She sipped her drink, pointed her foot, scuffed her toe on

the carpet. She said, "I expect you've been to a lot of houseparties."
He said, "One or two."
She said, "Richard, are they . . ."
"Are they what?"
She said, "I don't know. You can't help hearing things."
He said, "You'll be all right. One's very much like the next."
She said, "Are you honestly OK?"
"Sure."
She said, "You're all thumbs. Here, let me." She reached up, knotted deftly. Her eyes searched his face for a moment, moving in little shifts and changes of direction. She said, "There. I think you just need looking after."
He said carefully, "How's James?"
She stared a moment longer. She said, "I don't know. He's in Nairobi. I haven't seen him for months."
He said, "I am a bit nervous, actually."
"Why?"
He said, "Escorting a rather lovely blonde."
She tossed her head, and laughed. She said, "You need a drink as well then."
He poured whisky, said, "Cheers." The book, now, seemed to be burning into his shoulderblades.
She said, "As a matter of fact you're looking rather fetching yourself."
He thought, 'This is the night when all things come together. There should be a word for it.' Then he remembered about Till Eulenspiegel.
She said, "We'd honestly better go down."
Lights gleamed in the Great Hall, reflecting from polished boards, dark linenfold panelling. At the nearer end of the chamber a huge fire burned. Beneath the minstrels' gallery long tables had been set. Informal or not, they shone with glass and silverware. Candles glowed amid wreaths of dark evergreen; beside each place was a rolled crimson napkin.
In the middle of the Hall, its tip brushing the coffered ceiling, stood a Christmas tree. Its branches were hung with apples, baskets of sweets, red paper roses; at its base were piled gifts in gay-striped wrappers. Round the tree folk stood in groups, chatting and laughing. Richard saw Muller the Defence Minister, with a striking-looking blonde he

took to be his wife; beside them was a tall, monacled man who was something or other in Security. There was a group of GSP officers in their dark, neat uniforms, beyond them half a dozen Liaison people. He saw Hans the chauffeur standing head bent, nodding intently, smiling at some remark; and thought as he had thought before how he looked like a big, handsome ox.

Diane had paused in the doorway, and linked her arm through his. But the Minister had already seen them. He came weaving through the crowd, a glass in his hand. He was wearing tight black trews, a dark blue roll-neck shirt. He looked happy and relaxed. He said, "Richard. And my dear Miss Hunter. We'd nearly given you up for lost. After all, Hans Trapp is about. Now, some drinks. And come, do come; please join my friends. Over here, where it is warm."

She said, "Who's Hans Trapp?"

Mainwaring said, "You'll find out in a bit."

A little later the Minister said, "Ladies and gentlemen, I think we may be seated."

The meal was superb, the wine abundant. By the time the brandy was served Richard found himself talking more easily, and the Geissler copy pushed nearly to the back of his mind. The traditional toasts—King and Fuehrer, the Provinces, the Two Empires—were drunk; then the Minister clapped his hands for quiet. "My friends," he said, "tonight, this special night when we can all mix so freely, is *Weichnachtabend*. It means, I suppose, many things to the many of us here. But let us remember, first and foremost, that this is the night of the children. Your children, who have come with you to share part at least of this very special Christmas."

He paused. "Already," he said, "they have been called from their crèche; soon they will be with us. Let me show them to you." He nodded; at the gesture servants wheeled forward a heavy, ornate box. A drape was twitched aside, revealing the grey surface of a big tv screen. Simultaneously, the lamps that lit the Hall began to dim. Diane turned to Mainwaring, frowning; he touched her hand, gently, and shook his head.

Save for the firelight, the Hall was now nearly dark. The candles guttered in their wreaths, flames stirring in some draught; in the hush, the droning of the wind round the great facade of the place was once more audible. The lights would be out, now, all over the house.

"For some of you," said the Minister, "this is your first visit here. For you, I will explain.

"On *Weihnachtabend,* all ghosts and goblins walk. The demon Hans Trapp is abroad; his face is black and terrible, his clothing the skins of bears. Against him comes the Lightbringer, the Spirit of Christmas. Some call her Lucia Queen, some *Das Christkind.* See her now."

The screen lit up.

She moved slowly, like a sleepwalker. She was slender, and robed in white. Her ashen hair tumbled round her shoulders; above her head glowed a diadem of burning tapers. Behind her trod the Star Boys with their wands and tinsel robes; behind again came a little group of children. They ranged in age from eight and nine-year-olds to toddlers. They gripped each other's hands, apprehensively, setting feet in line like cats, darting terrified glances at the shadows to either side.

"They lie in darkness, waiting," said the Minister softly. "Their nurses have left them. If they cry out, there is none to hear. So they do not cry out. And one by one, she has called them. They see her light pass beneath the door; and they must rise and follow. Here, where we sit, is warmth. Here is safety. Their gifts are waiting; to reach them, they must run the gauntlet of the dark."

The camera angle changed. Now they were watching the procession from above. The Lucia Queen stepped steadily; the shadows she cast leaped and flickered on panelled walls.

"They are in the Long Gallery now," said the Minister. "Almost directly above us. They must not falter, they must not look back. Somewhere, Hans Trapp is hiding. From Hans, only *Das Christkind* can protect them. See how close they bunch behind her light!"

A howling began, like the crying of a wolf. In part it seemed to come from the screen, in part to echo through the Hall itself. The *Christkind* turned, raising her arms; the howling split into a many-voiced cadence, died to a mutter. In its place came a distant huge thudding, like the beating of a drum.

Diane said abruptly, "I don't find this particularly funny."

Mainwaring said, "It isn't supposed to be. Shh."

The Minister said evenly. "The Aryan child must know,

from earliest years, the darkness that surrounds him. He must learn to fear, and to overcome that fear. He must learn to be strong. The Two Empires were not built by weakness; weakness will not sustain them. There is no place for it. This in part your children already know. The house is big, and dark; but they will win through to the light. They fight as the Empires once fought. For their birthright."

The shot changed again, showed a wide, sweeping staircase. The head of the little procession appeared, began to descend. "Now, where is our friend Hans?" said the Minister. "*Ah . . .*"

Her grip tightened convulsively on Mainwaring's arm. A black-smeared face loomed at the screen. The bogey snarled, clawing at the camera; then turned, loped swiftly toward the staircase. The children shrieked, and bunched; instantly the air was wild with din. Grotesque figures capered and leaped; hands grabbed, clutching. The column was buffeted and swirled; Mainwaring saw a child bowled completely over. The screaming reached a high pitch of terror; and the *Christkind* turned, arms once more raised. The goblins and were-things backed away, growling, into shadow; the slow march was resumed.

The Minister said, "They are nearly here. And they are good children, worthy of their race. Prepare the tree."

Servants ran forward with tapers to light the many candles. The tree sprang from gloom, glinting, black-green; and Mainwaring thought for the first time what a dark thing it was, although it blazed with light.

The big doors at the end of the Hall were flung back; and the children came tumbling through. Tearstained and sobbing they were, some bruised; but all, before they ran to the tree, stopped, made obeisance to the strange creature who had brought them through the dark. Then the crown was lifted, the tapers extinguished; and Lucia Queen became a child like the rest, a slim, barefooted girl in a gauzy white dress.

The Minister rose, laughing. Now," he said, "music, and some more wine. Hans Trapp is dead. My friends, one and all, and children; *Frohe Weihnacht!*"

Diane said, "Excuse me a moment."

Mainwaring turned. He said. "Are you all right?"

She said, "I'm just going to get rid of a certain taste."

He watched her go, concernedly; and the Minister had

his arm, was talking. "Excellent, Richard," he said. "It has gone excellently so far, don't you think?"

Richard said, "Excellently, sir."

"Good, good. Eh, Heidi, Erna . . . and Frederick, is it Frederick? What have you got there? Oh, very fine . . ." He steered Mainwaring away, still with his fingers tucked beneath his elbow. Squeals of joy sounded; somebody had discovered a sled, tucked away behind the tree. The Minister said, "Look at them; how happy they are now. I would like children, Richard. Children of my own. Sometimes I think I have given too much . . . Still, the opportunity remains. I am younger than you, do you realize that? This is the Age of Youth."

Mainwaring said, "I wish the Minister every happiness."

"Richard, Richard, you must learn not to be so very correct at all times. Unbend a little, you are too aware of dignity. You are my friend. I trust you; above all others, I trust you. Do you realize this?"

Richard said, "Thank you, sir. I do."

The Minister seemed bubbling over with some inner pleasure. He said, "Richard, come with me. Just for a moment. I have prepared a special gift for you. I won't keep you from the party very long."

Mainwaring followed, drawn as ever by the curious dynamism of the man. The Minister ducked through an arched doorway, turned right and left, descended a narrow flight of stairs. At the bottom the way was barred by a door of plain grey steel. The Minister pressed his palm flat to a sensor plate; a click, the whine of some mechanism, and the door swung inward. Beyond was a further flight of concrete steps, lit by a single lamp in a heavy well-glass. Chilly air blew upward. Mainwaring realized, with something approaching a shock, that they entered part of the bunker system that honeycombed the ground beneath Wilton.

The Minister hurried ahead of him, palmed a further door. He said, "Toys, Richard. All toys. But they amuse me." Then, catching sight of Mainwaring's face, "Come, man, come! You are more nervous than the children, frightened of poor old Hans!"

The door gave onto a darkened space. There was a heavy, sweetish smell that Mainwaring, for a whirling moment, couldn't place. His companion propelled him forward, gently. He resisted, pressing back; and the

Minister's arm shot by him. A click, and the place was flooded with light. He saw a wide, low area, also concrete-built. To one side, already polished and gleaming, stood the Mercedes, next to it the Minister's private Porsche. There were a couple of Volkswagens, a Ford Executive; and in the farthest corner, a vision in glinting white. A Lamborghini. They had emerged in the garage underneath the house.

The Minister said, "My private short cut." He walked forward to the Lamborghini, stood running his fingers across the low, broad bonnet. He said, "Look at her, Richard. Here, sit in. Isn't she a beauty? Isn't she fine?"

Mainwaring said, "She certainly is."

"You like her?"

Mainwaring smiled. He said, "Very much, sir. Who wouldn't?"

The Minister said, "Good, I'm so pleased. Richard, I'm upgrading you. She's yours. Enjoy her."

Mainwaring stared.

The Minister said, "Here, man. Don't look like that, like a fish. Here, see. Logbook, your keys. All entered up, finished." He gripped Mainwaring's shoulders, swung him round laughing. He said, "You've worked well for me. The Two Empires don't forget. Their good friends, their servants."

Mainwaring said, "I'm deeply honoured, sir."

"Don't be honoured. You're still being formal. Richard . . ."

"Sir?"

The Minister said, "Stay by me. Stay by me. Up there . . . they don't understand. But we understand . . . eh? These are difficult times. We must be together, always together. Kingdom, and Reich. Apart . . . we could be destroyed." He turned away, placed clenched hands on the roof of the car. He said, "Here, all this. Jewry, the Americans . . . Capitalism. They must stay afraid. Nobody fears an Empire divided. It would fall!"

Mainwaring said, "I'll do my best, sir. We all will."

The Minister said, "I know, I know. But Richard, this afternoon. I was playing with swords. Silly little swords."

Mainwaring thought, 'I know how he keeps me. I can see the mechanism. But I mustn't imagine I know the entire truth.'

The Minister turned back, as if in pain. He said,

"Strength is Right. It has to be. But Hess . . ."

Mainwaring said slowly, "We've tried before, sir . . ."

The Minister slammed his fist onto metal. He said, "Richard, don't you see? It wasn't us. Not this time. It was his own people. Baumann, von Thaden . . . I can't tell. He's an old man, he doesn't matter any more. It's an idea they want to kill, Hess is an idea. Do you understand? It's *Lebensraum*. Again . . . Half the world isn't enough."

He straightened. He said, "The worm, in the apple. It gnaws, gnaws . . . But we are Liaison. We matter, so much. Richard, be my eyes. Be my ears."

Mainwaring stayed silent, thinking about the book in his room; and the Minister once more took his arm. He said, "The shadows, Richard. They were never closer. Well might we teach our children to fear the dark. But . . . not in our time. Eh? Not for us. There is life, and hope. So much we can do . . ."

Mainwaring thought, 'Maybe it's the wine I drank. I'm being pressed too hard.' A dull, queer mood, almost of indifference, had fallen on him. He followed his Minister without complaint, back through the bunker complex, up to where the great fire burned low and the tapers on the tree. He heard the singing mixed with the wind-voice, watched the children rock heavy-eyed, carolling sleep. The house seemed winding down, to rest; and she had gone of course. He sat in a corner and drank wine and brooded, watched the Minister move from group to group until he too was gone, the Hall nearly empty and the servants clearing away.

He found his own self, his inner self, dozing at last as it dozed at each day's end. Tiredness, as ever, had come like a benison. He rose carefully, walked to the door. He thought, 'I shan't be missed here.' Shutters closed, in his head.

He found his key, unlocked his room. He thought, 'Now, she will be waiting. Like all the letters that never came, the phones that never rang.' He opened the door.

She said, "What kept you?"

He closed the door behind him, quietly. The fire crackled in the little room, the curtains were drawn against the night. She sat by the hearth, barefooted, still in her party dress. Beside her on the carpet were glasses, an ashtray with half-smoked stubs. One lamp was burning; in the warm light her eyes were huge and dark.

He looked across to the bookshelf. The Geissler stood

where he had left it. He said, "How did you get in?"

She chuckled. She said, "There was a spare key on the back of the door. Didn't you see me steal it?"

He walked toward her, stood looking down. He thought, 'Adding another fragment to the puzzle. Too much, too complicated.'

She said, "Are you angry?"

He said, "No."

She patted the floor. She said gently, "Please, Richard. Don't be cross."

He sat, slowly, watching her.

She said, "Drink?" He didn't answer. She poured one anyway. She said, "What were you doing all this time? I thought you'd be up hours ago."

He said, "I was talking to the Minister."

She traced a pattern on the rug with her forefinger. Her hair fell forward, golden and heavy, baring the nape of her neck. She said, "I'm sorry about earlier on. I was stupid. I think I was a bit scared too."

He drank, slowly. He felt like a run-down machine. Hell to have to start thinking again at this time of night. He said, "What were you doing?"

She watched up at him. Her eyes were candid. She said, "Sitting here. Listening to the wind."

He said, "That couldn't have been much fun."

She shook her head, slowly, eyes fixed on his face. She said softly, "You don't know me at all."

He was quiet again. She said, "You don't believe in me, do you?"

He thought, 'You need understanding. You're different from the rest; and I'm selling myself short.' Aloud he said, "No."

She put the glass down, smiled, took his glass away. She hotched toward him across the rug, slid her arm round his neck. She said, "I was thinking about you. Making my mind up." She kissed him. He felt her tongue pushing, opened his lips. She said, "*Mmm . . .*" She sat back a little, smiling. She said, "Do you mind?"

"No."

She pressed a strand of hair across her mouth, parted her teeth, kissed again. He felt himself react, involuntarily; and felt her touch and squeeze.

She said, "This is a silly dress. It gets in the way." She

reached behind her. The fabric parted; she pushed down, to the waist. She said, "Now it's like last time."

He said slowly, "Nothing's ever like last time."

She rolled across his lap, lay watching up. She whispered, "I've put the clock back."

Later in the dream she said, "I was so silly."

"What do you mean?"

She said, "I was shy. That was all. You weren't really supposed to go away."

He said, "What about James?"

"He's got somebody else. I didn't know what I was missing."

He let his hand stray over her; and present and immediate past became confused so that as he held her he still saw her kneeling, firelight dancing on her body. He reached for her and she was ready again; she fought, chuckling, taking it bareback, staying all the way.

Much later he said, "The Minister gave me a Lamborghini."

She rolled onto her belly, lay chin in hands watching under a tangle of hair. She said, "And now you've got yourself a blonde. What are you going to do with us?"

He said, "None of it's real."

She said, "*Oh . . .*" She punched him. She said, "Richard, you make me cross. It's happened, you idiot. That's all. It happens to everybody." She scratched again with a finger on the carpet. She said, "I hope you've made me pregnant. Then you'd have to marry me."

He narrowed his eyes; and the wine began again, singing in his head.

She nuzzled him. She said, "You asked me once. Say it again."

"I don't remember."

She said, "Richard, please . . ." So he said, "Diane, will you marry me?" And she said, "Yes, yes, yes," then afterwards awareness came and though it wasn't possible he took her again and that time was finest of all, tight and sweet as honey. He'd fetched pillows from the bed and the counterpane, they curled close and he found himself talking, talking, how it wasn't the sex, it was shopping in Marlborough and having tea and seeing the sun set from White Horse Hill and being together, together; then she pressed fingers to his mouth and he fell with her in sleep past cold and loneliness and fear, past deserts and unlit places, down maybe to where spires reared gold and tree leaves moved and dazzled and white cars sang on roads and suns burned inwardly, lighting new worlds.

He woke, and the fire was low. He sat up, dazed. She was watching him. He stroked her hair awhile, smiling; then she pushed away. She said, "Richard, I have to go now."

"Not yet."

"It's the middle of the night."

He said, "It doesn't matter."

She said, "It does. He mustn't know."

"Who?"

She said, "You know who. You know why I was asked here."

He said, "He's not like that. Honestly."

She shivered. She said, "Richard, please. Don't get me in trouble." She smiled. She said, "It's only till tomorrow. Only a little while."

He stood, awkwardly, and held her, pressing her warmth close. Shoeless, she was tiny; her shoulder fitted beneath his armpit.

Halfway through dressing she stopped and laughed, leaned a hand against the wall. She said, "I'm all woozy."

Later he said, "I'll see you to your room."

She said, "No, please. I'm all right." She was holding her handbag, and her hair was combed. She looked, again, as if she had been to a party.

At the door she turned. She said, "I love you, Richard. Truly." She kissed again, quickly; and was gone.

He closed the door, dropped the latch. He stood a while looking round the room. In the fire a burned-through log broke with a snap, sending up a little whirl of sparks. He walked to the washstand, bathed his face and hands. He shook the counterpane out on the bed, rearranged the pillows. Her scent still clung to him; he remembered how she had felt, and what she had said.

He crossed to the window, pushed it ajar. Outside, the snow lay in deep swaths and drifts. Starlight gleamed from it, ghost-white; the whole great house was mute. He stood feeling the chill move against his skin; and in all the silence, a voice drifted far-off and clear. It came maybe from the guardhouses, full of distance and peace.

"Stille Nacht, heilige Nacht,
"alles schläfte, einsam wacht . . ."

He walked to the bed, pulled back the covers. The sheets were crisp and spotless, fresh-smelling. He smiled, and turned off the lamp.

"Nur das traute, hochheilige Paar.
"Holder Knabe im lochigen Haar . . ."

In the wall of the room, an inch behind the plasterwork, a complex little machine hummed. A spool of delicate golden wire shook slightly; but the creak of the opening window had been the last thing to interest the recorder, the singing alone couldn't activate its relays. A micro-switch tripped, inaudibly; valve filaments faded, and died. Mainwaring lay back in the last of the firelight, and closed his eyes.

"Schlaf' in himmlischer Ruh,
"Schlaf' in himmlischer Ruh . . ."

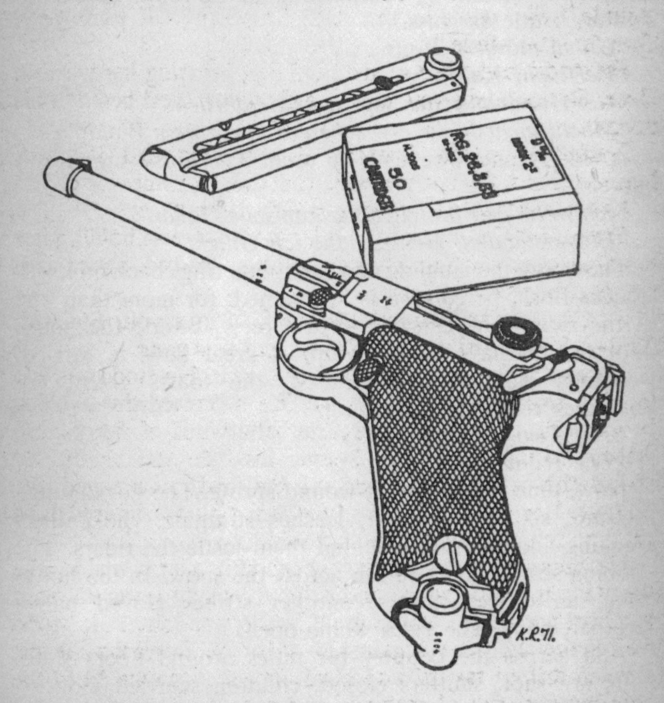

2.

Beyond drawn curtains, brightness flicks on.

The sky is a hard, clear blue; icy, full of sunlight. The light dazzles back from the brilliant land. Far things—copses, hills, solitary trees—stand sharp-etched. Roofs and eaves carry hummocks of whiteness, twigs a three-inch crest. In the stillness, here and there, the snow cracks and falls, powdering.

The shadows of the riders jerk and undulate. The quiet is interrupted. Hooves ring on swept courtyards or stamp muffled, churning the snow. It seems the air itself has been rendered crystalline by cold; through it the voices break and shatter, brittle as glass.

"Guten morgen, Hans . . ."

"Verflucht Kalt!"

"Der Hundenmeister sagt, sehr Gefährlich!"

"Macht nichts! Wir erwischen es bevor dem Wald!"

A rider plunges beneath an arch. The horse snorts and curvets.

"Ich wette dier fünfzig amerikanische Dollar!"

"Einverstanden! Heute, habe ich Glück!"

The noise, the jangling and stamping, rings back on itself. Cheeks flush, perception is heightened; for more than one of the riders, the early courtyard reels. Beside the house door trestles have been set up. A great bowl is carried, steaming. The cups are raised, the toasts given; the responses ring again, crashing.

"The Two Empires . . !"

"The Hunt . . !"

Now, time is like a tight-wound spring. The dogs plunge forward, six to a handler, leashes straining, choke links creaking and snapping. Behind them jostle the riders. The bobbing scarlet coats splash across the snow. In the house drive, an officer salutes; another strikes gloved palms together, nods. The gates whine open.

And across the country for miles around doors slam, bolts are shot, shutters closed, children scurried indoors. Village streets, muffled with snow, wait dumbly. Somewhere a dog barks, is silenced. The houses squat sullen, blind-eyed. The word has gone out, faster than horses could gallop. Today the Hunt will run; on snow.

The riders fan out, across a speckled waste of fields. A check, a questing; and the horns begin to yelp. Ahead the dogs bound and leap, black spots against whiteness. The horns cry again; but these hounds run mute. The riders sweep forward, onto the line.

Now, for the hunters, time and vision are fragmented. Twigs and snow merge in a racing blur; and tree-boles, ditches, gates. The tide reaches a crest of land, pours down the opposing slope. Hedges rear, mantled with white; and muffled thunder is interrupted by sailing silence, the smash and crackle of landing. The View sounds, harsh and high; and frenzy, and the racing blood, discharge intelligence. A horse goes down, in a gigantic flailing; another rolls, crushing its rider into the snow. A mount runs riderless. The Hunt, destroying, destroys itself unaware.

There are cottages, a paling fence. The fence goes over, unnoticed. A chicken house erupts in a cloud of flung crystals; birds run squawking, under the hooves. Caps are lost, flung away; hair flogs wild. Whips flail, spurs rake streaming flanks; and the woods are close. Twigs lash, and branches; snow falls, thudding. The crackling, now, is all around.

At the end, it is always the same. The handlers close in, yodelling, waist-high in trampled brush; the riders force close and closer, mounts sidling and shaking; and silence falls. Only the quarry, reddened, flops and twists; the thin high noise it makes is the noise of anything in pain.

Now, if he chooses, the *Jagdmeister* may end the suffering. The crash of the pistol rings hollow; and birds erupt, high from frozen twigs, wheel with the echoes and cry. The pistol fires again; and the quarry lies still. In time, the shaking stops; and a dog creeps forward, begins to lick.

Now a slow movement begins; a spreading-out, away from the place. There are mutterings, a laugh that chokes to silence. The fever passes. Somebody begins to shiver; and a girl, blood glittering on cheek and neck, puts a glove to her forehead and moans. The Need has come and gone; for a little while, the Two Empires have purged themselves.

The riders straggle back on tired mounts, shamble in

through the gates. As the last enters a closed black van starts up, drives away. In an hour, quietly, it returns; and the gates swing shut behind it.

Surfacing from deepest sleep was like rising, slowly, through a warm sea. For a time, as Mainwaring lay eyes closed, memory and awareness were confused so that she was with him and the room a recollected, childhood place. He rubbed his face, yawned, shook his head; and the knocking that had roused him came again. He said, "Yes?"

The voice said, "Last breakfasts in fifteen minutes, sir."

He called, "Thank you," heard the footsteps pad away.

He pushed himself up, groped on the sidetable for his watch, held it close to his eyes. It read ten forty-five.

He swung the bedclothes back, felt air tingle on his skin. She had been with him, certainly, in the dawn; his body remembered the succubus, with nearly painful strength. He looked down smiling, walked to the bathroom. He showered, towelled himself, shaved and dressed. He closed his door and locked it, walked to the breakfast room. A few couples still sat over their coffee; he smiled a good morning, took a window seat. Beyond the double panes the snow piled thickly; its reflection lit the room with a white, inverted brilliance. He ate slowly, hearing distant shouts. On the long slope behind the house, groups of children pelted each other vigorously. Once a toboggan came into sight, vanished behind a rising swell of ground.

He had hoped he might see her, but she didn't come. He drank coffee, smoked a cigarette. He walked to the television lounge. The big colour screen showed a childrens' party taking place in a Berlin hospital. He watched for a while. The door behind him clicked a couple of times, but it wasn't Diane.

There was a second guests' lounge, not usually much frequented at this time of the year; and a reading room and library. He wandered through them, but there was no sign of her. It occurred to him she might not yet be up; at Wilton, there were few hard-and-fast rules for Christmas Day. He thought, 'I should have checked her room number.' He wasn't even sure in which of the guest wings she had been placed.

The house was quiet; it seemed most of the visitors had

taken to their rooms. He wondered if she could have ridden with the Hunt; he'd heard it vaguely, leaving and returning. He doubted if the affair would have held much appeal.

He strolled back to the tv lounge, watched for an hour or more. By lunchtime he was feeling vaguely piqued; and sensing too the rise of a curious unease. He went back to his room, wondering if by any chance she had gone there; but the miracle was not repeated. The room was empty.

The fire was burning, and the bed had been remade. He had forgotten the servants' pass keys. The Geissler copy still stood on the shelf. He took it down, stood weighing it in his hand and frowning. It was, in a sense, madness to leave it there.

He shrugged, put the thing back. He thought, 'So who reads bookshelves anyway?' The plot, if plot there had been, seemed absurd now in the clearer light of day. He stepped into the corridor, closed the door and locked it behind him. He tried as far as possible to put the book from his mind. It represented a problem; and problems, as yet, he wasn't prepared to cope with. Too much else was going on in his brain.

He lunched alone, now with a very definite pang; the process was disquietingly like that of other years. Once he thought he caught sight of her in the corridor. His heart thumped; but it was the other blonde, Müller's wife. The gestures, the fall of the hair, were similar; but this woman was taller.

He let himself drift into a reverie. Images of her, it seemed, were engraved on his mind; each to be selected now, studied, placed lovingly aside. He saw the firelit texture of her hair and skin, her lashes brushing her cheek as she lay in his arms and slept. Other memories. sharper, more immediate still, throbbed like little shocks in the mind. She tossed her head, smiling; her hair swung, touched the point of a breast.

He pushed his cup away, rose. At fifteen hundred patriotism required her presence in the tv lounge. As it required the presence of every other guest. Then, if not before, he would see her. He reflected, wryly, that he had waited half a lifetime for her; a little longer now would do no harm.

He took to prowling the house again; the Great Hall, the

Long Gallery where the *Christkind* had walked. Below the windows that lined it was a snow-covered roof. The tart, reflected light struck upward, robbing the place of mystery. In the Great Hall, they had already removed the tree. He watched household staff hanging draperies, carrying in stacks of gilded cane chairs. On the Minstrels' Gallery a pile of odd-shaped boxes proclaimed that the orchestra had arrived.

At fourteen hundred hours he walked back to the tv lounge. A quick glance assured him she wasn't there. The bar was open; Hans, looking as big and suave as ever, had been pressed into service to minister to the guests. He smiled at Mainwaring and said, "Good afternoon, sir." Mainwaring asked for a lager beer, took the glass to a corner seat. From here he could watch both the tv screen and the door.

The screen was showing the world-wide linkup that had become hallowed Christmas afternoon fare within the Two Empires. He saw, without particular interest, greetings flashed from the Leningrad and Moscow garrisons, a lightship, an Arctic weather station, a Mission in German East Africa. At fifteen hundred, the Fuehrer was due to speak; this year, for the first time, Ziegler was preceding Edward VIII.

The room filled, slowly. She didn't come. Mainwaring finished the lager, walked to the bar, asked for another and a packet of cigarettes. The unease was sharpening now into something very like alarm. He thought for the first time that she might have been taken ill.

The time signal flashed, followed by the drumroll of the German anthem. He rose with the rest, stood stiffly till it had finished. The screen cleared, showed the familiar room in the Chancellery; the dark, high panels, the crimson drapes, the big *hakenkreuz* emblem over the desk. The Fuehrer, as ever, spoke impeccably; but Mainwaring thought with a fragment of his mind how old he had begun to look.

The speech ended. He realized he hadn't heard a word that was said.

The drums crashed again. The King said, "Once more, at Christmas, it is my . . . duty and pleasure . . . to speak to you."

Something seemed to burst inside Mainwaring's head. He rose, walked quickly to the bar. He said, "Hans, have you seen Miss Hunter?"

The other jerked round. He said, "Sir, *shh* . . . please . . ."

"Have you seen her?"

Hans stared at the screen, and back to Mainwaring. The King was saying, "There have been . . . troubles, and difficulties. More perhaps lie ahead. But with . . . God's help, they will be overcome."

The chauffeur licked his mouth. He said, "I'm sorry, sir. I don't know what you mean."

"Which was her room?"

The big man looked like something trapped. He said, "Please, Mr. Mainwaring. You'll get me into trouble . . ."

"*Which was her room?*"

Somebody turned and hissed, angrily. Hans said, "I don't understand."

"For God's sake, man, you carried her things upstairs. I saw you!"

Hans said, "No, sir . . ."

Momentarily, the lounge seemed to spin.

There was a door behind the bar. The chauffeur stepped back. He said, "Sir. Please . . ."

The place was a storeroom. There were wine bottles racked, a shelf with jars of olives, walnuts, eggs. Mainwaring closed the door behind him, tried to control the shaking. Hans said, "Sir, you must not ask me these things. I don't know a Miss Hunter. I don't know what you mean."

Mainwaring said, "Which was her room? I demand that you answer."

"I can't!"

"You drove me from London yesterday. Do you deny that?"

"No, sir."

"You drove me with Miss Hunter."

"No, sir!"

"*Damn your eyes, where is she?*"

The chauffeur was sweating. A long wait; then he said, "Mr. Mainwaring, please. You must understand. I can't help you." He swallowed, and drew himself up. He said, "I drove you from London. I'm sorry. I drove you . . . *on your own.*"

The lounge door swung shut behind Mainwaring. He half-walked, half-ran to his room. He slammed the door behind him, leaned against it panting. In time the giddiness passed. He opened his eyes, slowly. The fire glowed; the Geissler stood on the bookshelf. Nothing was changed.

He set to work, methodically. He shifted furniture, peered behind it. He rolled the carpet back, tapped every foot of floor. He fetched a flashlight from his case and examined, minutely, the interior of the wardrobe. He ran his fingers lightly across the walls, section by section, tapping again. Finally he got a chair, dismantled the ceiling lighting fitting.

Nothing.

He began again. Halfway through the second search he froze, staring at the floorboards. He walked to his case, took the screwdriver from the pistol holster. A moment's work with the blade and he sat back, staring into his palm. He rubbed his face, placed his find carefully on the side table. A tiny earring, one of the pair she had worn. He sat awhile breathing heavily, his head in his hands.

The brief daylight had faded as he worked. He lit the standard lamp, wrenched the shade free, stood the naked bulb in the middle of the room. He worked round the walls again, peering, tapping, pressing. By the fireplace, finally, a foot-square section of plaster rang hollow.

He held the bulb close, examined the hairline crack. He inserted the screwdriver blade delicately, twisted. Then again. A click; and the section hinged open.

He reached inside the little space, shaking, lifted out the recorder. He stood silent a time, holding it; then raised his arms, brought the machine smashing down on the hearth. He stamped and kicked, panting, till the thing was reduced to fragments.

The droning rose to a roar, swept low over the house. The helicopter settled slowly, belly lamps glaring, down-draught raising a storm of snow. He walked to the window, stood staring. The children embarked, clutching scarves and gloves, suitcases, boxes with new toys. The steps were withdrawn, the hatch dogged shut. Snow swirled again; the machine lifted heavily, swung away in the direction of Wilton.

The Party was about to start.

Lights blaze, through the length and breadth of the house. Orange-lit windows throw long bars of brightness across the snow. Everywhere is an anxious coming and going, the pattering of feet, clink of silver and glassware, hurried commands. Waiters scuttle between the kitchens and the Green Room where dinner is laid. Dish after dish is borne in, paraded. Peacocks, roast and gilded, vaunt their plumes in shadow and candleglow, spirit-soaked wicks blazing in their beaks. The Minister rises, laughing; toast after toast is drunk. To five thousand tanks, ten thousand fighting aeroplanes, a hundred thousand guns. The Two Empires feast their guests, royally.

The climax approaches. The boar's head, garnished and smoking, is borne shoulder-high. His tusks gleam; clamped in his jaws is the golden sun-symbol, the orange. After him march the waits and mummers, with their lanterns and begging-cups. The carol they chant is older by far than the Two Empires; older than the Reich, older than Great Britain.

"*Alive he spoiled, where poor men toiled, which made kind Ceres sad . . .*"

The din of voices rises. Coins are flung, glittering; wine is poured. And more wine, and more and more. Bowls of fruit are passed, and trays of sweets; spiced cakes, gingerbread, marzipans. Till at a signal the brandy is brought, and boxes of cigars.

The ladies rise to leave. They move flushed and chattering through the corridors of the house, uniformed link-boys grandly lighting their way. In the Great Hall, their escorts are waiting. Each young man is tall, each blond, each impeccably uniformed. On the Minstrels' Gallery a baton is poised; across the lawns, distantly, floats the whirling excitement of a waltz.

In the Green Room, hazed now with smoke, the doors are once more flung wide. Servants scurry again, carrying in boxes, great gay-wrapped parcels topped with scarlet satin bows. The Minister rises, hammering on the table for quiet.

"My friends, good friends, friends of the Two Empires. For you, no expense is spared. For you, the choicest gifts. Tonight, nothing but the best is good enough; and nothing but the best is here. Friends, enjoy yourselves. Enjoy my house. *Frohe Weihnacht* . . !"

He walks quickly into shadow, and is gone. Behind him, silence falls. A waiting; and slowly, mysteriously, the great heap of gifts begins to stir. Paper splits, crackling. Here a hand emerges, here a foot. A breathless pause; and the first of the girls rises slowly, bare in flamelight, shakes her glinting hair.

The table roars again.

The sound reached Mainwaring dimly. He hesitated at the foot of the main staircase, moved on. He turned right and left, hurried down a flight of steps. He passed kitchens, and the servants' hall. From the hall came the blare of a record player. He walked to the end of the corridor, unlatched a door. Night air blew keen against his face.

He crossed the courtyard, opened a further door. The space beyond was bright-lit; there was the faint, musty stink of animals. He paused, wiped his face. He was shirtsleeved; but despite the cold he was sweating.

He walked forward again, steadily. To either side of the corridor were the fronts of cages. The dogs hurled themselves at the bars, thunderously. He ignored them.

The corridor opened into a square concrete chamber. To one side of the place was a ramp. At its foot was parked a windowless black van.

In the far wall, a door showed a crack of light. He rapped sharply, and again.

"*Hundenmeister* . . ."

The door opened. The man who peered up at him was as wrinkled and pot-bellied as a Nast Santa Claus. At sight of his visitor's face he tried to duck back; but Mainwaring had him by the arm. He said, "*Herr Hundenmeister,* I must talk to you."

"Who are you? I don't know you. What do you want . . ."

Mainwaring showed his teeth. He said, "The van. You drove the van this morning. What was in it?"

"I don't know what you mean . . ."

The heave sent him stumbling across the floor. He tried to bolt; but Mainwaring grabbed him again.

"*What was in it* . . ."

"I won't talk to you! Go away!"

The blow exploded across his cheek. Mainwaring hit him again, backhanded, slammed him against the van.

"Open it . . . !"

The voice rang sharply in the confined space.

"*Wer ist da? Was ist passiert?*"

The little man whimpered, rubbing at his mouth.

Mainwaring straightened, breathing heavily. The GFP captain walked forward, staring, thumbs hooked in his belt.

"*Wer sind Sie?*"

Mainwaring said, "You know damn well. And speak English, you bastard. You're as English as I am."

The other glared. He said, "You have no right to be here. I should arrest you. You have no right to accost *Herr Hundenmeister.*"

"What is in that van?"

"Have you gone mad? The van is not your concern. Leave now. At once."

"*Open it!*"

The other hesitated, and shrugged. He stepped back. He said, "Show him, *mein Herr.*"

The Hundenmeister fumbled with a bunch of keys. The van doors grated. Mainwaring walked forward, slowly.

The vehicle was empty.

The Captain said, "You have seen what you wished to see. You are satisfied. Now go."

Mainwaring stared round. There was a further door, recessed deeply into the wall. Beside it controls like the controls of a bank vault.

"What is in that room?"

The GFP man said, "You have gone too far. I order you to leave."

"You have no authority over me!"

"Return to your quarters!"

Mainwaring said, "I refuse."

The other slapped the holster at his hip. He gut-held the Walther, wrists locked, feet apart. He said, *"Then you will be shot."*

Mainwaring walked past him, contemptuously. The baying of the dogs faded as he slammed the outer door.

'It was among the middle classes that the seeds had

first been sown; and it was among the middle classes that they flourished. Britain had been called often enough a nation of shopkeepers; now for a little while the tills were closed, the blinds left drawn. Overnight it seemed, an effete symbol of social and national disunity became the *Einstazegruppefuehrer* and the wire for the first detention camps was strung . . .'

Mainwaring finished the page, tore it from the spine, crumpled it and dropped it on the fire. He went on reading. Beside him on the hearth stood a part-full bottle of whisky and a glass. He picked the glass up mechanically, drank. He lit a cigarette. A few minutes later a new page followed the last.

The clock ticked steadily. The burning paper made a little rustling. Reflections danced across the ceiling of the room. Once Mainwaring raised his head, listened; once put the ruined book down, rubbed his eyes. The room, and the corridor outside, stayed quiet.

'Against immeasurable force, we must pit cunning; against immeasurable evil, faith and a high resolve. In the war we wage, the stakes are high; the dignity of man, the freedom of the spirit, the survival of humanity. Already in that war, many of us have died; many more, undoubtedly, will lay down their lives. But always beyond them, there will be others; and still more. We shall go on, as we must go on, till this thing is wiped from the earth.

'Meanwhile, we must take fresh heart. Every blow, now, is a blow for freedom. In France, Belgium, Finland, Poland, Russia, the forces of the Two Empires confront each other uneasily. Greed, jealousy, mutual distrust; these are the enemies, and they work from within. This, the Empires know full well. And, knowing, for the first time in their existence, fear . . .'

The last page crumpled, fell to ash. Mainwaring sat back, staring at nothing. Finally he stirred, looked up. It was zero three hundred; and they hadn't come for him yet.

The bottle was finished. He set it to one side, opened another. He swilled the liquid in the glass, hearing the magnified ticking of the clock.

He crossed the room, took the Luger from the case. He found a cleaning rod, patches and oil. He sat awhile dully, looking at the pistol. Then he slipped the magazine free, pulled back on the breech toggle, thumbed the latch, slid the barrel from the guides.

His mind, wearied, had begun to play aggravating tricks. It ranged and wandered, remembering scenes, episodes, details sometimes from years back; trivial, unconnected. Through and between the wanderings, time after time, ran the ancient, lugubrious words of the carol. He tried to shut them out, but it was impossible.

'Living he spoiled where poor men toiled, which made kind Ceres sad . . .'

He pushed the link pin clear, withdrew the breech block, stripped the firing pin. He laid the parts out, washed them with oil and water, dried and re-oiled. He reassembled the pistol, working carefully; inverted the barrel, shook the link down in front of the hooks, closed the latch, checked the recoil spring engagement. He loaded a full clip, pushed it home, chambered a round, thumbed the safety to *GESICKERT*. He released the clip, reloaded.

He fetched his briefcase, laid the pistol inside carefully, grip uppermost. He filled a spare clip, added the extension butt and a fifty box of Parabellum. He closed the flap and locked it, set the case beside the bed. After that there was nothing more to do. He sat back in the chair, refilled his glass.

'Toiling he boiled, where poor men spoiled . . .'

The firelight faded, finally.

He woke, and the room was dark. He got up, felt the floor sway a little. He understood that he had a hangover. He groped for the lightswitch. The clock hands stood at zero eight hundred.

He felt vaguely guilty at having slept so long.

He walked to the bathroom. He stripped and showered, running the water as hot as he could bear. The process brought him round a little. He dried himself, staring down. He thought for the first time what curious things these bodies were; some with their yellow cylinders, some their indentations.

He dressed and shaved. He had remembered what he was going to do; fastening his tie, he tried to remember why. He couldn't. His brain, it seemed, had gone dead.

There was an inch of whisky in the bottle. He poured it, grimaced and drank. Inside him was a fast, cold shaking. He thought, 'Like the first morning at a new school.'

He lit a cigarette. Instantly his throat filled. He walked to the bathroom and vomited. Then again. Finally there was nothing left to come.

His chest ached. He rinsed his mouth, washed his face again. He sat in the bedroom for a while, head back and eyes closed. In time the shaking went away. He lay unthinking, hearing the clock tick. Once his lips moved. He said, "They're no better than us."

At nine hundred hours he walked to the breakfast room. His stomach, he felt, would retain very little. He ate a slice of toast, carefully, drank some coffee. He asked for a pack of cigarettes, went back to his room. At ten hundred hours he was due to meet the Minister.

He checked the briefcase again. A thought made him add a pair of stringback motoring gloves. He sat again, stared at the ashes where he had burned the Geissler. A part of him was willing the clock hands not to move. At five to ten he picked the briefcase up, stepped into the corridor. He stood a moment staring round him. He thought, 'It hasn't happened yet. I'm still alive.' There was still the flat in Town to go back to, still his office; the tall windows, the telephones, the khaki utility desk.

He walked through sunlit corridors to the Minister's suite.

The room to which he was admitted was wide and long. A fire crackled in the hearth; beside it on a low table stood glasses and a decanter. Over the mantel, conventionally, hung the Fuehrer's portrait. Edward VIII faced him across the room. Tall windows framed a prospect of rolling parkland. In the distance, blue on the horizon, were the woods.

The Minister said, "Good morning, Richard. Please sit down. I don't think I shall keep you long."

He sat, placing the briefcase by his knee.

This morning everything seemed strange. He studied the Minister curiously, as if seeing him for the first time. He had that type of face once thought of as peculiarly English; short-nosed and slender, with high, finely shaped cheekbones. The hair, blond and cropped close to the scalp, made him look nearly boyish. The eyes were candid, flat, dark-fringed. He looked, Mainwaring decided, not so much Aryan as like some fierce nursery toy; a Feral Teddy Bear.

The Minister riffled papers. He said, "Several things have cropped up; among them I'm afraid, more trouble in Glasgow. The fifty-first Panzer division is standing by; as yet, the news hasn't been released."

Mainwaring wished his head felt less hollow. It made his own voice boom so unnecessarily. He said, "Where is Miss Hunter?"

The Minister paused. The pale eyes stared; then he went on speaking.

"I'm afraid I may have to ask you to cut short your stay here. I shall be flying back to London for a meeting; possibly tomorrow, possibly the day after. I shall want you with me of course."

"*Where is Miss Hunter?*"

The Minister placed his hands flat on the desk top, studied the nails. He said, "Richard, there are aspects of Two Empires culture that are neither mentioned nor discussed. You of all people should know this. I'm being patient with you; but there are limits to what I can overlook."

'Seldom he toiled, while Ceres roiled, which made poor kind men glad . . .'

Mainwaring opened the flap of the case and stood up. He thumbed the safety forward and levelled the pistol.

There was silence for a time. The fire spat softly. Then the Minister smiled. He said, "That's an interesting gun, Richard. Where did you get it?"

Mainwaring didn't answer.

The Minister moved his hands carefully to the arms of his chair, leaned back. He said, "It's the Marine model of course. It's also quite old. Does it by any chance carry the Erfurt stamp? Its value would be considerably increased."

He smiled again. He said, "If the barrel is good, I'll buy it. For my private collection."

Mainwaring's arm began to shake. He steadied his wrist, gripping with his left hand.

The Minister sighed. He said, "Richard, you can be so stubborn. It's a good quality; but you do carry it to excess." He shook his head. He said, "Did you imagine for one moment I didn't know you were coming here to kill me? My dear chap, you've been through a great deal. You're overwrought. Believe me, I know just how you feel."

Mainwaring said, "You murdered her."

The Minister spread his hands. He said, "What with? A gun? A knife? Do I honestly look such a shady character?"

The words made a cold pain, and a tightness in the chest. But they had to be said.

The Minister's brows rose. Then he started to laugh. Finally he said, "At last I see. I understood, but I couldn't believe. So you bullied our poor little *Hundenmeister,* which wasn't very worthy; and seriously annoyed the *Herr Hauptmann,* which wasn't very wise. Because of this fantasy, stuck in your head. Do you really believe it, Richard? Perhaps you believe in *Struwwelpeter* too." He sat forward. He said, "The Hunt ran. And killed . . . a deer. She gave us an excellent chase. As for your little Huntress . . . Richard, she's gone. She never existed. She was a figment of your imagination. Best forgotten."

Mainwaring said, "We were in love."

The Minister said, "Richard, you really are becoming tiresome." He shook his head again. He said, "We're both adult. We both know what that word is worth. It's a straw, in the wind. A candle, on a night of gales. A phrase that is meaningless. *Lächerlich."* He put his hands together, rubbed a palm. He said, "When this is over, I want you to go away. For a month, six weeks maybe. With your new car. When you come back . . . well, we'll see. Buy yourself a girlfriend, if you need a woman that much. *Einen Schatz.* I never dreamed; you're so remote, you should speak more of yourself. Richard, I understand; it isn't such a very terrible thing."

Mainwaring stared.

The Minister said, "We shall make an arrangement. You will have the use of an apartment, rather a nice apartment. So your lady will be close. When you tire of her . . . buy another. They're unsatisfactory for the most part, but reasonable. Now sit down like a good chap, and put your gun away. You look so silly, standing there scowling like that."

It seemed he felt all life, all experience, as a grey weight pulling. He lowered the pistol, slowly. He thought, 'At the end, they were wrong. They picked the wrong man.' He said, "I suppose now I use it on myself."

The Minister said, "No, no, no. You still don't understand." He linked his knuckles, grinning. He said, "Richard, the *Herr Hauptmann* would have arrested you last night. I wouldn't let him. This is between ourselves. Nobody else. I give you my word."

Mainwaring felt his shoulders sag. The strength seemed drained from him; the pistol, now, weighed too heavy for his arm.

The Minister said, "Richard, why so glum? It's a great occasion, man. You've found your courage. I'm delighted."

He lowered his voice. He said, "Don't you want to know why I let you come here with your machine? Aren't you even interested?"

Mainwaring stayed silent.

The Minister said, "Look around you, Richard. See the world. I want men near me, serving me. Now more than ever. Real men, not afraid to die. Give me a dozen . . . but you know the rest. I could rule the world. But first . . . I must rule them. My men. Do you see now? Do you understand?"

Mainwaring thought, 'He's in control again. But he was always in control. He owns me.'

The study spun a little.

The voice went on, smoothly. "As for this amusing little plot by the so-called Freedom Front; again, you did well. It was difficult for you. I was watching; believe me, with much sympathy. Now, you've burned your book. Of your own free will. That delighted me."

Mainwaring looked up, sharply.

The Minister shook his head. He said, "The real recorder is rather better hidden, you were too easily satisfied there. There's also a tv monitor. I'm sorry about it all, I apologise. It was necessary."

A singing started, inside Mainwaring's head.

The Minister sighed again. He said, "Still unconvinced, Richard? Then I have some things I think you ought to see. Am I permitted to open my desk drawer?"

Mainwaring didn't speak. The other slid the drawer back slowly, reached in. He laid a telegram flimsy on the desk top. He said, "The addressee is Miss D.J. Hunter. The message consists of one word. 'ACTIVATE.' "

The singing rose in pitch.

"This as well," said the Minister. He held up a medallion on a thin gold chain. The little disc bore the linked motif of the Freedom Front. He said, "Mere exhibitionism; or a deathwish. Either way, a most undesirable trait."

He tossed the thing down. He said, "She was here under surveillance of course, we'd known about her for years. To them, you were a sleeper. Do you see the absurdity? They really thought you would be jealous enough to assassinate your Minister. This they mean in their silly little book, when they talk of subtlety. Richard, I could have fifty blonde women if I chose. A hundred. Why should I want yours?" He shut the drawer with a click, and rose. He said, "Give me the gun now. You don't need it any more." He extended his arm; then he was flung heavily backward. Glasses smashed on the sidetable. The decanter split; its contents poured dark across the wood.

Over the desk hung a faint haze of blue. Mainwaring walked forward, stood looking down. There were bloodflecks, and a little flesh. The eyes of the Teddy Bear still showed glints of white. Hydraulic shock had shattered the chest; the breath drew ragged, three times, and stopped. He thought, 'I didn't hear the report.'

The communicating door opened. Mainwaring turned. A secretary stared in, bolted at sight of him. The door slammed.

He pushed the briefcase under his arm, ran through the outer office. Feet clattered in the corridor. He opened the door, carefully. Shouts sounded, somewhere below in the house.

Across the corridor hung a loop of crimson cord. He stepped over it, hurried up a flight of stairs. Then another. Beyond the private apartments the way was closed by a heavy metal grille. He ran to it, rattled. A rumbling sounded from below. He glared round. Somebody had operated the emergency shutters; the house was sealed.

Beside the door an iron ladder was spiked to the wall. He climbed it, panting. The trap in the ceiling was padlocked. He clung one-handed, awkward with the briefcase, held the pistol above his head.

Daylight showed through splintered wood. He put his shoulder to the trap, heaved. It creaked back. He pushed head and shoulders through, scrambled. Wind stung at him, and flakes of snow.

His shirt was wet under the arms. He lay face down, shaking. He thought, 'It wasn't an accident. None of it was an accident.' He had underrated them. They understood despair.

He pushed himself up, stared round. He was on the roof of Wilton. Beside him rose gigantic chimney stacks. There was a lattice radio mast. The wind hummed in its guy wires. To his right ran the balustrade that crowned the facade of the house. Behind it was a snow-choked gutter.

He wriggled across a sloping scree of roof, ran crouching. Shouts sounded from below. He dropped flat, rolled. An automatic clattered. He edged forward again, dragging the briefcase. Ahead, one of the corner towers rose dark against the sky. He crawled to it, crouched sheltered from the wind. He opened the case, pulled the gloves on. He clipped the stock to the pistol, laid the spare magazine beside him and the box of rounds.

The shouts came again. He peered forward, through the balustrade. Running figures scattered across the lawn. He sighted on the nearest, squeezed. Commotion below. The automatic zipped; stone chips flew, whining. A voice called, "Don't expose yourselves unnecessarily." Another answered.

"*Die kommen mit dem Hubschrauber . . .*"

He stared round him, at the yellow-grey horizon. He had forgotten the helicopter.

A snow flurry drove against his face. He huddled, flinching. He thought he heard, carried on the wind, a faint droning.

From where he crouched he could see the nearer trees of the park, beyond them the wall and gatehouses. Beyond again, the land rose to the circling woods.

The droning was back, louder than before. He screwed his eyes, made out the dark spot skimming above the trees. He shook his head. He said, "We made a mistake. We all made a mistake."

He settled the stock of the Luger to his shoulder, and waited.

ATTACK-ESCAPE

AN ARTICLE ABOUT ALFRED BESTER BY

CHARLES PLATT

"Begin with your second-best anecdote, to attract the attention of the reader," he told me. "Next pose a question, about the subject of your article: what makes him tick? To answer this you work around every aspect of him, the same kind of technique used in TV soap opera, where they examine a situation from a succession of different viewpoints, then resolve it. If possible, you should illustrate your points with more anecdotes—they are the crux of a piece. At the end of it, the summation: you say, *this* is Alfie Bester, this is what accounts for the writing he does. And you use your best anecdote, to illustrate the whole thing."

This is the Alfred Bester system for writing about a personality and I shall follow it closely. You will note, in fact, I have already used it, as my Second-Best Anecdote.

And soon, we shall Pose the Question.

Alfred Bester was born in December 1913. *The Broken Axiom* was his first published story, in *Thrilling Wonder* (1938). It won a $50 competiton prize, after the contest's judges had helped him re-work his original draft. Between then and the mid-fifties (when he stopped writing science fiction altogether) he produced two science fiction novels and a couple of dozen short stories—less work than any other well-known sf writer, yet of equal or higher consistent quality. Recently, almost all his sf has been re-published in paperback in the USA (the two novels and two collections), offering an opportunity for serious critical attention which, strangely, his work has seldom received. Most of what

Bester wrote was excellent; why didn't he write more? How did he start, why did he stop, and has he stopped for good?

* * *

In the early 1950's the awkward crudities of the Gernsback- and Campbell-dominated periods were being moderated with traces of sensitivity and maturity, in *Fantasy and Science Fiction* and *Galaxy* magazines. At the same time, the precepts of science fiction (alien cultures, hyperspace, telepathy) were still fresh to allow some truly imaginative forays.

The Stars My Destination (first titled *Tiger, Tiger*) epitomizes that period. It is probably the best science fiction of its kind ever written; by definition, this also means that it is the best that ever will be written, for the worth of such science fiction lies in its ideas, and the number of possible new ideas within the self-imposed strictures of the field really is limited. *The Stars My Destination* is a summation of what had been so far achieved, and a catalogue of what then remained available within those terms. After it, everything seems at least a little derivative. Innovation has been succeeded by permutation. Bester gave up writing sf and perhaps some of his contemporaries should have followed his example. True creativity these days exists only outside the field, in areas such as speculative fiction, where the rules, and the mood, are different.

The protagonist in *The Stars My Destination* is a hero-figure probably most used (and least explored in human terms) by A. E. Van Vogt: the common man who finds he has super-powers which enable him to alter the entire course of human history. This myth-figure dates back to before even John Carter of Mars; but seldom has it been so sympathetically described, and with such depth, as in Bester's novel. Gulliver Foyle, Mechanic's Mate Third Class, transcends not only the apparent limits of his abilities, but also the limitations of his archetype.

Stranded alone on a wrecked space ship for six months, his possessions are a *faceless clock which he kept wound just to listen to the ticking, a lug wrench with a hand-shaped handle which he would hold in lonely moments, an egg slicer upon whose wires he would play primitive tunes . . .*

His employee-classification lists *EDUCATION: NONE. SKILLS: NONE. MERITS: NONE. RECOMMENDATIONS: NONE.* It takes a stimulus—being left to rot, by a potential rescuer—to *turn the key in the lock of his soul . . . the door was opened. What emerged expunged the Common Man forever.*

Later in the book, a woman tells Foyle "*You've got nothing inside you . . . but hatred and revenge.*"

"*It's enough.*"

But by the end, having achieved his goal and found it empty—having gained control of a super-weapon, holding the fate of the world in his hands—Foyle has no answers, only questions: "*Am I to turn PyrE over to the world and let it destroy itself? Am I to teach the world how to space-jaunte and let us spread our freak show from galaxy to galaxy through all the universe? . . . Will you turn my name into a common anathema, like Lynch and Boycott?*"

The concerns are simplistic rather than subtle, and the book's power is in its melodrama rather than its messages. But Foyle is memorable—even lovable—and this is undoubtedly because Bester believes in him.

"I've always been attracted to the Henry V protagonist—man of direct action. I don't know whether it's because I wish to be like that, or because I *am* like that . . . I'm told I suffer from attack-escape: Any time I'm faced with a situation I attack it, to get it over with. And generally, I'm a great believer in *people*, and their untapped potential. It's obvious we can't all be a Gully Foyle, but most of us energize at such a low level, so far short of our real capabilities, we could all be more, do more. Today, in America, I think everyone needs a good kick in the ass, to get them *doing* things. This is the message at the end of the book, Tell 'em, kick 'em in the ass, make 'em *do*."

At the end of the book, when Foyle hands the super-weapon out to the general public, he indeed says "*I believe in them. I was one of them before I turned tiger. They can all turn uncommon if they're kicked awake like I was.*"

Bester still clearly believes in his "make 'em *do*" philosophy, and applies it to himself. But this aggressive energy is tempered by a relaxed, affable outlook toward people he meets, and by a quiet, thoughtful interest in the arts. He clearly values 'culture' highly, and literary and musical references abound in his conversation. "My writing always runs to the same pattern, and I'm aware of that. I write in terms of tempo. I say to myself, the feel of this script or story is, I need the attack of Beethoven in the first movement of the Eroica. Or as I move to a climax I'll say, presto, presto, Rossini, *Rossini*!"

Regardless of the comparability of Beethoven to science fiction, certainly one of the prime qualities of Bester's work is its excellent control and pacing. Much of this must be attributed to his early training in comic book writing (in the 1940s he wrote The Green Lantern, Star Spangled Kid, Captain Marvel and others) and radio scripts (Nick Carter, Charlie Chan and The Shadow, listened to regularly by millions of Americans). From there, he moved to TV.

All these mass-entertainment fields impose an obligation on the writer to be quick, to the point, exaggerating and simplifying human emotion and tying it all to a strong plot. A writer who does a lot of work of this kind can end up feeling extremely intolerant of fiction which 'breaks the rules' and makes fewer concessions to the reader. Bester prefers not to speak of 'rules', and yet he implies that such rules do exist: "You must tell a story. In order to tell a story you must have a point of view. In order to have a point of view you must have characters, your characters must be in conflict, and there must be a resolution one way or the other, or if there is no resolution, then *non*-resolution is the point. But there must *be* a point."

The plot of *The Stars My Destination* is beautifully engineered ("Largely based on *The Count of Monte Christo,*" says Bester, "surely that's obvious?") but its appeal is broader than that of a mere adventure yarn. There is great social and political awareness, equalled in science fiction only by the work of Cyril Kornbluth. The book is based on a situation where a reactionary industrialist is reluctant to disclose to a liberal regime the fruits of his firm's weapon research. Sociologically, too, the scenario is all too plausible: in a society where almost everyone can teleport, it is natural for the status-conscious upper classes to adhere to costly, antiquated mechanical transportation; for women to be relegated to the status of possessions, locked safely away from the privacy-invading potential of wish-responsive travel; for quack psychiatrists to offer double-your-teleporting-power-or-double - your - money back; for unscrupulous industrialists to employ the tiny minority who lack the teleporting faculty, to put them to work as virtual slave labour.

Most of all, this is a book of thrown-away ideas, any one of which might have been used by a less energetic writer for a short story or an entire novel on its own. The asteroid home of the Scientific People (reminiscent of some present-day hippie communes) who mate Foyle to a girl of his choice ('Natural Selection') and inocculate her with "something old, something new, something borrowed and something blue"—most scientific—in their drifting warren of trashed space ships, welded together; the decadent grandeur of the industrial clans, treasuring hereditary surnames such as Buick, Westinghouse, Kodak; the freak farm where monstrosities are manufactured for the entertainment world and the underworld; Olivia Presteign, the beautiful albino whose vision operates only in the infra-red; Robin Wednesbury, one-way telepath doomed only to broadcast her thoughts, unable ever to receive those of others; the Cellar Christians, furtively practising religion in suburban homes protected by the Lethal Defense Corp. of Sweden . . . every image is vivid, and perfectly part of the decadent scenario.

Bester clearly works by collecting such various ideas and images over a period of time, before he knows how they will be used. Only after he has established the basic structure are they slotted into place as embellishments in the collage.

The opening, space-wrecked situation, for example, was derived from something he read in an old *National Geographic Magazine*: "A Phillipine Cook's Assistant had been shipwrecked during the war, and survived on a raft for several months . . . he was sighted several times by merchant ships, but none of them would alter course to pick him up, because it had been a Nazi practice to set decoys of this kind. The idea stayed with me for three or four years, while I was thinking, how to *use* it . . ."

Such assorted imagery and peripheral ideas play a similarly large part in Bester's other science fiction book, *The Demolished Man.* His first novel (winning, incidentally, the first Hugo ever awarded), it was written in response to the promptings of Horace Gold, then the editor of *Galaxy* magazine, Bester was initially reluctant: "I told Horace, there were all these other *great* writers, I knew I wasn't in their class. Ted Sturgeon, Henry Huttner, Cyril Kornbluth. I said he should get one of *those* cats to write him his novel."

Eventually, he simply sent a bundle of ideas to Gold. In particular: "I had passed through the English 'closed' or 'whodunnit' format of mystery writing, to the 'open' American style in which you know everything except how they're going to catch the bad guy. I thought perhaps I could do an open mystery using science fiction to set up the most insuperable obstacles . . . when you write, you always present yourself with problems. It's the writer's job to set up a problem and then crack it; if you don't have a problem, then you ain't writin'."

The problem in *The Demolished Man* is how to commit a successful murder, when a large section of the public (including many police) are telepathic. Between them, Gold and Bester worked out a plausible scenario for what is, as Bester says, basically a mystery novel.

Though it has the pace and some of the colour of his other book, it is never quite as successful, as imaginative, or as satisfying, and the 'open' mystery format must take some of the blame. The plot relies heavily on psychology which is disappointingly glib and shallow: *"Every man is a balance of two opposed drives . . . the Life Instinct and the Death Instinct. Both drives have the identical purpose . . . to win Nirvana. The Life Instinct fights for Nirvana by smashing all opposition. The Death Instinct attempts to win Nirvana by destroying itself. Usually both instincts fuse in the adapted individual. Under strain they defuse."* If only it ever were really as simple as that. One is similarly unconvinced when the hero, out of guilt feelings, sets booby traps designed to kill himself, meanwhile hiding from his conscious mind the knowledge of having done so. (Unhappily, this self-assassination idea is also used in Bester's only other book, *Rat Race,* a mainstream novel whose film rights he later sold to Hollywood.)

Despite these flaws, *The Demolished Man* remains a tour de force, with some wild and colourful backdrops and some pleasing *intuitive* sympathy for human psychology, even if the formal approach seems rather simplistic. Most ingenious idea in the book is the manic rhyme which the would-be murderer picks up, with the aim of having it constantly running through his head, to camouflage from telepaths his homicidal intentions. Supposedly a one-time TV jingle, it runs, as every science fiction fan knows: *Eight sir; Seven, sir; Six, sir; Five, sir; Four, sir; Three, sir; Two, sir; One! Tenser, said the Tensor; Tenser, said the Tensor; Tension, apprehension and dissension have begun. Its* meaninglessness surely adds to its authenticity.

A similar rhyme is used in one of his short stories. *Fondly Fahrenheit*, an engaging, slightly manic case history of a psychotic android suffering from synesthesia (which, incidentally, is another Bester idea used elsewhere—in the climax of *The Stars My Destination).* Excessively hot weather triggers the android's psychotic tendencies; he murders his victims after singing: *"Oh, it's no feat to beat the heat. All reet! All reet! So jeet your seat. Be fleet, be fleet, cool and discreet, Honey . . ."*

It sang in a strange, halting voice, and its accomplished fingers were clasped behind its back, writhing in a strange rumba all their own. Dallas Brady was surprised.

"You happy or something?" she asked.

"I must remind you that the pleasure-pain syndrome is not incorporated in the android synthesis," I answered.

—This story being narrated in part in the first person by the android, also in the third person, and also (by turns, switching at times in mid-paragraph) in the first person from the viewpoint of the android's owner. The purpose is to convey the blurring of identities of man and machine, as each is influenced by the other's neurosis; or, as the narrator puts it, *"If you live with a crazy machine long enough, I become crazy too. Reet!"*

The technique reflects Bester's continual interest (shared by few of his contemporaries) in experimenting with form as well as content. The typographic 'pictures' in *The Demolished Man*, to convey the feel of telepathic word-images; the flamboyant effects at the end of *The Stars My Destination,* a kind of comic book concrete poetry; the text patterns in his short story *The Pi Man,* whose protagonist is obsessed with symmetry and order;—all are unusual and unexpected, and yet they are legitimate, and they work.

The experimentation is used always within the bounds of

the formal rules of storytelling, however, and Bester remains critical of writers whose inventiveness moves outside them. Of Burroughs' *The Naked Lunch,* he says "There are moments of such inspired brilliant writing it's not to be believed. There are also moments of such incredible dullardry, that, well, where was that boy's *editor*?" He laughs, but only half in fun. He feels that an editor has an important, if awkward, part to play: "There are certain ingredients that must be in a story. There must be a beginning, a middle and an end—" how often we have heard that phrase "—and there must be a structure. Really, it should be the author's structure; but how does an editor explain that there *must be one,* without imposing his own on the author? That is the difficulty." And of Brian Aldiss, he says, still half in fun, "I think Brian is the best science fiction writer today—or he would be, if he would just let me *edit* him."

Bester's only piece to go outside the limits of his formal approach is, despite its trite title, *They Don't Make Life Like They Used To.* His most subtle short story, it builds a creeping sense of unreality and fear, through the irrationality and possible delusions of a man and woman alone in a post-holocaust New York. Insanity is implied, but never stated; conversations are punctuated by the occasional crash of collapsing skyscrapers—at least, one supposes this is the source of the noise; and at the end, a sudden suspicion of a totally surreal, alien menace leaves the situation still less resolved. Although, conceivably, in Bester's own words, "non-resolution is the point".

Similar post-bomb scenarios are used in other Bester stories, but always with great originality. He advocates the lighter touch: "When you feel things badly, you have a tendency to get serious about them, and what you want to do is denounce. But you must never do that. You have to spoof. You can't be over-serious, unless you're writing hard action and adventure; that has to be done with grim intensity."

The Flowered Thundermug is a spoof. In the story: "*It seems after that war nearly everything was wiped out. When they started building a new civilization, all they had for a pattern was the remains of Hollywood. It was comparatively untouched in the war.*"

"Why?"

"I guess nobody thought it was worth bombing."

In this post-war world, the characters are all named after movie stars, and America is one big Los Angeles. *They passed the teardrop swimming pool, the book-shaped library, the heart-shaped heart clinic and came to the faculty-shaped faculty building.* Such structures necessitate a pinnacle expediter: *". . . a specialist whereby when the firm builds like a shoe-shaped building for a shoe store, he ties the laces on top; also he puts the straws on top of an ice cream parlor; also he . . ."*

"What was your last job?"

"The Memory Institute at 30449 Louis B. Mayer Boulevard."

"What did you do?"

"I put the veins in the brain."

In another story, *The Starcomber,* five classic science fiction wish-fulfilment situations are satirized by exaggeration. One seems directly comparable to the opening of his own novel. *The Stars My Destination: His assets were his convict clothes, a helmet, one cylinder of O_2, his grim fury at the injustice that had been done to him, and his knowledge of the secret of how the Grssh could be defeated in their maniacal quest for solar domination . . . they were irresistible, for they possessed the power of simulkinesis—the ability to be in two places at the same time!*

Another uses the post-holocaust New York background for ludicrous, rather than horrific, effect. The last man meets the last woman: *"I'm the daughter of the unfortunate Professor Field whose well-intentioned but ill-advised experiment in nuclear fission has wiped mankind off the face of the earth with the exception of you and me who, no doubt on account of some mysterious mutant strain in our makeup which makes us different, are the last of the old civilization and the first of the new . . . I'm a beautiful woman with at IQ of 141, which is important for the propagation of a brave new beautiful race of men to inherit the good green earth," she said.*

Unfortunately, not all of Bester's writing follows his own advice to spoof rather than sermonize. The ending of *The Demolished Man* is a little heavy-handed: *In the endless universe there has been nothing new, nothing different.*

What has appeared exceptional to the infinite Eye of God . . . coincidences of environment, opportunity and encounter . . . all of them have been reproduced over and over on the planet of a sun whose galaxy revolves once in two hundred million years and has revolved nine times already. There has been joy. There will be joy again. True, no doubt, but a little reminiscent of the ending of a Hollywood biblical epic. Again, at the end of the short story Hobson's Choice: *Through the vistas of the years every age but our own seems glamorous and golden. We yearn for the yesterdays and tomorrows, never realizing that we are faced with Hobson's Choice . . . that today, bitter or sweet, anxious or calm, is the only day for us. The dream of time is the traitor, and we are all accomplices to the betrayal of ourselves.* A pity, for the rest of the story shows none of this heavy approach.

The other area in which his writing sometimes shows weakness is that of human relationships. In The Pi Man: *"It happens," she said in a low voice. "I never believe it, but it happens. You fall in and out of love, and each time you think it's for real and forever. And then you meet somebody and it isn't a question of love any more. You just know he's your man, and you're stuck. I'm stuck."* It seems that the techniques of soap opera have applications in fiction, as well as in the writing of articles.

But to be fair, Bester is aware of his relative lack of empathy for his female characters (who are almost always beautiful, unthinkingly dedicated to the male hero, and altogether delightfully ineffectual). He says he is principally interested in writing about male characters, and "I don't believe in love as a motivation at all. I dislike love stories intensely."

Hence the simplification and codification of most of the love relationships in his work. It is probably his greatest weakness although, of course, it is a weakness shared with almost every other science fiction writer working in the 1950's and before.

* * *

During the past fifteen years Bester's preoccupation has been his work on the American magazine *Holiday*. He wrote regular features, conducted interviews and, finally, became an editor. Before this period, he found that his work writing scripts for TV (and before that, radio) limited him. Some of his ideas—such as synesthesia—were considered too far-out by the networks, and so he wrote science fiction, as an escape and as a means of using the more imaginative images about which he wished to write.

Strangely, the need for this escape disappeared when he began writing articles (for *Holiday*) about, as he puts it, "the fascination of reality—nothing could be more fascinating than that." This being the reason for his prolonged absence from the sf field.

However, his association with *Holiday* magazine ended recently, and "I have a pile of notes for stories, and ideas I'd like to do, but we'll see. Alternatively, a new magazine called *Travel and Leisure* wants me to work for them; I'm not sure yet." He also has what he calls a "contemporary" science fiction novel lying around one-third completed, but seems disinclined to finish it, fearing that he will be unable to sell it anywhere. He has some grounds for this suspicion. *The Demolished Man,* he says, "was turned down by every publisher in New York" at first. And he has another novel titled *Tender Loving Rape,* which he wrote six years ago and considers the best work he has ever done, and yet has proved unsaleable.

Either way, he is adamant that "No author should live off science fiction alone. That way, you produce a lot of damn bad science fiction. My point is, don't write unless you've got something to say. I do love science fiction, very deeply; God knows there are guys who write rotten stories because they haven't got any talent, but there are also talented men who have to meet monthly bills and they grind out stuff which they should never have considered writing. I say, for Christ's sake get into additional lines of writing so that science fiction becomes just one aspect of your work."

I'm using this as my Best Anecdote, because it sums up Alfred Bester's entire approach to writing science fiction: an approach which sometimes has resulted in his mass-entertainment writing adversely influencing his good work, but which, more often, has meant that his good work has maintained a quality of sustained innovation unmatched by any other science fiction writer of the 1950s.

THE AUTHORS

BARRY BAYLEY is a regular contributor to NW and NWQ. He has also sold sf to *Nebula, The British Science Fiction Magazine, Authentic, Science Fantasy and Science Fiction Adventures.* He is currently working on his third sf novel. His last story in NWQ was *The Four-Color Problem* (No. 2).

WILLIAM WOODROW's first sf story, *The Meek,* appeared in NWQ 2. He has also contributed to *Animals, Wildlife and the Countryside* and *The Countryman.* He is a biologist, currently working on a book of techniques in field ecology.

MAREK OBTULOWICZ's first published story appeared in NW monthly. Since then he has appeared a second time in NW and has also sold work to *Orbit.* Hs is currently living in a cottage in Herefordshire with his wife and daughter and working on his second novel.

THOMAS M. DISCH is a well-known contributor to NW since the days of our very first paperback format issues in the mid-sixties. He has contributed stories, criticism, essays and poems to NW and to most of the best literary magazines and poetry journals and is currently living in Rome, working on a non-sf novel about Middle America. His last story in the '334' series (of which the story in this issue is the last) was *Angouleme* in NWQ 1. He has appeared in all issues of NWQ.

ALAN AUMBRY was born near Birmingham, lived in Dublin for some years, and plans to be living in London shortly. *Man in Transit* is Aumbry's first published story.

JOHN T. SLADEK is a favourite contributor to NW and NWQ. He reviews for *The New Scientist*, has appeared in most of the American sf magazines and several anthologies, and is currently working on a book dealing with modern myths to be called *The New Apocrypha*.

KEITH ROBERTS divides his time between writing and illustration (and in NWQ manages to combine both talents). His last story in NWQ was in No. 3, *The Grain Kings*. *Weihnachtabend* is the first story in a new series. His latest novel is *The Boat of Fate* (Hutchinson, U.K.) a massive historical novel set during the last phases of the Roman Empire.

CHARLES PLATT currently spends his time between London and New York. He has published several sf novels, including *Garbage World*, which was serialised in NW monthly. He has also written novels for Essex House and Olympia Press, has worked as a book- and magazine-designer and contributes regularly to the *L.A. Free Press*.

LANGDON JONES has been associated with NW and NWQ for many years and has contributed many stories, articles and reviews to its pages. His first collection of stories will be published shortly by Macmillan in the U.S. and will be called *The Eye of the Lens*.

M. JOHN HARRISON received great praise from *The Daily Telegraph, The Sunday Telegraph, The New Statesman* and many other papers and journals for his first novel *The Committed Men* (New Authors, U.K., Doubleday, U.S.A.). His second novel was recently published in paperback by NEL and has also been very well-received. It is a fantasy of the far future and called *The Pastel City*. It is about characters who appeared in his short story *The Lamia and Lord Cromis* in NWQ 1. His most recent story in NWQ was *The Causeway* and he has contributed criticism regularly to NW and NWQ since 1968.

R. GLYN JONES has worked for *Cyclops, I. T.* and *Frendz,* doing design and comic strips, including half the Jerry Cornelius strip in *I.T.* (part of which was reproduced in *The Nature of the Catastrophe,* Hutchinson). Jones recently completed his doctors theses in psychology at London University.

MICHAEL MOORCOCK has edited NW and NWQ off and on since 1964. He published the magazine from 1968 to 1971 when various pressures resulted in insuperable distribution difficulties and it became practical to publish on a quarterly schedule.